WOMEN
TOGETHER,
WOMEN
ALONE

WOMEN TOGETHER, WOMEN A·L·O·N·E

The Legacy of the Consciousness-Raising Movement

ANITA SHREVE

VIKING

VIKING
Published by the Penguin Group
Viking Penguin, a division of Penguin Books USA Inc.,
40 West 23rd Street, New York, New York 10010, U.S.A.
Penguin Books Ltd, 27 Wrights Lane,
London W8 5TZ, England
Penguin Books Australia Ltd, Ringwood,
Victoria, Australia
Penguin Books Canada Ltd, 2801 John Street,
Markham, Ontario, Canada L3R 1B4
Penguin Books (N.Z.) Ltd, 182–190 Wairau Road,
Auckland 10, New Zealand

Penguin Books Ltd, Registered Offices:
Harmondsworth, Middlesex, England

First published in 1989 by Viking Penguin,
a division of Penguin Books USA Inc.

1 3 5 7 9 10 8 6 4 2

LIBRARY OF CONGRESS CATALOGING IN PUBLICATION DATA
Shreve, Anita.
Women together, women alone.
1. Feminism—United States—History—20th century.
2. Women—United States—Social conditions.
3. United States—Social conditions—1980–
I. Title.
HQ1421.S57 1989   305.4′2   88–40478
ISBN 0–670–81910–7

Printed in the United States of America
Set in New Baskerville
Designed by Jo Anne Metsch

For my daughter, Katherine

ACKNOWLEDGMENTS

I would like to thank Barbara Balliet, former coordinator of the Women's History Program at Sarah Lawrence College, for preparing a bibliography for me during the research phase of this project.

I am very grateful to both Amanda Vaill, my editor at Viking, and to Ginger Barber, my agent, for their advice, encouragement and support.

And I would like to convey a special thanks to all those women who allowed me to interview them and who were so forthcoming with their personal stories.

The italicized portions of this book portray a consciousness-raising group containing composite characters partially drawn from real-life experience, but not intended to portray real events or real people. In the rest of this book, all of the women are real, although in some cases their identities have been withheld because they have requested anonymity.

CONTENTS

WOMEN
TOGETHER,
WOMEN
ALONE

ONE

A Reunion

*A misty September evening. The east side of Washington Square
Park, Greenwich Village, New York City. Seven o'clock.*

*Catherine adjusts the strap of her carry-on luggage. She looks
down the street and up at a fifth-floor window, where she can just
make out the edge of a haze of light. She has had the taxi driver let
us off a block short, out of sight of the doorway to Jane's building
on Washington Place. She tells me, a reporter who has asked to tag
along, that she's not exactly sure why she has done this, except that
she knows she's not ready yet to see the other women—the women of
her consciousness-raising group, the women she knew inside out as
they did her, the women who changed her life.*

*She remembers this neighborhood from years ago, recalls walking
down this very block many evenings such as this, and she wonders
how safe it is today. It's been three years, no four, since she has been
in New York City—nearly fifteen since she has been at this address.
A fine, gentle mist begins to cover her hair and face and clothes. A
young man in a hooded sweatshirt walks past her, looks at her ap-*

1

praisingly. A woman wearing the headphones of a small radio jogs past her and around the corner. An older woman across the street stoops over her dog and picks him up. Looking at Jane's building, Catherine admits to a craving for a cigarette. She is certain she will probably be the only one who still smokes, and she says she'd better have one now before she goes up. When she takes the pack out of her purse, however, her hand is trembling.

"If my own life has changed so much since I left the group," she asks, "won't this be true for the other women as well?"

Catherine has her own business now in another city; her daughter is grown and off at her first year at Harvard. Catherine says she feels proud about this fact and will enjoy telling it to the other women. But there are other facts about her life, she confesses, that she would just as soon gloss over. She has still not married again. Almost all of her long-term relationships with men in the years since she left the group have ended badly—whether in this city or in another. It bothers her to have to tell the other women this, to have to account for herself, for all those years.

She looks down at the navy blue silk dress beneath her raincoat and winces. "It's too dressy," she says. She touches her hair at the nape of her neck. It is sandy blond and cut short. The last time the other women saw her she had hair below her shoulders.

"My God," she says, "they still think of me as Cathy!*"*

There'd been ten, sometimes twelve in the group at a time, but always there was the core of seven: Jane, Sandi, Maryanne, Felicia, J.J., Daphne, and herself. For two years, in the early 1970s, Catherine was closer to these women than to anyone but her daughter.

"Who are they now?" she wonders aloud.

When Jane called a month ago to tell her of the reunion, Catherine knew her voice at once, even though it had been more than a decade since she'd heard it. Jane had been the matriarch, the organizer of

2

the group, though in truth there had never really been any leader at all after that first meeting. Jane was the aspiring artist with a disintegrating marriage and four children. Even seventeen years ago, when the group first met, and Jane was only thirty-two, she'd seemed so much older, wiser than the rest.

Then there was Sandi, who was twenty-eight then, the Jewish princess married to Alan, the rich TV producer, who wanted a doll for a wife. Sandi, who chafed and bristled at her role, who thought she was endlessly depressed and didn't know why, even as she continued to play the maddeningly saccharine part of the cute and bubbly housewife. Until the night in the group when it all clicked for Sandi, and her life seemed to change overnight. Did that marriage survive? Catherine wonders. She remembers a round face framed in long, black, lacquered curls, a tendency to plumpness, a penchant for huge bright-colored sweaters.

Felicia must be coming, of course, says Catherine. Jane had said she was still living in New York. Felicia will have done well for herself, Catherine muses. She remembers Felicia's taut ambition and restless drive, and how being in the group seemed to put it all together for her. Felicia must be thirty-nine. Catherine wonders if she ever married, ever had children. Felicia was, of all of them, the most striking: Catherine remembers her thick blond hair, her somber gray eyes, her serious mien.

They were all so different, Catherine remembers—different religions, different classes, different ethnic backgrounds, even different races. J.J. was the only black woman in the group—with them and separate from them, sometimes politically edgy, sometimes, without warning, challenging them on issues of race. Yet she was always sharp and witty, a tease, her laugh exploding when something tickled her. J.J. was then a graduate student in political science at New York University. Catherine remembers a tiny woman who loved music and lived alone. She remembers that J.J. had a special fondness for Beethoven—even in that era of Stevie Wonder and Diana Ross.

Maryanne, Catherine recalls, liked to listen to classical music too. It was something that she and J.J. shared. Maryanne was a brunette like Sandi, but thin and wispy, seemingly insubstantial, the perennial graduate student—science? Catherine can't remember—always fragile, in her personality and in her mannerisms. Catherine remembers with a shudder the night Maryanne told them of the horrifying rape. "It was right here, in this neighborhood," she says, glancing at the darkened park, where today junkies and dealers conduct business.

And will Daphne come? she wonders. Daphne, the would-be poet with the Botticelli face and hair, and her gold granny glasses. Who could forget Daphne? She was both the most radiant and the most radical of them all—out nights to Progressive Labor meetings, organizing union protests. And then, halfway into their first year together, she announced that she was a lesbian, and all of them had been struck nearly dumb for the first time in the history of their meetings. Whatever had become of Daphne?

And then, of course, there was herself: a single parent at twenty-four, even as she is now, and struggling then to make it on her own with an infant in the city. She'd been a substitute English teacher because her father had insisted she get a teaching certificate in college and she, a refugee from a hideous early marriage, didn't know how else to make money. Well, she's a businesswoman now, with her own bookstore just off Harvard Square in Cambridge, and her child is grown—a tall, intelligent daughter in her first year of college. But Catherine often thinks to herself that if it hadn't been for the group, she'd have gone under for certain.

She drops her cigarette to the sidewalk, steps on it, puts her hands in the pockets of her raincoat, and walks down the block to the old graceful building.

"I used to love these women," she says.

In the early years of the 1970s—the beginnings of the "Me" decade, the era of Nixon and Watergate, the desperate last years of Vietnam—a phenomenon known as consciousness-raising swept the country. Tens of thousands of women came together in small groups to find out exactly what it meant to be female in America. They sought to identify, through the principle of commonality, the ways in which they were defined by a sexist culture. In doing so, they attempted to resolve emotional as well as practical conflicts, to educate themselves as feminists, and, in some cases, to become politically active in the Women's Movement.

Imagine, if you will, a darkened landscape with two or three small fires burning in New York City, Cambridge, Massachusetts, and Berkeley, California. Then picture these tiny fires spreading, seemingly igniting on their own, to Santa Fe, New Mexico; St. Paul, Minnesota; and Portland, Maine. And then envision the entire country igniting in one great whoosh to become a blaze—and you will then have some idea of the magnitude and speed of the consciousness-raising phenomenon and the pivotal part it had to play in the feminist movement.

It is important to realize at the outset that the essentially grass-roots phenomenon of consciousness-raising (or "CR," as it came to be called) and the Women's Movement, an amalgam of both radical and mainstream organizations, ideas and advocates, were not synonymous. While both shared a common goal of liberating women in a sexist culture, one was a political movement, while the other (CR) was a process. Although most members of the Women's Movement did at one time or another try CR (and although many CR groups were composed of committed feminists), some women who joined CR groups never considered themselves part of the Women's

Movement at all. Many thought of themselves as merely getting together with other like-minded women, with no pressing political agenda. Others were threatened by the more sensational aspects of the Women's Movement as reported in the media (such as the advocacy of all-female communes or bra-burning, the latter of which apparently never actually took place), but not by the idea of women meeting in living rooms. Still others were drawn into the movement through the process of CR.

Yet though the two were not synonymous, CR's impact on the movement was extraordinary. Although CR did not develop until four years after the publication of Betty Friedan's *The Feminine Mystique* in 1963 (a milestone loosely regarded as the beginning of the Women's Movement) and did not become widespread until 1970, it is nevertheless accurate to say that without CR, the movement simply would not have been as powerful. It would not have entered so quickly into the mainstream, nor would it have harnessed the large numbers of middle-class women that it did. In the year 1973 alone, some 100,000 women belonged to CR groups nationwide—making it one of the largest ever educational and support movements of its kind for women in the history of this country.

Where the very first small fire of CR was kindled is largely a matter of debate—but first it is necessary to understand the conditions that made CR possible, indeed so desirable.

The Second Sex by Simone de Beauvoir had been published in America in 1953, and the birth control pill had been approved for mass-market use in 1960, but it wasn't until *The Feminine Mystique* appeared that large numbers of American women were galvanized by the notion of their own liberation from the stultifying and limiting adult role into which they had been cast. In her book, Friedan identified the "feminine mystique" as a potent but hollow image that had trapped women within the confines of their homes, relegated them to tasks that were not valued by society at large, and which, in turn, caused women to doubt their self-worth and to find expression through fatigue and depression. She called it "the problem that ha[d] no name" because it had been kept silent for decades.

With the publication of her book, Friedan tapped into a rich vein of frustration. The job description of the American housewife had, almost since its inception, been dismissed by society. According to any standard of measure by which we value occupations—assigning a salary, title, or status—that of the housewife would seem to have no value at all. (In one official Labor Department ranking of jobs according to the complexity of tasks required, homemaker got the same ranking as parking-lot attendant.) Even when the job was the norm among women, women said they suffered from a lack of self-esteem. Studies from the 1950s showed housewives to be a distressed group, vulnerable to depression and feelings of uselessness.[1]

Historically, the notion of the middle-class home, in which the woman's role is primarily that of a support to her husband and children, is a relatively recent phenomenon, having developed in the mid-nineteenth century. Although many women, ever since the Industrial Revolution, have never been able to leave the factories (and there has always been a significant portion of women from the working class who have worked outside the home in low-paying jobs), the exclusive job of middle-class women became that of caring for men and children in the home. So entrenched did this notion become that a peculiar ideology arose: Women, and women only, were uniquely qualified to raise children and protect the home from the corruption of society.

Despite this new ideology, however, women could be shuttled in and out of the labor force if needed. The World War II propaganda image of Rosie the Riveter comes to mind. Women were hired during both World Wars to fill jobs vacated by men and to take on the increasing number of "pink-collar" jobs (clerks, typists, secretaries, and receptionists) that were developing as a result of post-industrial capitalism.[2] But, particularly after World War II, women were sent home— this time to a landscape specifically designed for the post-war family: suburbia. They were not needed and not wanted in the work force—except in pink-collar jobs—and the old ideology that women's place was in the home, which had proved so successful in keeping them there in Victorian society, once again became a nearly patriotic imperative for American women.

For these women, Friedan's book was a powerful catalyst. But it is doubtful it would have so inspired women if certain important social and economic factors were not already in place by 1963: the rise of a consumer society and the subsequent inability of one paycheck to pay for appliances, furniture, and two cars—not to mention college educations for growing children; runaway inflation; the post–World War II higher-educational attainment of women; and the tendency, made possible by the discovery and marketing of oral contraceptives, to delay childbearing and to have fewer children.

Also occurring nearly simultaneously was the emergence of the radical left on college campuses, growing out of the Civil Rights Movement of the early and turbulent 1960s— and, in particular, the splintering off from this radical left of leftist women's groups. As early as 1965, female members of the Student Nonviolent Coordinating Committee (SNCC) had begun publicly to bristle at their subservient role within the Civil Rights Movement. Many of the women interviewed for this book recalled that their own political educations began in college with membership in campus leftist groups, such as SNCC or SDS (Students for a Democratic Society), only to discover that women and women's issues were often dismissed out of hand, or worse, derided. Women were asked to make coffee, to type newsletters and to paint posters, but were often excluded from participation in important political matters. In 1966, women demanding equal rights were booed out of the national SDS conference. Expelled from the leadership of leftist radical groups (or feeling that their concerns would never be properly addressed), women began forming their own exclusively female groups.

Into this arena—that of the economic, social, and biological forces that were allowing women to leave the home; that of the recognition of "the problem that has no name"; and that of the emerging women's groups—came CR. As early as 1966 and 1967, groups of radical women were beginning to form what were then called "rap sessions" and "bitch sessions." These meetings evolved from the practice of self-critical sessions in small groups among the radical left. The radical left had themselves borrowed this technique from the Maoist Chinese practice: "Speak pains to recall pains." It is thought that this practice may have made the transition from radical politics to sexual politics on its way north from Tampa, Florida, to New York City, when a group of university women from Tampa (who were disenchanted with the male-dominated radical left) came to New York in 1967. There, the practice was adopted by a group known as the New York Radical Women.

9

The first formal introduction of CR into the Women's Movement appears to have taken place on Thanksgiving Day, 1968, when 200 women from thirty-seven states and Canada met in Chicago for the first national women's liberation conference. (By this date, nationwide, Congress had passed Title VII of the Civil Rights Act which forbade sex discrimination in places of employment; The National Organization for Women (NOW) had been formed; and women attending the March on Washington to protest the Vietnam War had marched under a banner that read "Sisterhood Is Powerful.") At this meeting in Chicago, a paper entitled "A Program for Feminist 'Consciousness Raising' " was presented. Already the New York Radical Women had found themselves the target of ridicule by other female members of the radical left for using CR in their meetings: Their sessions were called "hen parties" and were derided as being "trivial" and "nonpolitical" (as indeed the issues themselves had been called by men). The paper they delivered, then, was an attempt to defend themselves against these charges. In it they stated, among other things: "We assume that our feelings . . . mean something worth analyzing . . . that our feelings are saying something *political*. . . . Our feelings will lead us to ideas and then to actions."[3]

From the beginning, the practice of CR was controversial. Eventually it would split the New York Radical Women into two factions—those who defended the practice and those who dismissed it as being only partially effective. In 1969, the advocates of CR joined the newly formed feminist group Redstockings, which shortly became known primarily for its advocacy of CR and its articulation and promotion. By July 1969, the now-famous Redstockings Manifesto included the following statement:

10

"We regard our personal experience, and our feelings about that experience, as the basis for an analysis of our common situation. We cannot rely on existing ideologies, as they are all products of male supremacist culture. We question every generalization and accept none that are not confirmed by our experience.

"Our chief task at present is to develop female class consciousness through sharing experience and publicly exposing the sexist foundation of all our institutions. Consciousness-raising is not 'therapy,' which implies the existence of individual solutions and falsely assumes that the male-female relationship is purely personal, but the only method by which we can ensure that our program for liberation is based on the concrete realities of our lives.

"The first requirement for raising class consciousness is honesty, in private and in public, with ourselves and other women."[4]

The practice spread rapidly. By 1970, there were small women's groups, most of which met for the practice of CR, in every major city in the country. New York City alone had hundreds of such groups. Most universities were forming CR groups. Even high schools were organizing.

The practice harnessed not just urban radical women, but suburban women as well. Indeed, it is among suburban women that the phenomenon appeared to be needed the most urgently and attracted the greatest numbers. United by sex and by geography, women in groups of five to fifteen found their way to CR, either through the auspices of the National Organization for Women, through other feminist collectives, or by word of mouth. One woman might hear about CR from a friend; another might see a flyer announcing a general organizational meeting in a suburban storefront; still others heard of start-up meetings over the radio.

By 1972, the concept of CR had begun to come under the umbrella of the National Organization for Women, which clearly outlined CR's purposes: to break down the barriers between women, encourage open communication among them, and help them develop pride in their sex. Some individuals, it was understood, would use the insights gained in CR solely in their personal lives without becoming active in the Women's Movement. But from the beginning, one of the primary tenets of CR was *The personal is political.* By seeing the common threads that united all the women in the room, women would then begin to have some awareness—or *consciousness*—of the political nature of their problems. It was hoped that the collective experience of CR would radicalize many of the women and encourage them to become agents for change.

By and large, CR appealed primarily to white women of the middle class, although some groups formed in working-class neighborhoods. (One group that formed in a working-class neighborhood of the Jamaica Plain section of Boston in the early 1970s still continues to meet today.) There are several reasons why CR (and indeed, the Women's Movement itself) tended to be predominantly white and middle class. White middle-class women had more leisure time than women of the working class and underclass—many of whom were holding down full-time jobs to support themselves and their families. Also, CR often tended to spring up, as had the radical left movement before it, on college campuses—and the majority of women there were from the white middle class. And among older women, harnessed in suburbia, their population, too, tended to be predominantly white and middle class. They, more than the women of the working class and underclass, were familiar with "the problem that has no name."

Some black women and other minority women joined CR groups, but their numbers were limited—largely confined to black women on college campuses. For them, it was a matter of divided loyalties. Although black women's liberation groups did exist, they were, for the most part, concerned with issues of race.[5]

A number of CR groups quickly became radical in orientation; still others were primarily concerned with lesbian politics. Most groups, however, were composed of women from the mainstream—women who were actually fairly new to feminism.

Almost all successful CR groups followed a format—or something similar to a format—that had been finely tuned as the process passed from the New York Radical Women, to the New York Radical Feminists, to the Redstockings, and on to NOW. A topic from a prepared list was selected for each meeting. In order to establish trust and intimacy in their groups, the format advised that women begin with nonthreatening issues, such as childhood experiences, before moving into the heavies—first sexual encounters and feelings about abortion. Each woman was allowed "free space" to talk for as long as she liked without interruption. Women who were, by nature, reticent, therefore had as much opportunity to speak as women who were inclined to run the show. Sometimes there were tears and expressions of anger. Sometimes there was the release of communal laughter. Sometimes there were shocking revelations, when one or another confessed to having been abused as a child, or to having been raped. And occasionally, when the format was abandoned or when certain personalities in the group became dominant, CR meetings

13

degenerated into pseudo group-therapy sessions. But mostly there was, for women who had all their lives been told to be good and deferential, the freedom to say what was on their minds, and the comforting realization that they were all in this together.

By 1972 and 1973—the heyday of the CR experience nationwide—the Women's Movement was coming into its own. The term *sexism* had been coined; the Equal Employment Opportunity Commission (EEOC) had issued guidelines forbidding discriminatory want ads; *Ms. Magazine* had appeared; and the U.S. Supreme Court had legalized abortion, to name but a few of the many important milestones for women in that era. Women's history departments—following fast on the heels of black history departments—were emerging at college campuses all across the country. Women had marched in Washington and down Fifth Avenue in New York City for equal pay for equal work, and were demonstrating at suburban malls. After a period of dormancy beginning in the 1920s—including the devastatingly "silent" 1950s—the Women's Movement was rapidly becoming mainstream news.

And by 1972, the year that Catherine and Jane and the others were coming together to form their own CR group in New York's Greenwich Village, consciousness-raising—a woman-by-woman, systematic program of education—was among the Women's Movement's highest priorities. Social change was not possible, it was argued, until women clearly understood why they were oppressed and how. CR was viewed as a valuable, indeed, *essential* tool, that would, in turn, give individual women tools with which to go forward in their own lives. By realizing that an individual problem was in reality a common problem, and by discovering that the personal was really collective, a woman might begin to understand how a sexist society had limited her opportunities.

To a large extent, CR did what it was intended to do. Although each woman's experience in CR was unique, and although each group differed in character, goals, and composition, it is nevertheless accurate to say that the process was extraordinarily successful at the time. Not only did it transform the lives of most of the women who participated, but it also did so for millions of women who did not participate but who benefited from the phenomenon as feminist thinking began to pervade the culture. Indeed, much of the "basic training" that was accomplished in small consciousness-raising groups is now simply taken for granted. From the isolation of unhappy marriages, missed and lost opportunities, traditionally inhibiting expectations, and misinformation about a number of vital issues ranging from sex to self-esteem, women came together and found, in their commonality, the confidence to go out into the world and test new ways of being female. Critical areas of adulthood—sexuality, marriage, work, and motherhood—were forever changed for many of the women who emerged from CR.

■

Catherine rings the doorbell to Jane's apartment. Her breath is tight, her pulse is racing. The door opens a crack. Catherine sees the side of a face, an eye. Then the door opens wide and fast. Each woman says the other's name, and Catherine is immediately enveloped in a large green sweater. The two women stand back at arm's length to examine each other. Catherine searches for a spark of recognition in the familiar/not familiar face. Jane's hair is entirely gray now, still worn long in a bun at the nape of her neck, and it is evident to Catherine that she has aged a great deal over the last fifteen years. Her expression, however, is exuberant.

"You look great."

"You look great."

"Oh, look at you!"

"Cathy!"

"You haven't changed a bit!"

"Don't be silly. Of course, I have. But you. You haven't changed a bit."

They move into the hallway, and before Catherine even has her coat off, the doorbell rings again. Jane opens the door at once, eagerly anticipating who might be coming next. Catherine will later say that the next several minutes were a blur of short, sharp shocks. Daphne, in a long cape, towers over J.J. The two have met each other in the elevator. Now there is a chorus of greetings. Jane hugs Daphne, who is balancing a tray of hors d'oeuvres. J.J., who is carrying two bottles of wine, smiles broadly at Catherine. Suddenly J.J. hears a sound behind her and lets out a great whoop. "Holy shit!" she says. "Look at Maryanne! She's pregnant!"

The women back into Jane's hallway like a protective phalanx around Maryanne's protruding belly. Maryanne's once-thin hair is shoulder length and permed. She, too, is smiling hugely, as if she'd won a prize.

Then, without warning, Felicia is at the door behind Maryanne. She is wearing an expensive raincoat; her blond hair is expertly cut and tossed to one side. She has on mauve lipstick and calf-length wine leather boots. Jane turns and sees her. She walks toward Felicia, and the two women embrace. The women stand in the hallway in the throes of emotions they have anticipated for weeks, but now don't know what to do with.

The elevator door opens. Blue eyes peek out from under a fringe of black curls; a brilliant smile lights up the corridor. Sandi spreads her arms wide. For a moment, she seems not to recognize Felicia, who is standing in front of her, but when she sees Catherine, she lifts her into the air and dances with her for a moment in the hallway.

16

"I came to the apartment like a dog going home for supper."

"My heart was pounding in the elevator. I thought I'd have a heart attack."

"Am I thinner?"

"You've always been thin."

"I love your skirt."

"You cut your hair."

"When did you get a permanent?"

"We said we wouldn't talk about how we looked, and it's all we've said," says Jane, and everyone laughs.

The women form pods of twos and threes between the hallway and the kitchen, exchanging news of each other, hugging and touching spontaneously, and then changing partners, as in an intricate dance pattern. Like several of the other women, Catherine has pictures with her. She shows snapshots of both her daughter and her bookstore. The women, who have known Catherine's daughter only as a baby and then as a toddler, are astonished by the tall young woman in the photographs.

Catherine, giddy like the others, is talking too fast. She learns that J.J. has come up from Washington, D.C., where she works for a senator now. She's been married twice and has two young sons. Felicia is still in New York—she's an investment banker; her husband is a lawyer on Wall Street. The couple have a two-year-old son. Jane and her husband were divorced shortly after the group disbanded, and then they remarried ten years ago. She sells real estate part time now; and she no longer paints, she says. Catherine reels with this information, trying to process it, even as she's accosted by Sandi, who has more. Sandi has flown all the way from Los Angeles, where she and Alan—remember her husband Alan? she asks—live. She's a lawyer, an associate with a firm in Beverly Hills. Her children are teen-agers—one is grown, gone like Catherine's daughter. Catherine *hears someone exclaim "Cleveland!" and overhears Maryanne telling Felicia that she's been married just a year and is working as a computer analyst in Cleveland; her husband Bill owns his own construction company. In the kitchen, Catherine finds Daphne. Daphne still smokes, too, Catherine is relieved to see, and the two make disparaging jokes about each other, but when she tries to talk to Daphne, the other woman is strangely evasive, making only small nervous comments about how long it's been and about how much they've all changed.*

As if the dance had been choreographed, the women begin to make their way, with plates of food, into the sunken living room, where they settle themselves around a long, low coffee table, some on the floor, others on the sofa and in the deep armchairs. The room is a large one with high ceilings and with a view through the casement windows to Washington Place below. Later, Catherine will say that the room feels very different than it did fifteen years ago when the women sometimes met here—and as Catherine finds herself a chair, she tries to determine why: The hanging plants are still in the corner, and the red orientals are still on the floor, but there's no easel now by the window, no paintings of Jane's on the walls. No children's toys hastily stashed in the corners, either.

Nevertheless, sitting in this configuration reminds Catherine of being in this room fifteen years ago and of what they used to do here. Apparently it reminds several of the other women, too.

"Remember the discussions we had about sex?"

"Remember them! They changed my life. I'm not kidding. You ask my husband."

"Seriously, though," says Sandi, "the group really changed my life."

"Me, too."

"Absolutely."

"There was love in that group."

"*I used to think I might have died without it,*" *says Maryanne.* "*There's been nothing like it in my life ever since.*"

"*Women are more guarded now.*"

"*I think we're all more guarded now.*"

"*I don't think younger women today discuss the same things we did in the group.*"

"*I think the attitudes we questioned are still very much in place today.*"

"*I still feel I have to smile all the time.*"

"*I still feel that all of my life has to be positive.*"

"*It was because of the times.*"

"*I could definitely do it again.*"

"*I don't have* time *to do it again.*"

Several of the women laugh and nod their heads in agreement. Maryanne pours herself another glass of wine. Jane pulls her legs up under her on the couch. Felicia, balancing her plate on her knees, delicately cuts a piece of chicken. Catherine wants to light a cigarette, but doesn't.

"*I think we should pick a topic and have a meeting just like we used to,*" *says Sandi, breaking the silence.*

"*I don't see how we could have a real meeting,*" *says J.J.* "*I'm not sure I'd be able to do that after so many years.*"

"*Well, I have an idea,*" *says Jane.* "*After all, it was me who got you all here. And I'll tell you why. Aside from the sheer pleasure of seeing you all again, I've been thinking lately about the group and what it all meant. Recently I was talking about it to a friend and trying to describe it to her. She asked me what had happened to you all, and I realized I didn't know, and somehow that didn't feel good. I started to get very curious about what's happening now to all of us. So maybe we could talk about that? Perhaps we could each say a few words about how we feel about where we are right now.*"

19

The women think for a minute about Jane's suggestion, and there is a murmur of agreement.

Then there is a long silence.

And then an even longer silence.

"Well, we seem to have our same old problem," says Maryanne, laughing. "Who wants to start?"

"I'll start," says Felicia. "I've been thinking about this, too."

She puts her plate down and settles back into the chair. She is wearing a long, slim black wool-crepe suit with a white silk blouse and a string of pearls. She looks as though she has just come from an important meeting at a large investment-banking house, which is, in fact, the case. Catherine recalls the tie-dyed shirts and jeans Felicia used to wear, her hair parted in the middle and hanging to her shoulders. As if she is reading Catherine's thoughts, Felicia tilts her head to one side and runs her fingers through her hair. It is a nervous gesture Catherine recognizes at once. Some things, she thinks, never change.

"I'm operating as a woman on two fronts," says Felicia, "at work and at home. At work, I'm doing very well. I'm responsible for a three hundred fifty million dollar portfolio. I know I'm highly respected. But no matter how well I do, I'll tell you this—we're still shut out at the top. I've gone about as high as I can go. And I'm a little troubled, too, by what I see as a new kind of competition among women at my level. Sometimes I think we've bought into the masculine way of doing things perhaps a little too much. I don't have relationships with women where there's a lot of trust right now. I have professional, networking kinds of relationships, but it doesn't feel the same. In fact, until I walked into this room tonight, I think I'd forgotten just how very different it feels. And I've been realizing, as I've been sitting here, that I really do miss women. . . ."

She leans back and crosses her legs. Always, even in jeans years ago, there was an elegance and delicacy to Felicia's movements that

Catherine always admired, even envied. "At home," Felicia says, "my problem right now is trying to balance everything. I think this is a very difficult time for women." She sighs.

"When we were in the group, we all got very excited by all these new opportunities, and we began to really think, for the first time ever, about having serious and important careers. But we didn't get a chance to figure out what happens after you get the career. I have a full-time job. My husband has a full-time job. We have a home. And now we have a young child. When my son was born, I was afraid I'd resent my baby. That didn't happen. He comes first, and I love him more than my own life. But does that mean I should give up the career? I'm always torn. I feel like I never give anyone or anything enough: There's not enough time to be a mother; I have no time at all for my husband. Our marriage is stressful because of this. I feel sometimes like I'm cheating the people I work with. There's a lot expected of me."

Felicia turns slightly in her chair. "And the interesting thing is: I don't see men being expected to do all these same things," she says. "A lot has changed for women, and a lot hasn't. As far as I can see, women have simply taken on more. And more. And more. I'm happy I got to live in an era when I was allowed to achieve so much and to be so successful, but I'm not sure that we aren't submerged again because of the heaviness of the load."

A serious silence settles over the group. It is, however, a familiar silence—the same silence that came after each woman in the group, in the old days, gave her testimony. The rules were simple: Each woman could speak for as long as she liked. When she was finished, no one could comment or criticize. Each woman's statement was an entity unto itself, but Catherine was often amazed at the way in which, by the end of the evening, a tapestry had been woven.

In the silence someone says, "Next?"

"I'll go next," says Jane. She tucks her legs up even closer under

her body. She is wearing a denim skirt. Her feet are bare. Her face is heavily lined, and Catherine is suddenly worried for her health. Jane looks down at the floor. "When I was in the group," she says, "I was fighting for survival. The truth is, I'm still fighting for survival."

She looks up at them and coincidentally meets Catherine's eyes. "Richard and I got divorced, as some of you may know," says Jane, "but I just found it too difficult to raise four children by myself in the city with no real training, no real way to make any money. Being divorced was horrible; it was a very difficult time for me. So, ten years ago, Richard and I remarried—mostly for the children's sakes. When we remarried, I understood I was reentering a traditional marriage, and I agreed to that, so to speak."

Jane turns her head and looks out the window. "Sometimes this has been very difficult," she says quietly. "I don't think a lot of women would have made that decision. But I knew my limitations. I try to keep a sense of joy in my household. I have given of myself totally as a parent, and I don't regret a minute of it. I have given to Richard; he has needed a lot of attention and emotional maintenance. But I have a great deal of pain in the area of my career. There has been a lot of talk lately about the importance of careers for women and the importance of success. Success with a capital S. And I've failed. Pure and simple. I believe I had a gift, but I haven't channeled it. I couldn't pursue my art the way I wanted to do it, so I gave it up for a home and a family. Recently, I got my broker's license, and I've been doing some part-time real estate, to try to help put the kids through college. But it's not the same as having achieved something of your own. I know that.

"And yet," she says, turning back to the group, "even though I live this way of life—and maybe some of you will find this shocking— I still think of myself as a feminist. I'd even go so far as to say I'm

an ardent feminist. I will never give up my consciousness. I don't think you can. I've tried to impart my values to my children. We've been talking about the elections now for weeks—about who will do more for women. This is very important to me."

Jane stops. For a moment, Catherine finds it hard to meet her steady gaze. She is not used to this. She is amazed at the caliber of honesty, even after all these years. But she feels it, too—a kind of hunger finally to be able to say what she's been thinking. It's been so long since she's heard women share thoughts like this. She wonders if she'd have been able to make the same kind of accommodations as Jane, but she already knows the answer. She wouldn't have. If so, she'd have been married years ago.

"It's hard to go next after what Jane has just said," says Sandi, who is, typically, sprawled all over the rest of the couch. No longer the princess with the lacquered curls, Sandi, Catherine notices, has short wash-and-wear hair like most of the rest of them. Sandi has flown in from L.A. and is staying with her parents in the city. Although she is still plump, she has aged the least of all of them, Catherine is thinking. She barely looks a day older than when they disbanded the group.

"But since I'm sitting next to Jane," says Sandi, "I guess it's my turn." She takes a deep breath.

"My life did change," she says. "You were there. And my marriage changed. Dramatically. The way it happened was that I made the changes in my own life first, and then things sort of fell into place. I decided I would go back to school. I decided I would become economically independent. I decided I would never again be available nonstop for Alan and the kids. And I give Alan a lot of credit. A lot of marriages might have fallen apart: This wasn't what he bargained for, right? But he listened, and I think he saw the sense of it. Sure, we still have some of the old power struggles we always *had—I think we'll fight about money until we die—but* I'm *different, and so the marriage is different. I think it's a very good marriage; we've worked a lot out."*

Sandi, *by now lying on her back on the couch, looks up at the ceiling. "We have three children now," she says. "Two are still at home in high school. Our lives are very busy: Alan's work is demanding; I'm working as an associate in a law firm. Finishing law school with three kids wasn't that easy either. But I'd never give up that degree for anything. Our kids roll with the punches. They do their share. I think they're proud of their parents."*

Sandi *suddenly sits up. "Like Jane, I think of myself as an ardent feminist, though frankly, I can't tell you the last time someone mentioned feminism to me, and I'm sometimes amazed at how many people—women, too—think of feminism as a dirty word. But I have so much* gratitude.

"And what I really want to say is thank you. Thank you all.*" She spreads her arms wide. "If it hadn't been for this group, I honestly don't believe any of it would have happened."*

They spontaneously clap. This never happened before in regular meetings. But Catherine knows why they have applauded: She, like the rest of the women, feels very proud of Sandi. She remembers what Sandi was like when she first joined the group—a Barbie Doll with a massive inferiority complex. Sandi is a walking advertisement for the success of CR.

"Everything is stirred up in me hearing you talk," says Maryanne, who is sitting next to Sandi. Catherine looks at Maryanne. She can't get over how much she has changed. Maryanne—an anemic waif now blossoming with rude health and happiness.

"My life has been filled with struggles on so many fronts," says Maryanne, resting her folded arms over her large stomach. "Yet I feel I may be on track now. When I was in the group, I had such an uncertain sense of self. It's taken me years to begin to know myself.

24

A lot of things fell apart on me, and I've had to put them all back together. I thought I would be an academic, a professor, but after years of graduate school, the job just wasn't there. I can't say for sure if it wasn't there because I was a woman. I just don't know. I've taken a job in computers. It's okay, not great, but I can live with it. I was alone for a long time. I don't know if those of you who have husbands can know what that was like, but it was very difficult. Despite everything we talked about in the group, I always felt like something was wrong with me because I didn't have a man. I thought I would be alone forever. And then I met Bill, and finally, at thirty-nine, I got married. Now I'm pregnant. We even have a house: Me, *if you can believe it, settled down in a house. So even though there continue to be struggles, I think, hey, maybe this is it. Maybe everything's okay now."*

J.J. leans over and pats Maryanne's stomach. "Well, honey," she says in an exaggerated drawl she sometimes used to put on when she was teasing someone, "you sure are looking *okay." Everyone laughs. Catherine has always liked this supportive quality of J.J.'s—even though such comments weren't, strictly speaking, within the rules. The difficulty was, if you were supportive of one woman's testimony, but not of the next's, might not that second woman feel bad?*

"So," says J. J., leaning back as if for a deep think, "Where are we at?"

J.J. has put on some weight, Catherine sees. She is wearing a navy blue suit and a red blouse, as if she, too, had just come from work. She wears her hair natural as she did in 1972, but now it is parted on the side and shiny, like Michael Jackson's. J.J. has come up on the train and has said that she's staying with her family in Queens for the night.

"Well, personally *speaking," she says, "I'm at a good place. I'm on my second marriage, but my second marriage is a good one. I don't take any shit from him, and he doesn't take any from me either.*

We've got two beautiful boys—six and four, a handful, I don't have to tell some of you. I'm working. Life's okay. Personally, *I've got no problems. No complaints." She shakes her head back and forth and then stops.*

"But if you ask me how are things for women," she continues, "I'm gonna tell you right now, from where I see them, they're in pretty bad shape." She sits forward and enumerates the ways on her fingers. "I see a lot of single parents; I see a lot of women who can't make it economically; I see a lot of women with no child care; I see a lot of women who are being exploited by other women, women like us, for example; I see a lot of women who are losing it and abusing their kids. You ask me how things are for these women, and I have to tell you: I don't know if the Women's Movement has made a particle of difference in their lives. We still got a shitload of problems to solve."

Catherine notices that many of the other women are nodding their heads. J.J. has always had this way of reminding them of the bigger picture, and without her they'd have missed out on important political insights when they were in the group. She appears to have lost her edginess, however. Catherine wonders if it is age, the times, or simply having settled in with a family and children that has mellowed J.J.

Catherine is aware that the other women are watching her. She sits up a little straighter, puts her hand to the nape of her neck— her own nervous gesture. It is hard following J.J. It was always hard following J.J. Somehow J.J.'s concerns always seemed so much more global than the others, even though that, too, was against the rules. The point was to talk about oneself. The personal is political. *Though that doesn't seem to matter much now.*

"Okay," Catherine says, giving a little smile. "I'll go."

She hugs her knees. She looks at a point somewhere between the coffee table and the sofa.

"On many levels I feel I'm fighting the same battles I was fourteen years ago," she says. "I am a woman raising a child. I'm struggling.

26

I've always struggled. Now that my daughter has just left home, I'm beginning to have a sense of finishing my work. It was a lot of hard work, and a lot of aggravation, but I'm proud of what I've done."

Catherine is proud, and she had wanted to say that. It has been her most impressive accomplishment, she believes. But that work is mostly over.

"Now I don't know what I want anymore," she says, "as a woman. I'm alone now, and I like being alone, yet I still think, after all these years, that I should be in a relationship. I'm forty. I find that frightening. I read the statistics about the small percentage of women over forty who do get married. And yet I don't want to marry the men that I meet. I think about aging. I worry about losing my looks. Maybe I will be old and alone. I don't have a nest egg—all the money that I saved is going for my daughter's education."

She looks up at the other women. They are watching her intently. Felicia has her elbows on her knees, her hands folded under her chin. J.J. has her arms folded across her breasts. Sandi, with her feet up on the couch, is holding her ankles. Catherine can hear a siren.

"Sometimes I think about other women," she says, "but most of the time I don't anymore. I guess I'm too selfish, too caught up in my own little life: My daughter, the bookstore, managing the business. As I've told most of you earlier tonight, I'm co-owner of a bookstore near Harvard Square. It's been a huge undertaking for me. I got into it ten years ago when I had a relationship with a man who agreed to put up the money if I took on the responsibility of managing it. Gradually I've worked my way up to a half-share. The romantic relationship didn't work out (he's married now), but the business partnership has thrived. For ten years, I've been in charge and have built the store up from a little hole in the wall to a literary shop with a good reputation.

"Sometimes feminist issues crop up at work; I'm a boss, and I have men working for me, answering to me. It's interesting. But I don't

feel part of a cohesive group anymore. I don't worry about feminist issues the way I used to. I'll say straight out to anyone, with no hesitation, I'm a feminist—but I don't feel active and I don't really feel like I belong to any large important thing. In many ways, I think we're all isolated again. Perhaps not as desperately isolated as women used to be. But I don't think very many women I know think in terms of a common struggle anymore. I look at younger women, the women coming along in our wake, and they seem to take it all for granted. I think they regard the Women's Movement as historical, like we used to regard World War Two. And yet the problems, the issues are still there. It's all around us, everywhere we look. It's the women still giving up their jobs, not the men. It's the women at home with the sick kids, not the men. It's the women who are still making less money than their male co-workers. . . . The list goes on.

"I don't know what's happening with women right now. And I don't know what will become of me." She leans forward and flicks an imaginary speck off her shoe. She hasn't told them that she is just coming off yet another disastrous relationship and that she continues to be attracted to the wrong men. And she knows she won't. Perhaps if there were another meeting, another time. . . .

When she has finished, she sits quite still. She knows that no one will respond. That's the freedom—to be able to speak without fear of criticism. There is a rustle of cloth somewhere over by the sofa. The siren, actually two now, appears to be closer. Someone coughs— Maryanne? She hears the clink of silverware on a plate, the pouring of wine into a glass. She has always found it difficult to meet the gaze of the others when she has finished speaking, but when she looks up, she realizes that everyone is staring not at her, but at Daphne. She turns to look at the woman beside her and is momentarily stunned. Daphne, inexplicably, is tearing her napkin into dozens of tiny fragments. Jade-green tears—the color of Daphne's eyeliner—are making distinct rivulets along her cheeks.

"There's a feeling in my throat," Daphne says haltingly. "It's very special to me to be sitting here . . . . I feel we've all come so far, accomplished so much . . . but . . ." She looks up at the others, the pieces of the torn napkin at her feet.

Catherine feels the stillness in the room. It is a familiar stillness, one she felt dozens of times fifteen years ago. They are watching Daphne, but they are with her, too. No one moves or speaks. Daphne must finish her sentence.

"We've come so far," Daphne says simply, gesturing toward them with open palms. Then suddenly she clenches her fists, a flash of anger moving through her. "But sometimes," she says, taking them all in with a sweep of her gaze, "aren't you all just a little bit overwhelmed by how far we still have to go?"

■

They wore jeans and sat in a circle. They drank coffee and talked about anger. They spoke, for the first time, about body image and about sexism, and they realized, with relief, that they were not unique and were not alone. In shared details they found commonality; they learned to call themselves women and to trust women and to be women. And after a time, when they had said all of the things they needed to say in that time and in that place, they went away from each other and out into the world and got married and had children and found jobs and made money. Or didn't get married and didn't have children and didn't find the right job and didn't make enough money. Sometimes they were good at what they did and sometimes they were disappointed, but they all got older and busier and more tired and wiser—and sometimes happier than they thought they would be. Often they forgot about the struggles of other women and thought only of their own. At other times—like a wave moving in and out of their thoughts when there was room or when an issue demanded attention—they remembered the group and what it had felt like and who they had been and how much it had changed them.

By the mid-1970s, most CR groups had disbanded. Consciousness-raising was petering out, victim of a changing political climate, of expanding career opportunities for women, of shifting priorities on the part of the Women's Movement, and of a subsequent lack of a sponsor. As the country became more conservative, the quest for self-knowledge gave way to the pursuit of self-fulfillment. As jobs opened up for white middle-class women, and as they tried to combine careers with family life, the sheer struggle to succeed at mothering and working left little or no time for meeting with, or even thinking about, other women. The Women's Movement, having accomplished a preliminary stage of widespread education, moved reluctantly into a period of latency, shifting its attention from CR on a massive scale to activist issues on a smaller one. The dwindling number of women who have remained involved have found themselves at meetings to organize rape crisis centers or as members of Women Against Pornography. A personalized form of feminism, stemming from that initial basic training gained in CR, has invaded the home and the workplace.

The women who participated in consciousness-raising say they received an invaluable basic training. They developed a fluency about themselves and about women's issues—rather like the fluency a person who has been in therapy develops. They gained a certain kind of clarity about who they were and what they wanted and what the obstacles were to getting it. But most of all, they had respect and trust and love for women that grew out of that cauldron of shared experiences. Stripping away their preconceptions, they learned to have

30

enormous regard for the struggles of other women, even as they were learning to respect themselves.

But times change. And so have the women. In the fifteen or so years that have intervened since women belonged to CR groups, they have left behind them the support and the self-knowledge gained in consciousness-raising and gone out into the real world.

As Catherine wondered on a sidewalk in Manhattan: *What happened to these women? Who are they now?*

For two years, from the spring of 1986 to the fall of 1988, I set out to find the answer to that question. To do so, I tracked down and interviewed sixty-five women who had once belonged to consciousness-raising groups. The women, when I found them, ranged in age from thirty-four to fifty-five. (In 1972, they were between the ages of nineteen and forty.) Some were married; some had never married. Some were divorced; some were single parents. Most of the women had children, whether grown or small, and almost all of the women—with the exception of a few women with children under the age of three—were working. They live today all across the United States, from Los Angeles to Portland, Maine.

Only two women did not want to talk to me about their experiences in their consciousness-raising groups. The rest of the women were extraordinarily forthcoming—far more so, in fact, than has been true of my general experience as an interviewer of both women and men on other subjects. At first, during introductory phone calls to set up interviews, I would be surprised at the level of eagerness and enthusiasm. Later, it became commonplace for me to hear comments such as, "I've been dying to tell someone about this," or, "That group was so important to me; I have so much to say." I began to perceive, as the months wore on, that I had tapped into a mother lode of passion and feeling—one which was being touched by asking them to recall those early days and to speak about how that experience had altered or affected their lives.

The project began for me as an assignment for a magazine, and I confess I came to it through the back door: Its appeal for me was in the universality of that intriguing question—Where are they now? That same intriguing question that makes us go to high-school reunions and causes us to wonder whatever became of "Eleanor" on "Father Knows Best," or Lieutenant Calley. I have always been fascinated by how people's lives pan out after a pivotal event has occurred or a certain milestone has been passed. That the subject was women and feminism merely added to the appeal; it was not at first the point.

It quickly became the point, however. As I listened to the women speak—in their kitchens, in their living rooms, at their places of work—about where they'd been, where they are now, and where they think they're headed, I realized I was hearing heartfelt statements of enormous importance to all women, and that their collective statements were, in effect, a barometer of the legacy of consciousness-raising and of the fortunes of the Women's Movement. Insofar as a random sampling of sixty-five women, who once shared something in common and who once made an effort to educate themselves about women's issues, can tell us anything about women today (and I believe it can), this book is an answer to Catherine's question.

The personal testimony of each woman is as unique as is her personality—but certain disturbing and challenging

32

threads emerge with unmistakable clarity. The most significant and alarming of these is that women are again isolated—ironically, in part, by many of the opportunities made possible by their participation in CR. To be sure, it is not the stultifying isolation of the 1950s and early 1960s, but this new isolation may be no less inhibiting to personal and political growth. While the CR movement created opportunities for women on a widespread scale, it has also created new problems as a result of those very opportunities. Given confidence in their abilities and launched headlong into careers and economic independence as a result of those jobs, women now find they are dizzy with the demands of trying to succeed at work and at home simultaneously. Because simply trying to stay afloat in both endeavors takes nearly all their time, they are unable to join activist causes or meet with other women. Thus, they say they have turned away from a collective focus, coping with whatever conflicts arise on an *ad hoc* individual basis—boss by boss, husband by husband.

In addition to the isolation created by the difficulty of trying to balance work and family life, women today are alone for other reasons as well. Encouraged to demand from men equal participation in relationships, marriage, and family life, many women have subsequently discovered that a feminist perspective has a way of sabotaging relationships with men whose expectations are rooted in traditional roles, and that striving for across-the-board equality can lead to withering power struggles, even in the best of partnerships. The population of women in their thirties, forties, and fifties who are now divorced or never married—alone, some with children—is larger than it has ever been in our history.

While women have made tremendous progress since the early 1970s, many conflicts still remain unresolved. And new issues confront the women of this decade and of the future: the career-family merry-go-around; a search for relief from the burden of working more hours at both family and work tasks than one's mate does; emotional and sexual power struggles in marriage; finding good child care; coping with the role of the single parent; the dilemma of "the sandwich" (being expected, as a woman, to care for both your children and your aging parents at the same time); competition among women in the workplace; one's own aging; the moral dilemma of women exploiting women; and the feminization of poverty, to name but a few. These issues will almost certainly increase in intensity as we turn the corner into the 1990s. It may be that the unique isolation of the 1980s is particularly insidious not only because the lack of leisure time offers no respite from it, but also because, in adopting masculine modes of behavior in order to succeed in the male-dominated workplace, many women are losing much of their belief in the benefits of women's solidarity or women's common wisdom that would make coming together again desirable.

Near the end of my reporting, I interviewed one woman who seemed to me to strike the keynote of all the collective testimonies I'd been given. By the time I spoke with her, what she said was familiar to me—I'd heard it many times over from dozens of other women—but she had a way of putting it that seemed to me to sum up much of what had been said by others. "I don't think we have each other anymore," said Elaine R., a forty-one-year-old instructor of computer sciences at a junior college near her home in Belmont, Massachusetts. Elaine, who is the mother of two teenage girls, belonged to a CR group in Cambridge from 1971 to 1973. "I think that women are divided and alienated from each other now," she said. "Distrustful sounds strong, but I feel

it, and I'm confused. It's like we sit here doing whatever it is
that we as individuals do, wondering what is *she* doing, how
is *she* dealing with it, what does *she* want, what should *I* want.
We are not really talking to each other, except in certain little
isolated pockets: You meet someone you feel you have something in common with and you glom onto her, and for a time
it feels intimate and sympathetic, but it's not enough. It
doesn't let you grapple with these issues on a larger scale.

"Maybe we didn't have each other in the fifties—I wasn't
around then—but I sure feel we don't have each other now,"
Elaine said. "We are divided—the women who are supposedly
successful and career-oriented distrust the women who are
staying home with their kids, and vice versa. I think women
are pretty alienated from each other by issues like this. A lot
of women feel deserted by the women who want to be like
men, and those women, in turn, feel isolated from the women
in their own neighborhoods.

"The apparatus sort of wore itself out, didn't it?" Elaine
asked rhetorically. "There's a whole generation of younger
women coming along who don't have a clue. The women
behind us are not unified. They don't even have a *memory* of
a time when women could be together. I think they're really
in for it. I think they've got a very hard road ahead. They're
just coming up against the issues of motherhood and careers
and marriage and personal and financial power—all of that—
and they don't have anywhere to go to resolve these issues.
I don't know where we are right now, but we're foolish if we
don't come back together."

Come so far, said Daphne at the reunion. *But still so far to
go*. It is a measure of the success of the feminist activism of
the early 1970s that the lessons of CR are now an indelible

part of our lives and that an entire generation of American women have grown up in a society familiar with feminist doctrine. In culture and commerce, the contributions of women, both in general and in particular, are sought and recognized with greater consistency then they were a dozen years ago.

Yet as all idealistic causes must over time, feminism has yielded its intensity to other pressing issues, and it is evident that the Women's Movement has slipped into a period of political dormancy. Today, many of the women who were affected by CR still call themselves feminists; the term suggests a value system to which they still subscribe. But they also tend to divide their lives into three parts: before CR; after CR; and now. And for many of them, the "now" is a cornucopia of mixed blessings.

Consciousness-raising amounted to an organized life-support system that is largely unavailable to women in our society today. When the woman at the reunion says, "There has been nothing like it in my life ever since," she could be speaking for tens of thousands of women who struggle in their daily lives to be feminists but who do so without the once-a-week shot in the arm that characterized consciousness-raising.

In a way, it was a little like telling a child she should learn to ride a bike, buying the bike for the child, convincing her to get on it, then vanishing as she wobbled wildly down the street.

·

It is quarter to one in the morning, and each woman is tired. Daphne has told them her story—a difficult and troubling one of relationships with both women and men, a brief marriage, a son who lives with his father and whom she seldom sees, her part-time work in an art gallery, a nervous breakdown, a long sojourn to Sweden where she recuperated. When Daphne finished speaking, J.J. got up and hugged Daphne for a long time, and Catherine was glad. She thinks how vastly different each of their lives has turned out—Daphne's unhappiness, Jane's marital accommodations, Sandi's exuberance, Felicia's balancing act, J.J.'s no-nonsense success, Maryanne's late good fortune, her own private struggles and rewards—and yet she is struck by how the group seemed, at so many points in the evening, to find that old thread of commonality.

It has been a night of exhausting emotions, and tomorrow's responsibilities remind them that they are not as young as they used to be. Maryanne and Catherine each must catch an early morning flight to get back to work. Felicia has to be up at six with her son; J.J. has to be on a train to Washington by 8:30. It is very hard, however, to leave.

Felicia and Jane speak of starting up another group. Sandi, who must fly back to L.A. soon, proposes that they all write down their addresses. They head toward the hallway. They put on their coats. They embrace for the last time. They say there will be another reunion, but Catherine knows that this is unlikely. They look at their watches and toward the door. Already the pull and tug of their separate lives—of the reality that awaits them daily as mothers, wives, workers, and women—is crowding the edge of their good-byes.

TWO

The Click

Catherine is sitting on a daybed in her third-floor apartment on Marlborough Street in Boston. It is a handsome, tree-lined, Back Bay street, with wide graceful sidewalks and lovely three-storey, brick, bow-fronted townhouses. Catherine's apartment, however, with the exception of its bookcases, is remarkably spare and empty—decorated not much differently from that of a graduate student, the furnishings unmatched and looking decidedly secondhand.

It's noontime on a Saturday, and Catherine won't be going into her bookstore until about three o'clock. She is wearing a green cotton Shaker-knit sweater, a pair of jeans, black lace-up boots. She says that she has slept late, that she's read the paper, that she's been for a walk. Her life is quieter now than she's ever known it.

She was twenty-four, when she first joined her CR group. She had met Jane at a park near her apartment in Greenwich Village. Jane and she both had toddlers then. "That was how you met women when you didn't know anyone—at the park," she says. "Do women still do that?"

After the kids had played, Jane and Catherine would go to a coffee shop and treat themselves to a cup of tea and a muffin. Jane was, for Catherine, her only friend. Catherine and her husband had gone to Philadelphia for the first two years of their marriage—he was in school there, Catherine explains—but when she left him, she returned to New York. Her parents were living then in upstate New York, but she didn't see much of them. They didn't approve of Catherine's having left her marriage. "So Jane was very important to me," says Catherine. "Very, very important, like a lifeline."

Catherine remembers one particular day at the park when Jane seemed especially excited. "I asked her what was happening or something like that," says Catherine, "and she said, 'Everything. It's all happening.' She told me she'd joined a consciousness-raising group, and that there were all these women and they sat around and talked. I must have raised my eyebrows skeptically, because I remember she said, 'No, it's not like that. They really talk.' "

The group met on Tuesday evenings. Jane had told Catherine she thought she could still get in, even though there were nine or ten women already. Catherine, hedging, said she might go. "I remember that Tuesday night vividly," she says. "I had gotten a baby-sitter, and then an hour before the meeting I almost cancelled the baby-sitter. I thought, Why do I want to go do this? I'm not ready for this.

"But I went. I remember walking over very, very slowly. I got there late. And I'll tell you something interesting: It was the only time in the entire two years we met I ever got there late. I walked in and someone was talking. I remember the woman was talking about her breast size. It was very odd. And then the next woman started talking about how she'd always thought she was too fat. She was very beautiful, and I remember thinking, What's she got to complain about? But then, I began to notice, as the women talked, that it didn't matter how they actually looked—each of them thought there was something wrong with her. It was exactly *how I'd felt, how I was*

feeling then. I've always agonized over my breast size—they're tiny. I used to think that might be one of the reasons why I seemed to have such bad luck with men. It was incredible. There were all these women, all so very, very different, and yet we all had these same feelings.

"I said to myself, 'Hey, this is for me.'"

Some of the women who joined CR came from broken marriages; others were still in college. Many left husbands and children at home to fend for themselves, while others were all alone, unattached, drifting. Almost all of the women had grown up in traditional households, and many of them were trying to duplicate that way of life in their own homes. Although most had heard about the Women's Movement, and some had even demonstrated and marched, few clearly understood what was happening all around them or why their own lives and the lives of the women they knew seemed to contain so much turmoil.

"I had just had my last baby and I was thirty-one," says Patty C., who is now in her mid-forties and a Congregational minister in Burlington, Vermont. "I remember being dimly aware of Women's Movement rhetoric—the topic had been introduced to me—but as I look back on it now, I think I was in a stage of enormous denial of all kinds of issues because I had my hands full with these children." Raised in a traditional household in Vermont, Patty by then had three children, one of whom was ill and required a great deal of attention. "I certainly did not expect I would ever go back to work and become a professional woman," she says.

Then a friend suggested to Patty that she join a consciousness-raising group. "I can't remember the first night itself," says Patti, "but I do remember my early impressions of those times, which were that I was amazed at the way women were expressing themselves so openly and intimately about things that I had never talked to anybody about—probably not even my husband."

Eileen M., who was in a CR group in Cambridge, Massachusetts, in 1971, recalls a similar unease with the role that had been thrust upon her. As a bright young girl from Connecticut, Eileen had been groomed for Radcliffe—but no one had said much to her about life beyond Radcliffe. Consequently, like many of the young women of the early 1960s, she married shortly after college and stayed home to care for the children while her husband, who had gone to Harvard, pursued a more exciting career as a newspaper editor in Boston. "I hadn't wanted to be a wife and mother like my own mother had been," says Eileen, who now works as a fundraiser for a nearby college, "but there I was doing it. I didn't actively *mind* it; I was enjoying my children and the exciting social life we were having with all these interesting people connected with the newspaper. But I had started wondering how this had happened to me. I wasn't consciously discontented or anxious about it, but I was kind of wondering what was going to happen next. 'How did I wind up here?' I kept asking myself."

For Jeannette F., who was living on suburban Long Island in 1972, joining a consciousness-raising group was an act of salvation. She had three children under the age of seven, her husband had just left her, and having been a traditional housewife since the age of nineteen, she had no experience as a provider. Suddenly she found herself with a house and three young children to care for. Aware that women were meeting in "women's groups," she actively sought out such a group. She'd had one good experience with women in groups years earlier:

"We had lived in the city," recalls Jeannette, who today is a successful entrepreneur with her own public relations firm in Manhattan. "There was a group of young mothers who used to meet in the park, and they became an extension of my family. We saw each other more than we saw anybody else, more than we saw our husbands or our parents. We were just a park-bench group, but we were very solid. We were all young new mothers struggling with being at home, and we were lonely. Seeing each other in the park helped a great deal. If it rained, we would meet at each other's apartments. If a kid was sick, we would help each other with the baby-sitting. We were a very close group."

With that positive experience with women behind her, Jeannette called up NOW. "I said, 'I hear you have some groups,' and they sent me to the storefront in Hempstead. I walked into a room and there were all these women standing there. I used to be shy and retiring, but I didn't feel that way then. They talked about what consciousness-raising was. Everybody was there for the same reason. They needed some support just like me. They needed other women. And it was just an absolutely eye-popping experience for me. I didn't know that there were all these other women out there feeling just like me. I thought everybody was home, baking, and being happy about it."

Younger women, who were not yet married, not yet tied to husbands and families, often had different motivations for joining CR. Many joined simply because it sounded exciting and was, as one woman puts it today, "the thing to do."

"I joined because it was the cutting edge," says Darcy C.,

who is today a performing comedian living with her husband and children in Nyack, New York. "I had been very active in SDS at Yale, and I remember that sometime in the spring of 1970, I was at a demonstration in Washington and I saw this banner: FREE OUR SISTERS, FREE OURSELVES, POWER TO THE PEOPLE, and I realized that women now had their own political issue. For years I'd been fighting other people's struggles. Now *I* had a reason to feel oppressed. And CR was then just a very 'in,' hip thing to do. If you were really where it was at, you were doing CR."

Susan J., a psychiatrist from Chicago, also says she drifted into CR on the heels of other political commitments. "I'd had a boyfriend at the University of Chicago, and he was big in SDS, so consequently I was, too. We had a very political life together, but it was more antiwar types of things. I'd been hearing about women's issues, but it wasn't until my boyfriend and I broke up that I began to read and think about them seriously. Then I was just walking down the street one afternoon and a woman I'd gone to school with sort of said, in passing, 'We're starting a women's group; do you want to join?' and I said, sure. So that's basically how it happened. I didn't go out and seek it. It just walked into my life."

Most groups met once a week, usually through the academic year—that is to say, September through June. They would disband over the summer because of the travel plans of individual members. Generally, the meetings would take place in the evenings, after the children were in bed, in the homes of the different women. Meetings lasted two to three hours, although some women have said they often didn't go home until after midnight. It was the practice, in most groups, to rotate the homes where the meetings were held, so that each woman, in turn, had the responsibility for hosting the

meeting. Men were not invited; indeed, they were often encouraged to be absent when a meeting was taking place. Many
of the women recall the awkward tensions that would ripple
through the group if a woman's husband accidentally or ob-
tusely strayed into the living room while a meeting was in
progress. Interestingly, however, nearly all of the women recall at least one meeting at which men were intentionally
invited. Some of the women remember these occasions as
disastrous ("I was stunned at how each of the women changed
when there were men in the room," said one); while others
were pleasantly surprised ("I was delighted to see that men
could share, too," said another).

In most cases, some kind of refreshments were provided—
perhaps coffee and dessert, possibly chips and dip. Surprisingly few groups served alcohol at their meetings. As one
woman put it, "We didn't *need* to loosen up." Although some
women did serve wine, and occasionally a marijuana joint
would be passed around, in the main, the women stayed
straight and took the meetings quite seriously.

Almost all groups adopted the configuration of a circle to
sit in—whether that be on the floor or draped around the
furniture. In the published formats—from NOW or the New
York Radical Feminists—a circle was advised. A circle, according to the format, created a kind of "free space" that
would enable women to listen to each other and would break
down feelings of competitiveness.

In the format, women were encouraged to speak personally, specifically, and only from their own experience. Gen-
eralizations, theories, and abstractions were discouraged. The
idea was not to try to say what you thought was happening
to women as a whole, but only what was happening, or had
happened, to yourself personally.

Women were forbidden to interrupt each other. One could, if she had to, ask a specific informational question or request that a point be clarified, but she couldn't interject with a point of her own or with a judgment. If someone else's experience reminded a woman of something that had happened to her, she could, according to the generally accepted format, store it away in her thoughts until her own turn came. If her turn had come already, there was always the chance that she could mention the point at the end, when the group tried to sum up and find common elements in their collective testimonies. From the activist feminist point of view, the summing up— or this drawing of conclusions—was the most important part of the meeting: For it was then that the women might begin to discover the seeds of their common oppression.

Women were also prohibited from challenging another's experience. Even though one woman's comments might seem hopelessly misguided, other women were constrained from criticizing or confronting her in any way. Women were also told not to praise another's testimony, since this might lead to feelings of disappointment on the part of the women whose comments were not praised. This prohibition against criticizing or praising another's testimony was probably a pivotal element in the success of CR. Women who had never before had an opportunity to talk about themselves without being dismissed or interrupted by their husbands, boyfriends, or parents could now risk expressing themselves. And for many of the women, it wasn't until they were allowed to speak in these forums that their thoughts were finally crystalized.

It was also forbidden to give advice. The purpose of CR, the women were reminded, was not to offer specific help with day-to-day problems (with boyfriends, spouses, bosses) but rather to support each other in the knowledge that other women had thoughts and feelings similar to one's own. If a woman did come to a meeting with an urgent need to discuss a difficult current problem, the group might let her speak first, and then use her dilemma or her feelings as the topic for the evening. In this way, according to the format, the woman who brought the problem to the attention of the group might come to feel that her problem was shared by each of the other members.

Not every group followed a specific format with clear rules. Some women recall having no rules or topics whatsoever except what felt pressing on any given evening. But most groups adopted some kind of structure that closely resembled the published formats. Either they had come to these sensible and practical rules on their own, through trial and error, or the group might be a "second" or "third" generation CR group—that is, one of the members might have belonged to another CR group in which there was a specific format, and she might try to reproduce the general concept of the format for the new group. Those groups that did have some kind of formal or informal format were, by and large, and by their own reckoning, more successful than those that did not.

One rule that seemed to emerge in all groups—regardless of whether or not they used a format—was that of confidentiality. It was understood that what was said in the groups *would go no farther* than that particular room. Breeches of this rule were often treated harshly, with the occasional expulsion of a member who was careless or catty. Although friendships did surface outside the group—friendships during which other members and what had been said might be discussed—women seemed to honor this rule, even to the point, years later, when they found themselves occasionally tongue-tied when revealing to me what had gone on in their CR groups. The rule of confidentiality was vital, since it allowed women to speak without fear of reprisal from friends, boyfriends, or husbands.

Because of the rule of confidentiality, most CR groups were conducted on a first-name basis only. Although some members would, through previous contact, know the last names of the other women, women were introduced and referred to by first names only. It is in this spirit that the first names and last initials only of the women interviewed are used in this book.

The published formats of NOW and the New York Radical Feminists then went on to suggest topics. (The list of topics and the questions designed to stimulate discussions are reproduced at the end of this book in the Appendix.) The list of the topics had about it a chronological and autobiographical nature, beginning with early childhood notions about what it meant to be female, then moving on to puberty, first sexual experiences, and finally issues of adulthood: masturbation; orgasm; contraception; marriage; pregnancy and childbirth; motherhood; divorce; employment; aging; and "contemporary" issues, such as the way women were portrayed in the media. The questions attached to each topic were intended to probe the women further and get discussion going, but most women say that the mere mention of a topic was enough to set them off, or, in some cases, the testimony of the first woman that night would act as a trigger for the rest. In groups where there was no format at all and the discussion was more free-form, women say they remember a preponderance of discussions about men, marriage, relationships, and sex. Still other women recall a majority of discussions about work and careers. Where a format did exist, women were often asked at the end of a meeting to consider a particular topic for discussion the following week.

The chemistry of each group was unique. The dynamics among the women differed from group to group and from meeting to meeting. Some groups were harmonious from the outset; others were fraught with tensions, discomfort, and personality conflicts. Almost all of the women, however, remember a feeling of intimacy. "There was an extraordinary sense of closeness," says Janet P., now a math teacher in Oakland, California. "There was a period of time in my life when I was closer to these women than to anyone. I knew every little thing about them, the most intimate private details, and they knew every little thing about me, too. The feeling was incredible—to be that open, that free, that able to say what you were thinking without fear of reprisal, without worrying that someone would laugh at you. If we laughed, we laughed *with* each other, because we were all going through the same crazy things. It was wonderful, that feeling. I'm not sure I've ever had anything like it since. I'm not sure that most people have *ever* had it."

So compelling was this intimacy, and the relief that this intimacy afforded, that the meetings began to assume a large importance in the lives of the women. "Nobody, I mean *nobody*, ever missed a meeting that I can remember," says Jeannette F. of Manhattan.

"I always looked forward to the meetings," says Patty C. of Burlington, Vermont. "I always wanted to go, it was a real regular routine. I remember I'd always be offended if someone didn't show up."

"I looked forward to Wednesdays all week," says Carla W.,

the manager of a residential cleaning agency in St. Paul, Minnesota. "It was like food or water—you had to have it."

Often in the meetings there was among the women a rich panoply of emotions ranging from tears to laughter to anger to physical touching. Because of the painful nature of much of the testimony and reminiscences, tears, however, tended to predominate. "Things would be said that would touch on nerves that we didn't even know existed," says Edie G., a court reporter from Glenrock, New Jersey. "It was just realizing things about yourself and about your own character, your feelings, your frustrations, whatever, and it would be very shocking because you just didn't know they were there, and it would be a very emotional kind of thing. And then the tears would come. You couldn't stop them."

Toni L., an editor with a publishing house in Manhattan, recalls one meeting when she herself suddenly and unexpectedly broke down: "We were talking about our mothers. I had a lot of feelings about my mother being an oppressed woman and having had a hard life and how she had paid very dearly for being married to my father. And as soon as we began talking about this, I started to weep and I couldn't stop."

Laughter took the form of genuine hilarity at the comical stories some of the women might tell about mishaps in their relationships or adolescent lives, and nervous laughter about sex. There tended to be a lot of the latter. "Sometimes we'd be rolling, *rolling*, on the floor," says Laurel R., an administrator with a well-known financial institution in Manhattan. "I'm sure it was when we were talking about sex. There'd be a lot of laughing then because we were so nervous."

Anger and rage surfaced as well—generally not among

each other, but at events or people in their past. Feelings of rage that had lain dormant for years came out in an atmosphere of freedom and license. Women expressed anger at how they had been raised, at how their mothers had been treated, at how they had been shut out from certain opportunities in their childhood, at how pervasive and accepted was the sexism in their marriages and in the workplace. When the feelings were very strong, other women might offer their support. "When someone was getting really shaky or something, someone would come over and put an arm around you to comfort you, or just reach over and touch you somewhere," recalls Toni L. "And that felt very good."

Toni also recalls, however, the abrupt and brutal withdrawal of support in her group if the other members in the room didn't like a particular woman or didn't think she was pulling her own weight. "I didn't love everyone, and everyone didn't love me," she says. "Occasionally there would be some problems. There were some negative things, like jealousy and envy. There was a woman in the group who didn't change, who didn't grow, and she was ruining the group. It was decided to ask her to leave. I don't want to make too big a deal out of this—it was only one night out of many nights—but we all sat around, in our turns, and talked about her and how she didn't belong. She sat there on the floor at my feet, with both of her arms wrapped around my legs, and I felt so bad because I didn't say that I would leave, too, and be her friend. I didn't want to leave. I wanted to stay. It was a kind of cruelty, and it was shattering to this woman. It's something she will never forget. Eventually, she did get up and leave, and the group *did* improve a lot after she went."

Susan, the psychiatrist from Chicago, remembers that her group was nearly sabotaged because of tensions. "The group went through one very bad time when we found ourselves unable to confront each other about how we felt about each other. Specifically, there was one woman who was dominating us, and we all felt very controlled by her, but we were unable to speak up. The group nearly broke apart into subgroups because of this."

Still other women recall additional negative feelings associated with CR. One woman, a veteran of a highly successful and satisfying CR group, tried the experience again a year later and was astonished at the bitterness among the women of the second group. "It was 'fuck him,' and 'fuck this,' " says Joyce H., a forty-two-year-old social worker from Boulder, Colorado. "There was so much bitterness because of marriages, feeling really disappointed and cheated, emotions I hadn't gotten at all in the other group. I just didn't feel like participating anymore."

Although negative feelings did surface from time to time, as they might be expected to do among any intimate and intense group of individuals who meet over a long period of time, and although some groups were characterized by personality conflicts, most women speak very positively when remembering their groups and their participation in them. So much so, in fact, that one of the most prevalent feelings women today have about the groups they participated in is *gratitude*. "I owe those women so much," is an oft-repeated phrase.

It was common to belong to more than one group. Having had a successful experience in one CR group, a woman might want to continue or repeat that experience by joining another. Still other women went on to become "facilitators" in newly formed CR groups, using their experience with the format to guide new members. For those women who speak of having belonged to one or more groups (some women joined as many as four), they usually refer to one group in particular as having been the best, the most significant. Often it was the first one they'd ever joined.

The membership of CR groups tended to fluctuate. Although women were encouraged not to allow new members after the third or fourth meeting (because a new member might disrupt an already-developed intimacy among the women), groups did often evolve and grow and change their membership as the months progressed. Usually, however, there were six or seven women who remained the most committed to the group and who usually speak of themselves today as "the core."

Most groups tended to be organized by geography, though there were sometimes other reasons for gathering together. One group of women, for example, might be all Jewish or all Catholic, having met each other through a religious institution. One group in Boston was made up almost exclusively of nurses, since they had come together out of an already established health collective. Another group, in upstate New York, formed because they met each summer as part of a "bungalow" colony. On summer vacation with their children, with their husbands commuting up to see them on weekends, they found themselves thrust together during an era when group dynamics—T-groups, encounter groups— were in the air. Thus gathered together, with the children tucked in bed, they sat under the stars in chaises longues, forming a fledgling CR group. That group still meets today— though no longer in a bungalow colony. (Of the seventeen women in this group, the members of which are scattered all through the metropolitan Manhattan area, fifteen subsequently became divorced. Some have remarried, others have not. Most today are entirely self-supporting.)

Although there are a few ongoing groups like this one that continue to meet regularly today (see Chapter Thirteen), the average life of a CR group in the early 1970s was two years. Disbanding was often circumstantial: The group's meetings would come to a natural end that second June; no one would feel motivated to begin again in September. By the mid-1970s, however, groups were disbanding for other reasons. "The group did what it was meant to do," says Patty C. from Vermont. "And we all started working hard on jobs and careers. Then we didn't have any time to meet."

When women speak of their participation in consciousness-raising groups, they talk with a kind of reverence about the heady sense of sharing and expression of thoughts allowed them there. But as powerful as these activities may have been, they were merely the foundation on which the CR experience was based. The heart of the matter, say the women, was "the click"—the light bulb going off, the eye-popping realization, the knockout punch. It was the sudden comprehension, in one powerful instant, of what sexism exactly meant, how it had colored one's own life, the way all women were in this together. It was that awe-inspiring moment of vision and of commonality, when a woman was instantly and irrevocably transformed from naïve to knowing, from innocent to experienced, from apolitical to feminist. It is a moment that women recall with utter clarity, one link on their private chain of critically important milestones—such as the day they got their period or the day they first had sex or the day they first gave birth to a child.

"It was very early in the group," says Rhoda Z., a buyer for a department store in White Plains, New York. "And one of the women was talking about how in her family her older brother was taken more seriously than she was—he got the education and she didn't type-of-thing, and I realized I was sitting there nodding my head, finally understanding how incredibly sexist it all was, but more important, how I had just bought into it without thinking, without ever protesting. I remember my father explaining to me that it was more important for my brother to go to a good school because he would one day have a family he'd have to support, and, of course, I wouldn't, and I hadn't even questioned the premise of that notion. I'd just gone on to secretarial school, like I was supposed to. I hadn't given it a *thought* until that night and it all clicked. It was like this woman was opening my eyes."

Another woman remembers the click this way: "We were having a meeting in a woman's kitchen in Brooklyn," says Betty N., a legal secretary in Queens. "And she was talking about how her husband never took her seriously, about the tricks he had for doing this. I can't remember what all of them were, but one thing she said was how he seemed never to hear what she was saying, how an hour later, or days later, he'd say she hadn't told him the thing she'd said, when she knew she had. It was a way of dismissing her, of subtly suggesting that his mind was so full of *important* matters that he couldn't be expected to have to listen to the trivia she had to say. I remember that I brought my hands to my face, and I might have said something like, 'Oh, my God.' I'd been living for months in a state of constant confusion and bewilderment because my husband always did the same thing to me. I'd sometimes thought seriously that I was losing my mind, that he was right, that I *hadn't* actually said the thing to him. But here was this other woman, with the very same experience. And once that opened up, everything opened up. It changed my life. I'm not kidding."

The importance of "the click" cannot be overstated. Although it might be only a tiny moment, a split second of recognition, it was the door that opened onto large life-shattering, life-enhancing matters. It was the window that permitted a woman to see the big picture, that allowed her to realize she was not alone. Sometimes it happened only once, at one particular meeting; for other women it happened time and time again, renewing itself. Not surprisingly, women characterize that moment of "the click" as one of enormous relief.

"When I saw what was going on," says Betty, "when I realized how it all worked, it was like this huge, heavy burden was lifting off my shoulders. I literally felt lighter. I'd thought I was depressed, that there was something wrong with me. And then I realized none of this was my fault at all. There were things that had been done to me, been done to all of us, and we could get free if we wanted to. For the first time in my life, I felt like I was in the clear."

THREE

Female in America

Sandi is seated behind a large polished mahogany desk in her office overlooking the Westwood section of Los Angeles. From her perch high atop a neighborhood of small but expensive and expertly manicured houses neatly surrounding a university enclave, Sandi can see for miles out her floor-to-ceiling windows. It is an uncharacteristically sparkling clear day outside those windows on this October afternoon, the air "like champagne," she says. She is wearing a pair of red outsized glasses with tinted lenses that match her sweater. Dress is reasonably casual here in L.A., even for a corporate and commercial real estate lawyer, which is what Sandi has been for some years now. But Sandi hasn't always been a lawyer. Instead, she says, she was groomed to wear fur coats and give bridge parties—and she owes to her CR group her "rebirth" and salvation. Today she not only doesn't own a fur coat, but she hasn't played a game of bridge in fifteen years.

"I had a mother who was up at six o'clock in the morning," says Sandi, leaning over her desk and speaking confidentially. A man, a *male colleague, pokes his head in the door. Sandi, with a smile and a "Hi, Mark," waves him away. "And by the time the kids got up,"* she continues, *"the house was spotless, the breakfast was on the table, she had her makeup on, and her hair was done. She entertained my father's business people; she did it all. And she made it appear to be very easy."*

Sandi and her family lived in the Riverdale section of New York City. Her mother hadn't gone to college—it wasn't considered necessary then, explains Sandi. *"What was considered necessary,"* she says, *"was that she knows how to make a great cocktail party."*

She takes off her glasses and runs her fingers through her hair. *"I was raised as a very protected child. It was life in the suburbs, dancing lessons, Brownies, all of that. I come from an upper-middleclass Jewish home, and I had all the princess kinds of things that kids today talk about. I was a real stereotype."*

Sandi, however, did go to college. She says she had a good education, but no one ever mentioned to her what she was supposed to do with that education once it was completed. *"What you were supposed to do was get married,"* she says, *"and that's exactly what I did. I went right from my parents' home to living with my husband. I never lived on my own. It was very much your typical traditional pattern, except that when I got married, I found housekeeping totally overwhelming. My mother couldn't understand why. 'What's the big deal?' she would say to me. 'You wax the floor everyday, so what?'*

"But I didn't want to be waxing the floor everyday." Sandi laughs, then grimaces.

She didn't understand what was happening and, as a result, she was often depressed. *"It was a feature of my life. But it was hard to understand. Why should you be unhappy if your parents just got you a car, and your father just got you a fur piece and jewelry? You've got a husband. Everything is going well. Why should you feel depressed? You have all these things; you're being taken care of, right?*

So I would feel depressed and unhappy, because it felt to me as though something were profoundly wrong, *but there would seem to be no reason for it, so I would turn it inward and say, 'Well, okay, it must be because I'm crazy. It must be me that's making me feel this way.' "*

That she was crazy was an idea with which her husband Alan was willing to go along. "He'd be very quick to say, 'Oh, that's a very female thing, you're upset and hysterical as usual.' *And after awhile, you can start to buy any song and dance anybody gives you." As a consequence, Sandi went to several psychiatrists and had a history of headaches—a minor ailment that women have traditionally had without understanding why. "When I think back on it, a lot of my psychiatrists were reinforcing the idea that something was wrong with me, and that there must be something internally wrong with the female if she's not happy in the traditional role of being taken care of."*

Sandi stands up and walks to the window. She talks about how after the birth of her second child she entered a period of severe depression that lasted for two years. During this time she recalls subscribing to Ms. Magazine. *"I was roughly sensing something in the air, and I was obviously interested enough to be subscribing to* Ms.," *she says. "I was attracted to this idea I was hearing about, though if I'd been interviewed at the time, I probably couldn't have told you why."*

During this period, Sandi heard about a group starting up in the Village. It sounded like something she wanted to do, but she remembers at first being very frightened.

Once she went, however, she was hooked. "I remember the first night very clearly. I walked into this room. There were a dozen women there, none of whom I had ever seen in my life. I was struck immediately by how unlike each other we all were. I'd had a very narrow social life—all Jewish, all upper middle class. But there were women there of varying ages. Some clearly didn't look Jewish. There was one black woman, and some were not of the middle class—in short, they were women I'd never have met in a million years if I hadn't gone to this meeting.

"We sat in a circle, and I realized when it came to my turn, after a number of others had gone, that I could say things and try them out on the group and see how the group responded. It was the first time in my life that I could do that. I didn't have to protect myself. It was like coming out in a very safe place."

Sandi was most impressed by the commonality of all the women's problems. Issues she had previously felt were deeply personal problems she discovered were part of a common experience caused by the world at large and sexism in particular. She began to see that the other women had been carrying around the same burden as she had—the burden of depression. "And I thought to myself, Hey wait a minute, she is a thirty-year-old Irish woman who has had a completely different education and background from myself and this other women is a twenty-two-year-old woman who also has had a totally different cultural background from myself, and so how is it that we three are sitting here in this same room and the words that are coming out of their mouths are exactly what I feel?"

Sandi turns and comes back to her desk. She sits on the edge. She smiles. "You cannot imagine how wonderful that felt!" she exclaims. "It was absolutely my rebirth as a human being. Other people talk about being born-again Christians. Well, I was a born-again woman."

During those meetings in the group, Sandi's notions about what it meant to be female in America were turned upside down and shaken inside out. She realized she could not simply be taken care of. She saw she could not be put on a pedestal and worshipped with fur coats. "I realized for the first time in my life that I had choices," she says now, "and that the only person responsible for making those choices was me. Me and me alone. The changes began inside. I had to grow up. I had to become a person. And once I became a person that I

59

respected, then other people around me would look at me and see a person that they respected."

It was while Sandi was in the CR group that she overhauled her life. She first went back to school—to be trained as a paralegal—and worked in that capacity for a time. Then she took the plunge and went to law school. While she studied, she kept working for her law firm, and she also had three children at home. Then she and her family moved to L.A. for Alan's business, and Sandi got her job with her current firm.

"Today I have a very busy professional life and a very busy family life," Sandi says. "Our family is completely, totally different than it would have been if I hadn't made the changes inside myself. Our marriage is really good and solid. My husband was stymied at first by what had come over me, but he quickly saw that life was changing for the better, and he rolled with it."

Sandi slips off her desk and back into her chair. She leans back, studying her hands. A slight frown replaces the smile. "Where you could fault me is that I haven't done very much for the Women's Movement," she confesses. "I have every reason to be grateful to it— look what it did for me!—and I guess you could say I haven't repaid my debt. A big debt, and those kinds of debts you should repay. But I look at it this way. I went out and climbed the ladder. I didn't try to bring other women along with me. But I feel that if I tried to carry an entire movement around on my shoulders, I would not get very far. They would drag me down, instead of me dragging them up. So the only way to do it is go out and do it for yourself and get there.

"My ties to the movement ended the day I went out and got into law school," she says. "There wasn't any time for other women. I had to do it for myself. Maybe I can be a role model, not just for my daughters, but for other women. Because the biggest thing I learned in CR is that you are responsible for your own life and no one else's.

*And that's the only way you can survive in this world. Ultimately
you are all alone."*

Very early on in the CR group discussions, women talked
about their childhoods and about what they'd always imagined it meant to be female in this country. The format asked
very specific questions geared to stimulate discussion in this
direction: "Were you treated differently from boys?"; "Did
your parents have the same attitudes about education for girls
as they did for boys?"; "What did you think it was going to
be like to be a woman?" For many women, these discussions
were the foundation on which the CR experience was built.
By looking closely at and reevaluating what it meant to be a
girl and then a woman in America, one could begin to understand the roots of sexism in the culture.

It was common in that era just prior to the early 1970s—
and indeed such notions still exist in many American homes
today—to treat girl children differently from boy children
right from birth. This different treatment had the effect of
teaching girls that they were second best, dependent, and
passive individuals. Sex-stereotyping began as early as in-
fancy, with girls intuiting the idea that they were intended to
remain passive and that they would be cared for by their
parents until such time as Prince Charming, in the form of
a more active and decisive male, would arrive to sweep them
off their feet and take care of them for life. Such messages,
as we now know well, were not only debilitating for the emotional, intellectual, and social health of the female who believed them (girls who are encouraged to adopt a mode of
behavior that is devalued by society run the risk of devaluing
themselves), they could also be practically and economically

disastrous for the woman whose Prince Charming up and left her with three children and no income-producing training or job. Nearly all of the women who joined CR in the early 1970s had been taught these early impractical myths.

"*I* was taught the myth," says Margaret S., the vice-president of a wine firm in Manhattan. "I was brought up a Catholic and was very sheltered. I had a mother who believed in fairy tales and story-book endings. I was told that if you're a good, nice, sweet person, good things will happen to you. And God created only one you and only one man, and soon that one perfect man—your prince—would come and make your life fine. There was no thought of working. If you wanted something, you had to learn to be manipulative within the confines of your station in life. My mother was fairly manipulative. If she wanted the apple over there, she would find twelve ways to get it short of saying, 'I would like the apple over there.' No one ever told me I might one day have to take care of myself—or even that I ought to be able to take care of myself."

The myth of Prince Charming appears to have been ubiquitous and no respecter of geography. Joyce H., the social worker who now lives in Colorado, grew up in Georgia. She remembers the stultifying notion of womanhood passed on to her in her childhood. Males and females were always separate, recalls Joyce, now the mother of two children. The point of being female, as she was taught it, was to go to dances and balls and wait to meet the right man. And the point of that was to get married and be taken care of. The concept of having a real relationship with a man, one in which a woman and a man could be friends and share interests was never introduced to Joyce. "One of the things I remember most about my childhood," she says, "was the way you'd walk into a house and the men would be in one room and the women in another."

Many women remember the days before consciousness-raising vividly—an era in which being female meant a severe limiting of opportunities because a young woman was to keep herself ready and available for the Prince. They particularly recall being maneuvered into a "flexible" course of study or temporary jobs because such flexibility was thought not to be threatening to the concept of marriage. One could be a teacher or an artist or an English major no matter what one's husband's job was, no matter where one had to move to live.

Because of this, many women recall feeling that their educations were dead-ends. It was common in traditional households in the 1960s for girls to be encouraged to do as well as possible in school, and even to get into good colleges—but when those educations were finished, they were to be put aside in favor of finding and serving the Prince—whom, by the way, a young woman had better have met while she was still in college. It seems extraordinary today to think of the large numbers of women in the early 1960s who married either just before graduation from college, or immediately afterward. Those who didn't were often frightened and confused. One woman I interviewed—a single woman who teaches English at the college level in Worcester, Massachusetts—spoke of her bafflement once she graduated from college in Boston. The day after she graduated, when she realized she wasn't in school anymore, she nearly went into shock. She had never really thought beyond college, she says, and she had no idea what to do with herself. She wasn't married, she didn't have a boyfriend, she had no job and no prospect of one—she'd studied English literature in school. As a result, she found herself reduced to asking for loans from friends and family and trying (and failing because she couldn't type) to get work as an office temp. It was one of the most disturbing and humiliating periods of her life, she says today.

People who study the behavior patterns of teen-age girls and boys have noted that girls who have previously been encouraged to do well in school and participate in many different kinds of activities begin to withdraw from achievement in the mid-teen years; some even go so far as to sabotage their own competence. Barbara D., a forty-one-year-old nutritionist from Hartford, Connecticut, recalls that her teen-age years confused her. "When I think of myself as a little girl," says Barbara, who has been married three times and attributes at least two of those marriages to having too hastily attached herself to a man in panic at the thought of living alone, "I think of myself as strong, athletic, and gutsy. But when adolescence hit, it was a really big shock. Because then I became undeniably female, and that meant having to play the part of my mother and grandmother, which I translated into having to be a *femme fatale*. I wanted to be popular; I wanted all the boys to like me—and I had some success. Yet I was furious that somehow boys, in my mind, were dominant and girls weren't. I remember actually being told that the way to get a boy was to read the sports page, and never to let a man know what you were thinking. I was taught every single trick in the book."

Many women also recall the dearth of independent role models for young girls in that era before CR. Women who appeared to be free of the myth of the Prince and who were strong, appealing women on their own were scarce. And when one did meet such a woman, often preconceptions got in the way. "Her life would seem unbearably lonely, and I would run away in fear," says Barbara now. "I couldn't imagine how she existed, because women were supposed to be like alarm clocks—you only got wound up by the man. Men had the key and they wound you up, and you came alive and then you were fine."

Finding a man to "wind you up," however, was often only the beginning of a woman's conflicts—not the desired nirvana she'd been taught marriage would be. For marriage itself continued to perpetuate the sexist notion that there were two unequal beings in the partnership—the more dominant, stronger, economically independent male and the subservient, passive, and dependent female. In many cases, this master-servant notion of marriage led to abusive relationships—emotionally so, if not physically so. "I got married in the fifties," says Toni L., the editor in Manhattan. "You wore white gloves and sex was a sin. You had three kids right away. You lived in this nice house, and if your husband didn't actually beat you, and brought his paycheck home, you know, what was there to complain about?"

Burdened since childhood with these inhibiting beliefs, many women found their expectations shattered in CR. With the safety net of the group to support them, women explored, tested, and tried on new roles. This overhauling of the adult female role was among the more successful ventures of the CR process, in concert with the changing attitudes about women in the culture at large as a result of the activities of the Women's Movement. And as Sandi put it, once those women began to see themselves differently, others around them were forced into a new consciousness of who women were as well.

A number of the women recall today the frustration of their traditional ideas of what a wife and mother was supposed to be and how their CR groups helped to unravel those unworkable stereotypes. Nearly all of these women had been raised in households in which mothers did not go outside the home to work, and thus they grew up believing that's how it was to be for them, too. But many of them withered in the isolation of the housewife's role, and chafed, like Sandi, at the job description. Believing that they ought to be content with their role, they felt guilty if they weren't. For some, the relief of being able to share this confusion with other women, and to speak of their doubts within the safety of their CR groups was the first step—as it was for Sandi—in freeing themselves of unwelcome constraints.

Virtually none of the women interviewed for this book envisioned herself, when she was a girl, as being economically independent as an adult. Today, almost all of them are, and have what they refer to as jobs or careers. Even those women who are at home with young children think of themselves as returning to the office when their job raising their kids is finished. And although many of the women said they still often felt *emotionally* dependent on a man, and others worried about *not* being home with their young children, not one woman evinced any nostalgia for the rigid family roles of the 1950s and early 1960s.

Without question, the range of opportunities for women has expanded enormously since the early days of CR. Girls grow up today imagining that they will be pilots, not flight attendants; CEOs, not secretaries. As early as grade school, girls are encouraged to think in terms of making a lifelong commitment to work, a notion that used to be fostered only in boys. Instead of pressuring daughters to find the Prince as soon as possible, today's mothers caution daughters to wait to get married until the daughter has an income-producing job or career under way, and more importantly, has some sense of herself as an independent person. From birth, parents now make a conscious effort to treat girl babies with the same respect as they have always treated boy babies, and to avoid thinking of their daughters as passive individuals. Girls now have a wider range of adult females to model themselves after, and many young women espouse the idea of equal and shared partnerships in marriage—partnerships in which both men and women share the domestic and economic burdens equally.

Seen from the perspective of dozens of generations of women forced into traditional, subservient roles, the possibilities for women today appear to be head-spinning. Yet as is true in any era of extraordinary and rapid change, new roles aren't always comfortable. Nor are women certain that they haven't exchanged one ill-fitting role for yet another. Women today, fifteen years after CR, express concern about a number of troubling issues. Have they, they wonder, taken on too much of the male plumage and the corporate value system at the office in order to compete, succeed, and/or survive there? Why is it so difficult, they ask, to balance their new assertiveness with more traditional female qualities, such as nurturing? Why is it, they muse, that women's issues and women's things, such as child care, are still dismissed or devalued by society at large? And many are concerned by what they perceive as a new and disturbing wrinkle in the legacy of CR: competition among women at the workplace—an issue that may be, say women, an outgrowth of having so heavily adopted a masculine mode of operating.

"The problem with being female in America today is you're expected to be *male* in America," says Elise B., a trusts-and-

estates lawyer for a large firm in Denver. "We haven't learned
yet what it means to be female today. We're reinventing the
wheel, and I feel we've gone overboard. I see it every day in
the women around me. Look at how I'm dressed: Gray suit,
a scarf you could think of as a tie, short hair. You can't even
tell I have breasts. And that's just on the surface. I'm tough.
I've learned to be tough. I can give as good as I get. I have
four men under me, who work as my assistants. I'm tyran-
nical. They're afraid of me. I used to love it. I used to brag
about it. I make more money than most of the people in this
firm, except the senior partners. Now I'm scared. I've made
it, and now that I've made it, I'm not sure I know myself
anymore."

The last fifteen years have been a time, in the lives of many
women, when they have taken advantage of open doors previously closed to them, and have built their careers with all
the passion and fervor that used to be the nearly exclusive
domain of men. For many, the struggle has been all-
consuming and arduous, leaving little time for reflection and
self-scrutiny. And to succeed, as many have done, it has become necessary to adopt unquestioningly a number of characteristics traditionally associated with the way men operate
in business. While that taking on of a new set of seemingly
masculine practices has been empowering for women, enabling them to achieve their goals, allowing them to be the
competent and effective individuals they wanted to be, it has
also required the assumption of certain ill-fitting attitudes and
values: a cutting away of things evidently "feminine" at the
workplace; a new set of learned responses to stress, anxiety,
and fatigue; a new assumption of command, sometimes over
other females, sometimes over males; and for some, an adop-

tion of a ruthless manner on the job. While not all women are as concerned as Elise by what appears to be a complete reversal in personality, others are worried about how to merge the new behavior at the office with more nurturing behavior at home.

"My problem is switching back and forth," says Carol P., the sales manager of a pharmaceutical firm in New Hampshire. She and her husband, an electrical engineer, live in a large white Victorian house just outside Concord. Although Carol is nearly thirty-seven, neither she nor her husband has any desire for children. She is a tall, lithe, dark-haired woman, with a clear, direct manner of speaking. She says she first heard of consciousness-raising and joined a group on campus at the University of New Hampshire, where she majored in chemistry. Today she has a sales force of eighteen under her.

On the job, says Carol, she's as good as any man in the business. She describes herself as a fair boss and a hard worker. She enjoys her job and finds enormous satisfaction in her competence. Her problems begin, she says, not at work, but when she comes home.

"I walk in the door, and I'm still trembling from work," she says. "I'm still high over a big sale, or I'm bristling with energy and businesslike mannerisms, and I'd like to be kowtowed to once in a while. Hey, I'd like the glass of wine handed to me when I walk in the door sometimes. But instead, my husband wants a soothing, sympathetic ear, and I can't always give it, and he feels resentful. We both wind up feeling resentful. When he gets mad, he says I'm 'tough,' and it's understood that this is a real put-down. 'No one wants a tough woman,' he'll say to me. And I feel inside me this incredible mix of feelings. On the one hand, I don't want to be called 'tough' in that way: It sounds horrid. On the other hand, I *am* strong, and I'm proud of it. So I end up feeling enraged and confused."

Carol believes the conflict lies in the fact that most men don't really want women to be 'tough' or *strong*, a word she prefers. It's threatening, she says, but even more to the point is that she's not sure that women themselves are entirely comfortable with the description either.

Women speak of a dichotomy lodged deeply in their psyches, and of how they would like to be able to merge what feels like two disparate parts—the masculine and the feminine—more easily. For Carol, it is a daily struggle, one she sees as a part of the legacy of her consciousness-raising group. Her experience in the group allowed her, she says, to be a fully alive and vibrant person on the job—but not at home.

This merging of the two parts of one's being—the masculine and the feminine, as some women label them; or the non-traditional and the traditional, if you will; or the "assertive-on-the-job" and the "nurturing-at-home"—is among the most puzzling aspects of being female in America in the late 1980s. To be sure, many women have not felt this split, and others have (as Carol wished for herself) integrated the two modes of behavior. Women with men who appreciate strong, assertive women or women who are happier living with other women or by themselves, or single parents (for whom remaining strong both at work and at home may be a vital necessity and therefore not subject to the same kind of self-inquiry or self-scrutiny) have not found this issue so troubling. But other women worry about finding a comfortable way to blend what appear to be two distinct and, at times, antithetical parts of their personalities. This concern is particularly keen when hard-driving, hard-working, committed women have babies or young children at home.

"I would get in the car after work," says Tessa W., a reporter for a Boston paper, "and everything in my mind and body would be in high gear. Humming. Sometimes screaming high gear. And I would know that in twenty-five minutes exactly, I would have to walk into my house and hold and love my son, who was just a toddler then. And give him a bath, and make him dinner and read to him, and that I had only twenty-five minutes to get from where I was to where I could be with him. And I would use that twenty-five minutes very consciously to chill out. I'd do deep breathing. I'd work to put the paper behind me. If there were problems, I developed a technique to think of them as getting farther and farther away as I was driving. Basically, I was meditating. I had to do it. If I'd come in the house looking and acting the way I have to be to function at work, I'd have been useless in those two or three precious hours I used to have with him before he had to go to bed."

As Felicia pointed out at the reunion, trying simultaneously to go to work and to care for one or more children at home can cause a woman to feel torn—and not merely because of the shortage of time to do both comfortably. Although certain businesslike qualities of organization and good management may translate to the running of the home, and vice versa, that slow, quiet, drifting, going-with-the-flow-of-a-four-year-old mindset is rarely pertinent on the job. Nor do corporations have much use for nurturing at the workplace. A woman who is committed to proving herself may find she has to strip away or hide from view many of those characteristics that are vital in the home.

Even more stressful is the evident dismissal of traditionally female activities. In particular, women worry about the devaluation of *nurturing*, whether that be motherhood itself, or work in one of the "helping professions," or a job having to do with children. A number of them said bluntly: Nothing's changed but the date. Women and women's occupations are still scorned. One had only to look at child care in America or at what child-care workers are paid or to glance at the statistics—one in every four children in this country lives in poverty—to understand that female occupations, such as nursing, teaching, and even mothering, are still regarded as second rate, something outside the real pulse, the heartbeat of America. We applaud women every day who are better businessmen than men, and we say they're achieving what the movement meant for them to achieve. But one wonders if in doing so we haven't arbitrarily limited again the role of the adult female in our society.

Thus, the legacy of consciousness-raising is, for some women, one of intimate and personal confusion. "I don't know what it means to be a woman anymore," says Cassie S., a thirty-nine-year-old high-school guidance-department head from North Carolina. "I think that's good and that's bad. We're open to everything. We can be who we want to be. But we're confused, too. I think we may have cut away too much that was good about being women when we tried to be like men. Now we have to try to find our way back to what was valuable."

Women agree with this assessment and wish they could talk with other women about this issue. Some liken the last fifteen years to a "revolution," and the present era to one in which the revolutionaries must stand back and take stock of what has been accomplished and what has been lost. In particular, women in business are dismayed by the fact that by and large they have failed to bring to the workplace a more feminine, humanistic mode of operating that would, they say, make the workplace a better place to be. Some say they are beginning to move in this direction and that as more and more women assume positions of power, they will see more changes. But progress, they admit, has been slow—perhaps because capitalism itself is based on the desire for power, individualism, competition, and money-as-success, characteristics that may be "antifeminine" by nature.

Causing great dismay, for example, is a trend that women in business express a great deal of concern about: women competing with other women—something that is anathema to those women who came of age in CR. Yet, even so, many find themselves daily in such competitive situations. "I look at other women, and I worry about how many stories they've been assigned for a certain issue," says Marcia T., a senior editor of a weekly magazine in New York. Marcia "did CR," as she puts it, in New York City in 1973. "I worry about who's got the cover, what kind of coverage their stories are getting in the magazine. I watch who's going to lunch with whom; I get very anxious about the new talent coming up straight from school. There are a few top positions open to women in this business, and we're all fighting like dogs for them. I like women better than men—I always have. But if one of them is more successful than me, I get scared."

Some say this competition with other women is merely the same old competition women have always been encouraged to engage in with each other, now merely in another guise; and others see this as one aspect of the legacy of the Women's Movement. But it is especially troubling to feminists because such competition makes any kind of future solidarity, any kind of coming together again, much more difficult to achieve. In the 1950s, women were encouraged to compete for men; today they are encouraged to compete for jobs (*and* men). In both eras, an undercurrent of distrust taints women's relationships with each other, undermining the possibility of a second wave of unity in order to grapple with many of the larger issues of the 1990s that need attending to.

Obviously, not all women today perceive the taking on of both traditionally masculine and feminine roles as a difficulty. Perhaps it's a matter of feeling comfortable with a wide variety of behaviors; perhaps it's a matter of perception; or maybe it is simply a case of semantics. But many see the legacy of CR as nothing but positive. Regina M. is a commercial architect from Baltimore. She's a single parent with two preschool boys. When she's at home with the boys, she says, "I'm down on the floor, we're tickling each other, we're laughing, or I'm holding them and hugging them. It's all physical. It's all giving. But when I'm out on a job, and especially when I'm out with contractors or what-have-you, I'm strictly professional. I have no trouble giving orders. I have no trouble asking a lot of money for my time and work. I don't see being able to be one way at home and one way on a construction site as a split. Sure, I hide my natural self on the job, but don't we all? I'm a good, loving mother, and I'm sharp as a tack when I'm working. I think what CR gave me was the freedom to operate on many different levels. I think of myself as having range."

Call it range. Call it choice. Call it opportunity. No woman I interviewed denied that her life was richer for its expanded possibilities. But the women did seem perplexed about what it meant to integrate a new way of being female with the old.

Doors had opened, one by one, and the women had walked through them, shedding old ideas, taking on new—sometimes being scared by the new ideas and shedding them, too. Some women had walked through so many open doors they no longer were certain where they'd gone. Others recognized in themselves the pull and tug of the old and new.

One Sunday afternoon, I sat in the apartment of a woman who had not had what I would describe as an easy life. Her name was Erin and she was forty years old. She'd been married early, right out of high school, and had had a baby shortly after that. Despite her protests, she and her husband had moved from New York to Chicago, where he convinced her he'd have better luck getting a job in the steel industry. While he looked for work, Erin cared for her baby, and then almost immediately after the first, she cared for another. But three years after her wedding, her husband left her for another woman. Erin found herself without an income and with two babies to raise. She put her children and herself on a bus and made her way back to New York. She worked as a waitress for a time, then as a ticket taker in a movie theater. She traded off baby-sitting hours with other women so that when she wasn't working, she was nearly always baby-sitting. One of the women she baby-sat for told her of a CR group starting up on New York's Upper West Side. Erin, nearly blind with fatigue, went as a respite from her daily struggles. She says she was a vegetable when she went, and that the group "saved her life." It is a phrase one hears often from women in CR, but in this case, Erin believed it literally.

Today Erin runs a daycare center in the city. She doesn't make a lot of money, but is able to live in a decent apartment and to send her second child to private school. On this Sunday afternoon, she talked for a long time about the way in which she went from being a girl to a woman in CR, and the way those early lessons of dependency on a man had been not only unrealistic but destructive. She believes fervently in feminism, she says, and is unreservedly grateful to CR. But, she says, that doesn't mean that all her conflicts are resolved.

"When you become a feminist," says Erin, "I don't think you all-of-a-sudden become a totally different person. You regress and you advance. Though my consciousness was raised and it grew, and there were things that I could verbalize that I couldn't before, making emotional and intellectual changes are two different things. There is still this part of me that is growing, and there is still this part of me that would like to lie down on the floor and have somebody take care of me. It was so ingrained in me from such an early age that you're nothing without a man, I don't think you can excise those ideas totally, especially in a culture that still reveres the idea of the couple."

Erin's candor about the struggle inherent in the legacy of CR for those women who were children in the 1950s and 1960s makes one wonder about the younger women coming along today, those women in their early twenties who may have been spared the stifling message that a female is nothing without a male. Are these women free of those traditionally inhibiting notions?

Yes and no. While many young women today insist that they will not marry until their careers are well underway (the age most of them focus on for marrying is in their early thirties; they also say they will have children no sooner than that—some even think in terms of their mid- to late thirties for first babies), the myth of the Prince, it appears, is not dead and buried.

Recently, an interesting mutation of this myth—perhaps

the 1980s version of it—surfaced during a class discussion in a women's history class at Sarah Lawrence College. A group of students, all young women, were trying to identify women's problems and solutions. Not being part of any larger feminist movement, however, and not having experienced anything like CR, they tended to see both problems and solutions as belonging to the individual, and not a larger group. "The key is to find the right man," said one young woman, "one who will share the chores and the breadwinning." All of the other women in the class nodded energetically. Although the future husband this young, progressive woman envisioned for herself was a man of a different character than the man who inhabited the fantasies of women twenty years ago, once again, there he was—the Prince.

Find the right guy, she seemed to be saying, and all your problems will be solved.

FOUR

Sex and the Secret of Life

It is ten past nine in the evening, and Felicia has just gotten home from work. She has missed seeing her son tonight. Maria, Felicia's live-in housekeeper, has already put Sandy, who is two, to bed. Felicia is eating a small bowl of pasta in cream sauce, a meal that her husband Art hastily put together when he returned home from work at seven. Felicia says she normally doesn't get home this late, but pressure at work recently has been severe, and she's had more late nights this week than she'd like. She is wearing a black and white silk dress. A black suede blazer is flung over the sofa. Her blond waved hair is pulled to one side with a large onyx and gold barrette.

Her apartment on Manhattan's Upper East Side is cavernous and comfortably furnished in an English country-house style. Of all the women in her original CR group, Felicia has been the most successful financially. Not only does she make considerably more money than any of the other women—she makes more money than most men in America: close to $160,000 with bonuses last year. In fact, she *confesses at one point during the evening, she makes more money than her husband does. And has always done so.*

Tonight, however, Felicia is thinking and talking not about money, but about sex—a subject, she says ruefully, that sometimes seems like a distant and fond memory. And like many women her age who belonged to CR groups in the early 1970s, she divides her life— and, in this case, her sex life—into three time periods: before CR, after CR, and now.

"I was brought up Catholic and was extremely sheltered growing up," she says, kicking off her shoes. "By the time I had joined the CR group, I'd had one or two love affairs in college, and I was in one serious relationship at the time. His name was Bob, and we were living together near NYU. We'd been together, oh, I guess, about eighteen months when I remember quite clearly, I read a reprint of an article called 'The Myth of the Vaginal Orgasm.' I remember becoming very anxious after I'd read it. Because the truth is that I hardly knew anything at all about sex. It's hard to believe now— young women know everything about sex today, don't they?—but I was a virgin when I went to college, and I'd only had these couple of relationships."

In Felicia's family, sex was never discussed. Today she has no idea how she came to know about menstruation and the facts of life— probably, she thinks, through the osmosis of having girlfriends and giggling and talking about it. But she does know that she had a great deal of misinformation. "I didn't know," she says, "that women routinely had orgasms when they had sex with men. You may think that's incredible, but that's how sheltered I was. I knew there was this pleasurable thing you did in the bathroom alone by yourself, masturbating, but I never really connected it with intercourse in bed with a man. It wasn't that I thought you weren't supposed to feel it; I just never knew you were. I thought going to bed with a man was about romance for yourself and sexual pleasure for him."

After Felicia read the article about orgasms, she was full of ques-tions. How do you achieve orgasm in bed? she wanted to know. "I mean, he's there worrying about his thing," she explains, "and what do I say to him, and literally how do I get my arms and legs around him to do what I have to do? And then I heard about this CR group starting, and I said to myself: 'They know the secret of life.' "

Felicia isn't clear as to when sex first came up in the group. She had wanted to bring it up from day one, but was too shy. She believes it finally surfaced because of the format. Most of the women, says Felicia, were more savvy than she, but she does recall that everyone had certain misinformation and insecurities.

"At first, everyone was very nervous, and we giggled and laughed a lot. One woman became tongue-tied and couldn't speak at all. Another woman, and I can't tell you who because of our rule of confidentiality, had horrible stories about her husband: He liked to dominate and would tie her up and sort of hurt her, and she hated it, but was terrified of him. We talked about everything, I mean everything. *There was this one woman in the group, she was much more evolved than the rest of us—and she was just very lusty and matter-of-fact about sex: She'd say, 'What's the big deal about sex? You like wine? I like sex. It's the easiest thing on earth.' She'd tell stories about some guy who'd patted her on the fanny, and she'd turn right around and grab him by the balls. She made us aware of how men do sexual rip-offs all the time. And I believe she's the one who got us to bring our vibrators to one session. I didn't have one, of course. I didn't even know what they were. But the other women brought them, and we discussed technique. Real straightforward tech-nique. We didn't take our clothes off, or anything like that, but, in terms of discussion, we got down to the nitty-gritty."*

For Felicia, it was her first awareness that other women were enjoying sex. Somewhere, in the back of her mind, she'd always thought sex was dirty, and that she'd go to hell for enjoying it. "I knew I'd go to hell for masturbating," she says. "I'm sure I thought that. So the important part for me was finding out that sex was natural and a pleasure I deserved. You cannot today imagine how big a message that was then. Huge. And there was also the awareness that women cared about sex and were experimenting, and if things went wrong, it wasn't necessarily the fault of the woman; the man might have a part in it, too."

Felicia believes those discussions in the group about sex changed her life. Never again did she feel inhibited with a man, she says. Never again did she have any trouble telling a man what to do, or where to put what or what she felt like doing. "Once you get comfortable sexually, I don't think you can ever go backwards," she says. "It's like the toothpaste out of the tube. It freed me, liberated me, so to speak. I have a vibrator now—actually I have two. I know what I like, and I know what I don't like, and I have no trouble expressing myself. That was a fantastic thing the group did for me. I have absolutely no doubt, no doubt at all, that without the group, it would have taken me another ten, fifteen years to figure it all out."

But when you ask Felicia about now, today, she laughs. "Sure, I know what to do and how to do it—that's almost old hat now," she says. "My husband and I are very easy with each other. But the truth is, I seldom feel like doing it. I'm exhausted all the time. So I've got two vibrators? Frankly I can't remember when the last time I used them was. We make love now, maybe twice a month, if we're lucky. When I fall into bed, I crave sleep, not sex."

Felicia would like to make love more, or rather would like to feel the urge more. Her lack of lovemaking sometimes makes her wonder if her marriage is in trouble. "Sometimes I think I'd like to get at this problem. Do other couples stop making love like us? Is it age? Is it exhaustion? Is it work? Is it temporary? It must be an issue that bothers other women, too. But I have to laugh when I say that. There's no way that I could even consider talking with other women about this, sex life or no sex life. Look at me tonight—I didn't even get to kiss my son good night."

Of all the subjects that "took" during the era of consciousness-raising, sex was among the most successful—if not *the* most enduring benefit of participation in CR. In part this was because of the nature of much of the information shared: Practical techniques once learned are seldom forgotten. But primarily it was because of the sexual "click"—that realization that, as Felicia puts it, "sex was a pleasure I deserved." An intimate and forbidden subject was brought out into the open air. Women shared fantasies, knowledge, fears, and insecurities with more abandon than ever before and emerged from group meetings about sex with a completely new sense of entitlement and comfort about their own sexuality.

From the vantage point of the late 1980s, with our concern about the fallout and sometimes devastation of the sexual revolution—AIDS, herpes, children having children—we tend to forget just how very much was accomplished during the consciousness-raising sessions of the early 1970s. But the comments of one woman who was raised in the deep South and then found herself in a CR group in Colorado in 1972 tend to remind us: "I'd never been able to relax and enjoy sex," says Joyce H., a social worker. "As a teen-ager, I'd been uncomfortable with anything sexual or even sensual. I had to wear girdles all through high school just so I wouldn't shake at all—and I weighed nothing. It's just unbelievable when I think back on it. From the little bit that I gleaned from the ideal of Southern womanhood, I understood that sex was a subject that you never discussed at all; and when you finally had to actually *do* sex, in your marriage, you were supposed to be utterly passive. The only thing my mother ever told me about sex was that it wasn't any fun, so not to expect anything."

When Joyce joined her CR group, she was married. She had what she describes as a "passive" idea about sex, and when the subject first came up, she was too embarrassed to talk about it. But then she discovered that a number of the other women had passive notions about sex, too. "They weren't from the South," says Joyce, "but still they had those ideas. I don't think women got much of a sexual education then; at least most women I knew didn't."

The subject of sex, in most CR groups, generally did not surface until intimacy among the women had been established. "I can't remember which meeting it was that we talked about sex," says Emily V., a sculptor from Santa Fe, New Mexico, "but I do remember that it wasn't brought up for a very long time."

"We would have one big sex meeting a year," says Alexandra T., a psychologist from Newton, Massachusetts, "and it usually would be in candlelight or some atmosphere that invited greater intimacy. Often it would be sparked by a conversation begun by a smaller group of us."

"I remember bringing up sex at one meeting," says Diane A., a nurse from Baltimore, Maryland, "and I was quaking in my boots when I did it. It was such a big issue for me, and I needed so badly to discuss it, but it hadn't come up yet. But when it did, Wow! We really went to town on that one. I think everyone must have felt as I did—just waiting for some sucker to finally bring it up."

For most groups that had come together under the auspices of a larger women's organization, sex emerged as a topic as a natural progression through the format. Very specific questions were asked of the women to stimulate discussion: "How

often and under what circumstances do you masturbate?";
"Can you describe your feelings and sensations during orgasm?"; "Have you ever faked an orgasm?"

Assertiveness during sex, faking orgasms, and the differences between the "vaginal" and clitoral orgasms were discussed in detail. For many women it was the first time they
heard that all orgasms were clitoral, and vaginal orgasms were
indirect—a subject to which a great deal of political importance was attached at the time. If a sexist culture had per-
petuated the myth that female satisfaction could be achieved
only through a vaginal orgasm—one in which male partners
were supposed to have a critical part to play—might not the
realization that orgasms were clitoral be immensely liberating? The notion that a woman might be able to satisfy herself
independently of a man—in the same way she might be able
to support herself independently of a man—was thought to
be a vital political step in freeing oneself of the constraints
of a sexist culture.

Of equal importance to the message, however, was the
process. Many young women, bringing with them sheltered
notions of sexuality from their own 1950s girlhoods, found
the sharing of sexual matters to be both heady and liberating.
"There was a lot of talking about sex," says Toni L., the editor
from New York. "It certainly was an eye-opener. I discovered
that the anxieties that I had were common anxieties. We were
all different—there were women who had never climaxed
before; there were women who were leaving their husbands
because of unsatisfactory sexual relationships—but we all
found a commonality and we bonded together in the process."

In some groups, women brought sexual paraphernalia to
the meetings to demonstrate and investigate. Other groups
experimented with self-examination: Learning how to use

gynecological tools was a feature of some meetings. Still other groups explored sexual fantasies: "I remember we all got hold of that book, *My Secret Garden*, and read it before one meeting. It was the fastest book I ever read in my life," says Laurel R., the financial administrator in Manhattan. "We were a group of women who had never really talked about sex openly—there'd been no sex education in school, or whatever, and we lived in an environment where it wasn't talked about—and so we all read this book and we began to explore our sexual fantasies. Just to know that they were okay and that other women had sex fantasies, too. I remember being aware at the time that this was a little risky, but we all realized that we were sharing something that in some form we had all felt or thought about. And it made us feel more comfortable about who we were. It enabled us to move on in some form. Sexually, we were all at different stages—different ages, some married, some with a little more maturity and experience—and there was a kind of common wisdom that was passed down from the older women to the younger women in this atmosphere of openness we'd created. I think it was incredibly valuable. Sometimes I fear that's what's missing today—there's no passing on anymore of the wisdom of older, more experienced women. The younger women, they think they already know it all."

Other women recall that discussions about sex unmasked a wide and contradictory range of feelings. At first there might be a tremendous release of energy, during which women would exclaim how much they liked sex. It was the most important part of their lives, they would say, and they reveled in the opportunity to celebrate their sexuality. But in time—at that meeting or the next—one woman might shyly confess she'd never had an orgasm and that for her sex was a very painful subject. Her speaking up might act as a catalyst for the others, and suddenly many of the women would begin to speak about their own sexual difficulties. Most had questions and anxieties and problems, but it had taken the courage of one woman to allow these concerns to emerge.

The result of sexual discussions in CR groups was both personal and political. On the personal level, it is probably accurate to say that an entire generation of women became better educated about sexual matters. What they then did with that new education in their private lives is as varied as the women themselves. Although the primary objective on the part of the women was to educate themselves and expand their own sexual horizons, male partners in relationships with these women were often grateful recipients of the progress being made in CR: "The husband of one of the women in the group is very fond of us all," says Toni L., the editor, "because it changed his sex life. He's very much in love with his wife and still is, and their sex life just got better and better because of the group."

For some relationships, however, as was true in other domestic areas, the lessons being learned in CR were fundamentally and irrevocably threatening to male partners. In many cases, marriages and relationships, unable to accommodate this volatile information, disintegrated. "There were a number of women in our group who were either virgins when they got married or had only had a sexual relationship with one person in their life," says Laurel R., "so that when their sexual horizons were expanded, it was devastating for them as women. They all felt the grass would be greener— you know, there was something else out there—and they felt like they'd missed out. So they had affairs, and in some cases the affairs destroyed their marriages. Of the seventeen or so women in our group, myself and a couple of other women are the only ones still married to the same man that we were when we first met."

Before CR, after CR, and now. Indisputably, the lessons learned in CR about female sexuality were lessons that "took." But in the fifteen years since the women first met in their groups, much has changed on the American sexual landscape for both men and women. While some women, like Felicia, see their own personal sexual liberation coming to an end because of time constraints and the exhaustion of trying simultaneously to love a child and maintain a career, many other women have seen it come to an abrupt halt because of public health issues.

■

"Liberation is not the point anymore, is it?" asks Catherine, pouring a glass of Cabernet Sauvignon in her kitchen. "Expressing your sexuality is not the issue anymore," she says. "Staying alive is the issue. My sex life has taken a nose dive since the advent of AIDS. It's true of every woman I know who is single. It started on its way down about five years ago, when the herpes epidemic was big news and started to put the fear of God into us. But, pardon my bluntness, at least you could see that. Now it's plummeted into nonexistence with AIDS. How do you know that who you're with hasn't been with someone who's been with someone who's been with someone? It's endless."

"I'm forty," she says. "I'm still single. I meet men. And I'm scared. You can't imagine what it's like—the runaround, the etiquette. Do you ask? When do you ask? What do you say? It's mind-blowing. It's enough to make you say to yourself, 'I'd rather be at home reading

a mystery.' And it's not enough that I'm worried for myself: I'm terrified for my daughter. She's just beginning her sexual life. What will happen to her?"

•

For single women, AIDS looms as an enormous issue, curtailing whatever remnants might be left for them of the sexual revolution. Single women today are careful, circumspect, and cautious. Even those who do not express fear quite as openly as Catherine say that AIDS is an issue that confronts them immediately every time they contemplate a new sexual relationship. They are self-educated about AIDS, but they are often confused. Almost daily, new reports about the spread of this deadly disease contain contradictory bits of information. In the absence of clear answers and any foreseeable cure, prevention is the only sensible course of action. And in this atmosphere of alarm and caution, the notion of sexual liberation sometimes seems like a bitter and ironic historical concept, like the once-fashionable and hip aura surrounding the passing of a marijuana joint or of the taking of LSD.

And other women, like Catherine, express fears for their growing or grown children. "In the 1950s, you told your daughter not to sleep with boys because she would be ruined," says one woman with two teen-age daughters. "Now you tell your daughter not to sleep with boys because she might die. This is progress?"

While a life-threatening issue such as AIDS must, and should, take immediate precedence over sexual freedom, some women express alarm at what they see as growing conservatism in the country, a return to traditional values as a result of the new appeal of monogamy, and consequently, the potential for a backwards slide for women. Thus some wonder if women shouldn't explore these profoundly disturbing questions about female sexuality that have arisen in the late 1980s: the expression of sexuality in an era of caution, the new rules of etiquette surrounding the old mating rituals, and how to obtain accurate information about sex and disease to dispel fears and rumors. Simply learning that other women are struggling with these issues, too, and hearing how they handle ticklish situations would be a tremendous help.

Another issue that might be explored is one that bothers some women tremendously now, but one which most of them couldn't even conceive of in 1972: the issue of having a blossoming, beautiful, highly sexual teen-age daughter while a woman in midlife is just coming to grips with the imagined loss of her beauty and the reinventing of herself as a sexual being. Laura W., a forty-year-old public relations director from St. Louis, who is the mother of three girls, says she often feels guilty, chagrined, and confused over the issue of her eldest daughter's budding sexuality occurring simultaneously with what she feels to be the loss of her own beauty. Although the topics of aging and motherhood were separately included in most CR formats in the early 1970s, this particular issue was not identified—primarily because most of the women who participated in CR during its heyday were in their twenties and early thirties. The concept of the waning of one's sex appeal at the same time one is dealing with a daughter's burgeoning sexuality seemed then as alien and as foreign as distant old age.

"Based on what the Women's Movement was telling us," says Laura, whose eldest daughter, Caro, is thirteen, "we weren't supposed to have these feelings of rivalry with our own daughters. Well, I don't know if we were supposed to or not; it just wasn't mentioned. We were supposed to feel loving and giving toward them, and what I'm saying is I feel a lot of guilt at this time. I'm upset about getting physically older and having negative feelings about this beautiful young woman who is emerging in my family.

"Turning forty in this era is very difficult," she continues. "Maybe it's always been hard to turn forty, but I feel it's especially hard now. It's painful to lose your beauty—but it's almost as if it's illegitimate to have these feelings because we were told those were not the characteristics you were supposed to rely on for self-worth.

"So I wonder: How am I going to emerge as a strong woman in the second half of my life? Before, I had a lot going for me—my youth, my energy, my beauty, the prospect of giving birth and having children. It was all possible. Now it's behind me, and I'm struggling with how to be a valuable person to myself. I feel like I'm working like mad to come to terms with this."

Women's sexuality emerges as a highly paradoxical topic— one rife with contradictions, unexplored territory, and hidden land mines. Although sex was unquestionably a subject that "took" from the early days of CR, many issues need to be investigated: remaining a sexual being while simultaneously trying to balance the demands of children and careers; negotiating one's sexuality through the public health crisis of AIDS; protecting and educating one's daughters and sons; remaining a fully sexual being during midlife; and coping with feelings of rivalry with blossoming teen-age daughters.

"I believe we're all fighting," says Laura, "but it seems that we are fighting these very lonely personal battles."

On the political level, sex became an important battle-ground in the war against sexism. This was particularly true among lesbian women—those who were part of straight CR groups as well as those who formed their own exclusively lesbian splinter CR groups. The notion that women were responsible for their own sexual pleasure allowed them to experiment with their sexuality. While some women simply were gay by preference and inclination, others explored what they felt was an emerging bisexual nature. Still others entered into relationships with women as a gesture composed of both political and personal yearnings.

■

"For me, there were distinct political overtones to loving women," says Daphne, who is having a cup of tea in a SoHo café in lower Manhattan. It is a cold October afternoon, and even inside, she hugs her wool cape about her. Her hair, a faded light brown with threads of gray, falls loosely about her face, framing her remarkable sea-green eyes. "I learned that I could do without a man," she says. "That was thrilling, because I was furious at men. In college, I would fall in love like Isadora Duncan. And I would resent it terribly when my male lovers would be cavalier about my feelings. It happened over and over again. As soon as a man found out I was really serious, he would leave."*

Daphne began to believe that what she wanted could not be had from a man. At the same time, she says, she was discovering that women could be very sensual and wonderful, and for her, she says, "that was terrific." It seemed logical to her to take on women as lovers. "I was thrilled that I could have a relationship with a woman, because then the personal and the political would merge. I'd always been very involved with radical politics, but this was an entirely new dimension."

Daphne began having women lovers when she was in the CR group. At first she didn't tell anyone, and then one night she "came out," as she describes it. It was an evening she will never forget. "No

91

one said a word. Not one word. Not then, not ever. It was the weirdest thing. It was as if I were the invisible woman. I said my piece. I waited for an explosion. Nothing happened. We went right on to the next person."

Other friends, however, were more outspoken. According to Daphne, they divided right down the middle. The most advanced politically were happy for her. Her best friend, however, was horrified. "She was very personally threatened," says Daphne.

Daphne left the CR group some months before it disbanded and became involved with lesbian separatists, a group that was ideologically separate from mainstream feminism, in that they believed that men were the oppressors and that women should not have relationships of any kind with them. For six years, Daphne had lesbian relationships only. She describes this as a very political time in her life. "We wanted to do something on a large scale," she says. "We were very radical, so radical you knew nothing was ever going to happen. We wanted to start a lesbian army. We wanted to find an island off Denmark, I remember, to start a totally women's community."

When Daphne was in her early thirties she had a serious love affair with another woman, who was ten years younger than she. "I wanted to spend every minute of my time with her. I changed jobs and moved up to Albany just so I could be near her. And then, after we had been together for about a year, she started seeing other women. I was shattered. It was a revelation to me that I could be mistreated by women."

Daphne swore off women forever, or so she thought. She met a man and, on the rebound, so to speak, she married him. The marriage, however, was disastrous. He was everything Daphne hated in men— macho, traditional, chauvinist. She wanted to leave, but by then there was a son.

"Sometime after my son was born, I just found my marriage in-

tolerable. It seemed natural at the time to turn again to women. And so I fell in love with another woman. I started seeing her, and my husband found out. He just hit the wall. He tried to destroy me because of it. He went to court and got custody of my son. I have visitation rights, and that's all. It really put me under for about two years," she says.

Now Daphne is confused about her sexuality. "I don't believe that lesbianism is primarily political," she says. "Lesbianism, for me, *was one of the forms taken as an outcome of the sexual revolution; I was not only encouraged to enjoy sex and have more of it, but to have more choice. As for actually doing it, obviously some women have a taste for it and others do not. But to be open to it, that seemed to be political.*

"Personally, I feel that I am probably bisexual, though I haven't been able to have any sexual relationships at all for a while now. I don't belong to any lesbian groups anymore—I don't feel the same kind of political urgency I did years ago—but I still can't say goodbye to my lesbian self. If you ask me what I want, it would be just to live alone and have my son back. I wouldn't ask for anything more. I know there are a lot of gay women out there who are strong, beautiful, together women. They have good, productive, happy and valid lives. But I'm not one of them. . . . At least, not yet."

■

In 1972, the year that Daphne's CR group first began to meet, lesbian separatist issues nearly split the Women's Movement. In September of that year, lesbian groups dominated the Women's March for Equality down Fifth Avenue in New York, sparking an intense debate about the rightful place of lesbians within the movement. Many feminists who had taken part in two previous marches did not attend that year in silent protest against what they felt was a takeover by radical elements.

The debate was fierce. Although few feminists rejected the notion of a woman's right to express her own sexuality, it was feared that if the movement was too closely identified with gays, it would alienate hundreds of thousands of still uncommitted women. Those who worried about the lesbian segment of the movement claimed that lesbian politics ignored sexual reality: Gays, they said, had given up on two essential aspects of womanhood—sexual feelings for men and childbearing.

The lesbian position, naturally, was quite the opposite: If a woman's loyalties were first to a man and a family, her emotions and her energies would necessarily go to them. Lesbians were thus freer to act out the independence that every woman should have as a person.

The National Organization for Women, not surprisingly, took on the role of peacemaker. Since lesbians were both women and homosexual, went the NOW position, they were doubly oppressed. NOW endorsed their civil rights and civil liberties and said that lesbianism was a legitimate concern of the Women's Movement. They made it clear, however, that they did not equate lesbianism with feminism.

From the vantage point of the late 1980s, such a debate may seem historical. The political and social gains made by homosexual women in America seem impressive when compared to that bleak era just prior to the early 1970s, when very few women indeed would dare even to come out of the closet, never mind become an advocate for lesbian rights. Yet interestingly, and rather alarmingly for the Women's Movement as a whole, that old debate is not over. On college campuses, which are now the most consistently fertile soil for the gathering of women's groups, often the most outspoken advocates for women's rights are lesbians. It is frequently the lesbian groups who engineer candlelight vigils for rape victims, who manage incest-abuse centers, and who still hold forums on women's issues in what often seems like a vestigial remnant of an earlier era. Although one can only be grateful to these young women for working so tirelessly to push important issues into the forefront of women's consciousness, their peers, who have not lived through an era when a broad spectrum of women were fighting for women's rights, often say they are "turned off" to women's issues. In their universe, women's rights are too closely allied with gays—a campus group with which they may not wish to be identified.

One confusing result of this is that many young women today have difficulty with the term *feminist*. "I wouldn't go so far as to say 'feminist' is a dirty word," says one young student. "I don't think we feel quite that strongly about it. But if there's a group of women having a speak-out or whatever for rape victims, and I find out that almost everyone who's going to be there is gay, I'm not going to show up. It's not the cause itself I mind (in fact, I think the issue is very important); it's that I'm not gay myself, and I don't want to be identified as gay. I have no problem with other gays; it's just that I'd have to explain myself afterward. So, I don't go to women's meetings, period."

While antilesbian bias is not as strong on college campuses as it was in previous eras when lesbians had no political power whatsoever and were shunned and humiliated, many young heterosexual women today remain ignorant and fearful about just who lesbians are and what they want.

"Before we discovered lesbianism in my CR group," says Leslye S., a lawyer in Pearl River, New York, "I had never really thought about the issue, and I thought lesbians were strange and deviant. But after we had talked the issue through, my feelings were quite different. One of the women

I met was a lesbian, and I remember she said: 'I get up in the morning, and I put on my lesbian sneakers, and I eat my lesbian cornflakes, and I get in my lesbian car, and I go to my lesbian job.' She made me laugh, and she just put it all into perspective—the only difference between her and me was sexual preference. And I understood why it was such an important issue to talk about and deal with in the open, because I could see the way the label was used as a slur—and more importantly, the way it was used to get women to disaffiliate themselves from the Women's Movement."

FIVE

Getting Launched

Jane is sitting at the wheel of a beat-up blue Chevy station wagon, double-parked in front of a loft on Mercer Street. She is waiting for her daughter, Simone, to finish her cello lesson and come lumbering down the stone steps, cello case in hand, backpack slung over her shoulder. Simone, a freshman at NYU, has chosen to live at home this first year of school not only because of the proximity of her home to the school, but also for the savings to her parents. Jane, who said at the reunion that she had once made a conscious decision to put her family before herself, has been ferrying Simone and her cello to lessons for five years.

It is raining hard outside, the rain drumming against the windshield as Jane waits with the engine running. She is wearing a tan raincoat and rainhat and a pair of gray rubber boots. With her other three children grown and out of the house, and her daughter in her first year of college, Jane says she has had more time this fall to think about what she might do with herself now that the children are leaving the nest. She has a broker's license and has made some money with

*that, but the broker's license, she says, was merely a pragmatic mea-
sure—a way for a woman with children to make some money on the
side to supplement her husband's income. While she says that the
years spent with her children were the happiest of her life, she also
speaks candidly about a tremendous sense of loss she experiences when
she thinks about what she might have done with herself.*

*"When I was my daughter's age," she says, "there was no thought
of a career. I did go to college, in a liberal arts program, and there
I got the idea I should be an artist. I had a bit of talent, but the
main thing about being an artist, I remember, was that you could
do it anywhere—so they said. It was like being a writer. You could
go where your husband wanted you to, and you could have kids, and
you could still be an artist. So if you didn't want to be a teacher or
an executive secretary, you thought about being an artist or a writer.
No one ever said anything to girls then about being lawyers or doctors
or business women. But, my God, when I think of all the jobs out
there, all the things that might have been possible . . ."*

*When Jane joined the CR group, she had four young children,
and she had already learned, "the hard way," that a woman couldn't
really be an artist "anywhere," especially if one had kids underfoot.
Although Jane and her husband had broken through to an adjacent
apartment to provide room for their growing family, Jane still had
to set up her easel in her living room. And in order for her to find
time to paint, the children had to be having naps or be at school at
the same time—or in bed for the night. "Being an artist is a selfish
endeavor, if you're going to do it right," says Jane. "A man who is
an artist doesn't have to stop every five minutes to pour the juice or
help a child find his sneakers. A man who is an artist leaves the
house and goes to a studio. A mother can't do that."*

*Despite her own inability to commit herself to her art, however,
Jane saw in her CR group that something extraordinary was happening all around her. Women, perhaps just a few years younger*

than herself, were radically changing their ideas about what they were going to do with their lives. "It was absolutely the most amazing thing," she says. "You had to live through it to see it. Take Sandi, for instance. A housewife like myself. But going crazy. When I think of her then, I think of that movie, Diary of a Mad Housewife. *But through the group, she broke free. I don't know how else to put it. She just broke free and took charge of her own life, and started to think about using all those talents she had that were dying on the vine.*

"And Felicia," adds Jane, remembering. "She was in college then, liberal arts, just like I'd been. And you could see when she entered the group, she was headed toward one of the traditional women's jobs—teaching, college teaching if she got her graduate degree. But I remember one night she was talking about being an English teacher and how she wasn't sure she wanted to do that, and someone in the group said, 'Felicia, you should go into business, you're so organized and fast.' And Felicia kind of looked surprised, as if to say, 'You've got to be kidding.' No woman then thought about going into business. You just didn't. But as the night wore on, and everyone got excited, there was this tremendous groundswell of energy, and I remember Felicia saying, 'I can do that.' And it became a kind of rallying cry for all of us: 'Yeah, I can do that.' *Whether it was learning how to change the oil in your car or driving across the country by yourself or telling your husband you were going back to school or simply* thinking *of yourself in a different light. And that's what happened to Felicia. Suddenly it was, 'Yeah, I can go to business school. I can do that.'"*

Jane laughs. "We said it so much," she says, "it became a joke. One of us would say to the other how we were thinking of getting our hair streaked, or heading off to Bloomingdale's for a new dress, and the other would say, 'Yeah, I can do that.'"

She smiles. Then she shakes her head. She looks away, out the window at the rain-soaked street. "It was too late for me," she says.

"I was just a little bit too old, too established already as a housewife. I tried leaving, but it didn't work out. I was too much a product of my childhood, my upbringing. I gave myself to my children, and I don't regret it."

As if on cue, the door to the loft building opens and Simone struggles through it with her cello case. She waves at her mother and smiles as she makes her way slowly down the steps.

"But Simone," says Jane. "She's the real recipient of it all. The world is wide open for her. She's going to medical school, she says. Can you imagine? And not to be a pediatrician or a psychiatrist— she wants to be a surgeon. She came to this all on her own. She looked out into the world, saw something she wanted to be, and never thought to herself for one second, 'Only a man can do that,' or 'Will I be able to pick up and move with this job if my husband has to relocate?' It's not part of her thinking. I have a son, and I saw the way he decided on architecture, and I watched the way Simone came to her decision to go to medical school, and I'll tell you, there was no difference between the two."

Simone opens the door to the back seat, slides her cello across, and slips in herself. She is a lithe young woman, with large dark eyes and short brown hair. She gives her mother a rub on the shoulder, settles back, and says with a sigh that she's got to do the Mozart again this week. Her teacher didn't like her timing.

Jane puts the car in gear and edges out into the street. "It all happened in CR," she says. "You could see it happening all around you, like popcorn popping. All these women getting energized and exploding into action. It was fantastic. . . ."

"Mom?" asks Simone from the back seat.

"What is it, sweetie?" Jane says, somewhat distracted by a taxi that's cut her off.

"What was CR again?"

■

If consciousness-raising was a spur to the sexual revolution, it was a veritable catapult to the working-woman revolution. The launching of large numbers of women from the interior, domestic world of the home into the outside world is the single most dramatic outcome of the consciousness-raising phenomenon. CR allowed women to expand their horizons, to become economically independent, and to increase their self-esteem to the point where they were able to envision themselves as ambitious, successful, and competent. Hundreds of thousands of women who had previously imagined for themselves lives of foreshortened horizons, emerged from CR sessions with a new way of thinking about their futures. Women who had once thought they would be stewardesses began to conceive of themselves as lawyers. Women whose ambitions had once stopped short at being an executive secretary started to think about running the company instead. Women who had been groomed to be nurses switched gears and went off to medical school. "I can do that," became the rallying cry of thousands, then hundreds of thousands, then millions of women, as they poured out of the home into the work force.

To be sure, certain economic factors were operating simultaneously to push women into the work force: the rise of a consumer economy, the inability to make ends meet with one paycheck, and the increased number of young women with college educations. But it was in CR that women became empowered. Something could be had in the workplace, they were discovering among themselves, that they were not finding at home: a sense of being valued by society, a newfound feeling of competence, a new respect hitherto never experienced, and a life that seemed to offer more rewards—both monetarily and emotionally—than washing diapers and cleaning toilets. Access to money and power need not be the exclusive privilege of the male gender, they were learning. Money and power—seductive, mesmerizing, and suddenly attainable (at least for the white middle class)—was within women's grasp.

But women in their groups did not confine themselves merely to launching themselves into the workplace; they also spoke of how to negotiate the workplace once there. In their CR groups, women shared anecdotes of sexual discrimination, and their anger rose to a crescendo. Women were paid less than men for the exact same job. Click. A woman in a company was shut out at the top. Click. A woman lawyer could not become a partner. Click. Among a group of peers, it would be the woman who would be asked to get the coffee. Click. Women were harassed in the professions, scorned by the old guard, and held in contempt for taking good jobs away from men with families. Click. Click. Click.

"While I was in the group," says one woman who in 1972 worked in a public relations firm, "I was called into my boss's office and told that while I was as equally qualified to get a promotion as a male colleague of mine, they were promoting him instead of me, simply because they needed a 'nominal' director. Before I'd joined the group, I wouldn't even have gotten angry. I would have gone home quiet and depressed, and I really wouldn't have understood that my depression hid my anger. But being in the group gave me insight—not courage *per se* (I'd always had courage)—but *insight*. I said to my boss, 'It's a lousy decision. Professionally, you're stymieing me, and politically, it stinks. The only thing this guy has got that I haven't is a fucking penis! You'll have my resignation in the morning.'

"As it happened, they didn't let me resign—in fact, they

promoted me. But that didn't matter as much to me as the fact that I went home feeling *great*. I felt so powerful! Without the group, it would have taken me twenty years to gain that insight."

Such power, opportunity, and insight were unarguably of tremendous benefit to women. Women today, fifteen years after CR, speak of pivotal moments and life decisions occurring because of what they were hearing in CR. "There was one woman in my group I'll never forget," says Susan J., a psychiatrist in Chicago. "She had gone to college and had started to be an artist. She thought she wanted to be a sculptor. She was the kind of person who did whatever she did seriously, but you didn't necessarily feel any passion when she talked about being an artist. There was something missing from her. And one time we were talking about ourselves as preadolescents. During the discussion, she started to remember how much she had loved science, and how much she had wanted to be a doctor. But at eleven years old, she said, she'd given that up in favor of a more suitably feminine occupation. Then, a couple of meetings later, she announced she had decided to try to go to medical school, which involved her going back to school with all premed courses. Subsequently, in the group, I watched her doing all this premed stuff, and I felt a complete radical shift of identity within her. Now she's a doctor, a gynecologist, and I'm sure that was because of the group."

Consciousness-raising encouraged women to become breadwinners, to enter into male-dominated professions, to push further ahead in chosen careers, to think beyond the myth of Prince Charming, to demand equal pay for equal work, and to begin to think of women as having the same rights as men not only in the workplace but to work at all.

In short, women in the CR groups learned that they had choices. Women in their CR groups gained the courage to go for it.

And go for it they did. From 1972, the heyday of the consciousness-raising movement, to 1982, the number of women lawyers alone increased fivefold. Today about 40 percent of management positions in the private sector are held by women, and in the public sector, 18,000 women hold elected office. Medical schools, which once had only one or two women students in each class, now boast that nearly half their students are women. Women now resemble male workers in the strength of their commitment to the workplace and in the nature of their steady, full-time employment. Today, work-life expectancy of women is less than ten years behind that of men. In 1959, work-life expectancy for women was nearly thirty years behind that of men.

No profession, no place of work has been untouched by this revolution. And no American family can ignore it. Even that minority of families that still operates in the traditional mode (the breadwinning father; the at-home mother) lives and works in a world of women mail carriers, construction workers, CEOs, and bank presidents. The full-scale entry of women into the work force has been historic, unprecedented, and revolutionary—changing the way an entire generation of young girls and boys now view the adult role of woman.

The headlong catapulting of women into the work force, however, has not been without its individual traumas and its difficulties. Although almost all women interviewed for this book say they have come much farther in their careers than they ever thought possible before they joined CR (and some extraordinarily so), nearly all are mindful of barriers, obstacles and pitfalls. Old problems remain unresolved. New problems, unforeseen a decade ago, threaten the gains made by women in the workplace. And, say the women, their heavy workload and their isolation because of that workload prevents the tackling of these problems on any widespread scale.

Chief among these unresolved difficulties is sex discrimination at the workplace. Women have narrowed the pay gap, but they still only make seventy cents to every man's dollar. They have narrowed the professional gap as well—actually surpassing men in the total number of positions held in the professions—but they remain shut out at the very top. Unable to penetrate what has been called "the glass ceiling," most top women still languish at middle and upper-middle management. And women still account for the overwhelming majority of clerical workers.

In addition to these longstanding areas of discrimination, however, women have recently been encountering a new kind of prejudice—that against working mothers. Women with young children who seek flexible schedules, part-time work, adequate maternity leaves—or even those who work full-time but who must return home each evening at five o'clock to make supper and care for their children—are finding that they are denied promotions, salary increases, and respect at the workplace. Among the professions where twelve- and fourteen-hour days are *de rigueur*, women who seek to modify their hours in order to care for families are regarded as having slipped off "the fast track" and are therefore thought to be uncommitted to the profession. In law, this translates to a closing off of access to partnerships; in business, to a denial of top management positions and the loss of thousands of dollars in potential income; and in medicine, to the encouraging of women to enter "softer" practices, such as research. At work, say women, is the old sexism, albeit in a new guise:

A man can give his all for his career and still be a decent father; a woman, however, cannot give everything to her career and still be a decent mother.

Beneath the placid statistics of increasing numbers of women in the work force, a crisis is simmering. Today more than 50 percent of women with children under the age of one year return to the work force (many because they *have* to). When they do, however, they often find themselves torn, unable to work the excessively long hours needed to compete with colleagues and stay on top. Worse, many are so grateful for any kind of flexible scheduling, including part-time work, that they quietly relinquish, without a fuss, whatever seniority they might previously have held. The result is a two-tier system—men on top, women on the bottom.

Discrimination is not confined, however, just to management. Women say that they feel resentment and hostility from colleagues as well. Elizabeth M., who belonged to a CR group in Manhattan in 1972 and who today is an editor for a New York publishing firm, says she fully expected to go back to work full time after her maternity leave. But as happens so often, Elizabeth fell in love with her daughter and requested part-time work instead. When she did so, she pointed out to her boss that she could make a valuable contribution during this temporary period in her life, and that she was prepared to commit herself to the company for many years. She was refused part-time work, but when it became clear that a full-time schedule was making no one very happy, her company allowed her to work part time as a free-lancer. As such, she lost all her benefits and her seniority, but she was still willing to give it a try.

As time went on, however, Elizabeth discovered that she

was regarded as a second-class citizen by her colleagues. She also felt a considerable loss of self-esteem as well as a good deal of guilt when watching others working long hours while she came and went. Thinking that perhaps a job change was in order, she sought and found a three-day-a-week schedule at another publishing firm. Yet again, the response from colleagues was unnerving. "People would make snide comments such as, 'Well, we'd like to go home early, too, you know,' or, 'If you were in here more, you'd know what was going on,'" says Elizabeth. "After awhile, my self-esteem plummeted to an all-time low. I just wasn't able to get the job done. I didn't feel a part of the team and I felt a lot of hostility from my co-workers."

Called "the maternity backlash," the discrimination against women with children in the workplace is an issue that women say needs to be tackled on a widespread scale. Tamara R., a lawyer with a large firm in Boston, recently gave birth to a son. When she returned from her maternity leave, she asked for and received part-time work. Part-time work in Tamara's firm, however, is unofficially defined as nine to five, five days a week. "You would think that would qualify as full-time work," says Tamara, "and probably in many occupations it would. But not in the law. Prior to having the baby, I would stay until ten at night on many occasions, and I was nearly always in the office by eight. But that kind of schedule is impossible with a family. So I got my part-time work—but I was made to understand that by requesting it and getting it, I'd be giving up any thought of making partner."

Maternity backlash is an urgent problem, but it may be, say many women, only part of a much larger problem: the complex nature of work and success in America today. "Do we want to teach our children that success in life means leaving the house at seven in the morning and coming home at ten at night?" asks Tamara.

"We've become obsessed with the idea of success," says Mayra K., a personnel manager in Houston. "I know women who have no personal lives anymore. They live, breathe, eat work. They might as well sleep there. In most companies, and in most professions, there's an unwritten code of behavior: Those who will make it to the top have to sacrifice a personal life. And making it to the top has become the be-all and the end-all. The pressures to be successful, and not to fail, are tremendous. I really don't believe that this is what men and women were meant to do at the workplace. It's spiraled out of control. And for women, it's especially difficult. I believe it goes against their natures to give up home and family. I don't believe that women have brought their values to the workplace. I think they've just bought in totally to male values."

In an era in which it was necessary to take by storm those previously male-dominated professions, adopting the values of the power elite may have been vital. But now that women have infiltrated most professions, perhaps it is time, they say, to rethink those values that women appear to have taken on for themselves. Might it not be possible, women ask, to change the nature of going to work in this country in order to better accommodate children and family life? Must women give up the joys of nurturing and of making a home merely to keep a job? Must a woman (or a man) be made to feel a failure if she or he chooses also to be a loving and committed parent? What does it say about us if we are willing to sacrifice our children, time spent alone, and friendships with other women in order to achieve "success"? Are promotions and salary increases, in fact, the true definition of success?

The heart of the problem may be, say many women, that in entering the male-dominated workplace, women felt compelled to identify with a masculine mode of being—in behaving, speaking, and dressing. In so doing, they devalued feminine modes of behavior and those preoccupations associated with females: homemaking, children and child care.

"To seek for equality alone, given the current male bias of the social values, is to assume that women want to be like men or that men are worth emulating," writes Jo Freeman in her book *Women: A Feminist Perspective*. "It is to demand that women be allowed to participate in society as we know it, to get their piece of the pie, without questioning whether that society is worth participating in. Most feminists today find this view inadequate. Those women who are personally more comfortable in what is considered the male role must realize that that role is made possible only by the existence of the female sex role; in other words, only by the subjection of women. Therefore, women cannot become equal to men without the destruction of those two interdependent, mutually parasitic roles."[6]

Women today, fifteen years after CR, have begun to question success as a value in itself, and to examine the ways in which they have unthinkingly adopted masculine values at the workplace. Indeed, they are asking themselves whether or not values can be characterized as either "masculine" or "feminine," and if so, what exactly those values are. In addition, they are wondering to what extent the premium placed on success has caused them to feel competitive with other women—and even with their spouses. Do they, for example, have enough time for spouses and children? Does super-achieving on the job lead to power struggles in a marriage? In the contemporary dual-career marriage, what determines power now? Job status? The higher salary? Time pressures? And in this contemporary dual-career marriage, who takes care of the home? Or the children?

For few doubt that the massive entry of women into the job market will eventually reshape the American workplace. "I think it's already happening," says Beth P., an account executive with an advertising firm in Manhattan. "Women have made many fundamental changes in the workplace. And perhaps through these changes, we are beginning to reassert our values. Look at the number of corporations nowadays that offer flex-time, part-time work, on-site daycare, or day-care subsidies. These changes all came about because of the large numbers of working mothers on the job who demanded them."

Another issue that concerns women today is that of sexual harassment on the job. Because it is an issue that while always present at the workplace, has only been labeled and critically examined in the last decade, it did not present itself in earlier CR groups. Yet sexual harassment, say many women, has been and continues to be an occupational hazard.

In November 1980 the Equal Employment Opportunity Commission (EEOC) defined sexual harassment as a violation of Title VII of the 1964 Civil Rights Act. Many state human rights laws today protect workers from discrimination. Despite this legal recourse, however, sexual harassment is prevalent in the workplace, with as many as 70 percent of all female workers, according to some studies, having experienced unwanted advances.[7] Although men can be victims of sexual harassment, the overwhelming majority of the abused are women—with women reporting everything from pats on the fanny to denial of promotion for refusal to sleep with the boss. The effects of sexual harassment can be debilitating for the female worker: humiliation, anxiety, loss of confidence and self-esteem, chronic stress, chronic absenteeism, and job loss.

At its most basic level, sexual harassment represents the abuse of power. A woman dependent upon her job for her livelihood may feel too vulnerable to resist the advances of a male superior. On another level, a male who feels threatened by powerful women colleagues may seek to reduce their power by resorting to sexual condescension—thus subtly "putting them in their sexual place." Sexual harassment has always been a potent tool to subjugate women at the workplace, and legal recourse alone has not eliminated the practice.

Also worrisome to women, however, is the flip side of the sexual harassment issue: What to do about the age-old practice of using one's sexuality to get ahead? While some women argue that trading sexual favors for work benefits is simply a pragmatic recognition of where power resides, others worry about how to separate an office romance from one's career. "For four months I was having an affair with my boss," says one woman, a reporter for a large metropolitan newspaper. "Part of the attraction on my part was the power. He was a very important editor and in a position to have a tremendous effect on my career. And for most of the time we were together, I was aware of having an enhanced status. I got the plum assignments. We went out to lunch regularly and talked over stories. There was even talk of promoting me to the editorial desk with the idea we'd be a team. It was a very complicated thing. The love affair was linked to the job, each one enhancing the other. If he hadn't been in the position he was in, I might not have found him so attractive. And the job itself definitely became more fun because of the affair. But when it ended, it was very awkward and painful. Here we were supposedly working together on all these stories, and we weren't even speaking. And I became a kind of pariah. My status plummeted. There was no more talk of promotion."

The Women's Movement gave women choices and opportunities and paved the way for them to enter the workforce in droves. In their CR groups, women became encouraged and empowered. But now, fifteen years later, many new difficulties have presented themselves. Many hard questions need to be asked and answered. In some places of work, women have formed networks to help solve pragmatic problems, but most of these networks are based on the male model of the "old boy" networks and are intended to increase women's access to power—not to question the basis of that power, or to ask how women might merge access to that power with the joys of home and family.

At issue today is nothing less than the very nature of work and love, and the opportunity for women to have both in their lives. Whether or not the difficulties at the workplace will be tackled and resolved is impossible to predict. But one thing *is* certain: Women cannot resolve these dilemmas as isolated individuals. Nor will anyone else do it for them.

SIX

The Age of Beauty

"It was a very large issue," says Catherine thoughtfully, as she sits behind the till at her book shop on a Saturday night. It is late— 10:45—and only a few browsers still remain. "We talked about it many times, and we covered a lot of territory," she says. "I believe at the time we did ourselves a great deal of good, but I think it's one of the few lessons we learned in CR that didn't take."

Catherine begins to wind a long roll of register tape. She has done the tally, and is pleased. It has been a good day. She is wearing a fashionably short peach-colored skirt and matching jacket with a white T-shirt underneath. She has on gold-colored earrings, a necklace and bracelet, and one can see that she uses several different kinds of makeup, albeit subtly and expertly.

Catherine is talking about appearance, body image, how she looks.

"I think for about six months we all had clarity on this issue, but I would have to say that for most of my life, I've been confused," she says.

When Catherine joined her CR group, she had already begun to

move away from the Barbie-Doll-and-girdle-look that had charac-
terized the 1950s and early 1960s. Most of the women she knew,
she says, were letting their hair grow long and natural, and had
taken to living in jeans and black turtleneck sweaters or tie-dyed
shirts. And in CR, she says, it became a political gesture to emphasize
the natural. "You remember how it was," she says, smiling. "You
didn't shave your legs, you didn't wear a bra, you didn't wear makeup.
You didn't dream of wearing a girdle or high heels and stockings.
The point was to liberate yourself from being a sex object," she says,
"but, of course, most of the guys found the natural look pretty sexy
then, too."

As liberating as the natural look was for the women in her CR
group, however, Catherine was amazed to discover just how complex
the issue of body image was for all of them. "Every woman in the
group had imagined for herself some serious flaw that she obsessed
about," recalls Catherine. "There were all these beautiful women,
and none of them thought so. They'd all been made to feel imperfect
because they didn't measure up to some Madison Avenue stereotype
of what beautiful and sexy was supposed to be. I remember one
woman was in agony because her breasts were too big; *I remember*
another hated being short. Another hated her nose; another said her
life had been ruined forever because she wore glasses. It was one of
those epiphanies that we were having on a regular basis back then.
You had thought you were the only one who felt flawed, until you
realized everyone did. And that told you something—that it wasn't
the women who were flawed, but the image of what a woman was
supposed to be."

A man comes up to the counter with an armful of books and asks
Catherine where he might find the new Jean Stafford biography. She
directs him and returns to her thoughts.

"So we had that epiphany," says Catherine, "and it felt good for
about a couple of months, but it didn't last. Look at me," she says.

"I'm wearing a skirt above my knees. I wouldn't dream of coming in here without my makeup on. I've got about seven or eight outfits I rotate, and none of them is even remotely what you'd call 'the natural look.' It would be ridiculous to say I dress for success; I don't. But I dress to look 'with it' in my job and I dress to be attractive. I can't say whether I'm doing it for men or not. I don't really know. It's as important to me to have a woman think I look good as a man. I spend a lot of time on my appearance. Too much time. I'm very confused on this issue. I don't like spending all that time. I think I ought to be able to come in here in a pair of jeans and eat a pizza if I want to and just be me. But when I see women who don't take care of themselves, or women who still wear the natural look it looks wrong to me, out of sync. Kind of silly, really."

In their CR groups, women talked about body image and their appearance. It was a subject that ignited passion. So important was the topic to women, in fact, that it seems to have surfaced in almost all groups whether or not the group had a format to follow. When they did have a format, the women were asked the following questions: "How do you feel about your body?" "How did you feel (in adolescence) about your bodily changes?" "How do the media present women?"

For years women had been told that they should look and act sweet, demure, sexy, soft, and vulnerable. They should also smile a lot. In short, they should appear to be at all times a perfect blend of Barbie and Grace Kelly. But the women chafed at the image. Why should they be sweet? they asked. Why should they have to smile all the time? Being sweet and smiling all the time placed a woman in an inferior position. Wearing high heels and having long fingernails rendered a woman useless, weak, and incompetent. Wearing pointy bras and high heels turned women into sex objects whose sole existence seemed to be for the pleasure of men. In their CR groups, women talked about their self-image, and about how their very identity had become so dependent upon the mirror of the men and the sexist culture that surrounded them that they no longer even knew who they really were.

"You were supposed to have this body language in order to attract a man," says Margaret S., a wine merchant in New York. "You were supposed to lower your eyes, and smile demurely, or bat your eyelashes and cross your legs. . . . It was as if women were supposed to be gooey, like marshmallows and Twinkies."

And if you didn't measure up, the rest of the message went, if you were unable to achieve the "marshmallow and Twinkie" demeanor, you were supposed to feel ashamed of your body, or, at the very least, inferior to all those other women out there who seemingly had it together.

For many women, the most important benefit of CR was the realization of how much they had despised their female bodies. Many were astonished to discover that others felt the same way. Tiny women said they felt like they were heifers. Voluptuous women wanted breast reductions. Women despised their hair, their thighs, their skin. "It was beyond the question of what men were going to think about you," says one woman. "It was just something so internal."

Because being vulnerable or attractive and "gooey" often meant being smaller than a man, weight was frequently the issue. Why was it, they asked, that women were trying to look like teen-age boys? And what did it really mean to want to diminish a strong woman's body? Wasn't refusing to be thin— or rather, flat and without hips and bellies—acknowledging that you didn't want or deserve to be put in the mold that men and the culture were trying to put you in?

Enraged by the insight that their appearance was not of their own making, many women began to eschew the artifice that had turned them into Twinkies.

"I was so upset when I learned who I was," says Margaret S., "that I cut my hair to within half an inch of my scalp, I threw away all the makeup, the bras, and the tight skirts. I started wearing pants. I didn't want something so ludicrous as the fact that my hair wasn't curled right or my eyeliner wasn't on straight to determine the state of my day."

For a time, CR allowed women to come to grips with awkward and confused feelings they had had for years about their body image. Women who felt they were spending too many precious hours a day on their appearance suddenly had awareness as to why they were doing so. Women who had bristled at being sex objects found support for relinquishing the apparatus that had created them. Women who minded being vulnerable and soft shed the accoutrements of helplessness and found a kind of tantalizing liberation in an image of strength. They learned, for the first time, that they had choices about how they wanted to look—and many of them chose to explore freedom rather than restraint.

They also learned that the issue of appearance was not a trivial one. Many of the women came to have understanding and compassion for themselves and for all those other women who had for years been trying to fit themselves into an acceptable mold. It was merely, they learned, a completely sensible and realistic survival tactic. As one Redstocking sister wrote in 1971: "There is a frequent putdown of women who wear makeup and bleach their hair. According to the brainwashing theorists, such a woman has blindly accepted the ad men's image of what she should look like. She must 'liberate herself' by learning to accept her natural beauty. Completely left out of the picture is the fact that a woman's appearance is her work uniform. If she shows up to work without the proper uniform her boss (or husband) can harass her or find a replacement."[8]

Once the women in CR groups gained awareness of the concept of appearance-as-uniform, they began to revolt. A woman could do the job of being a wife or a secretary without the traditional uniform, they said. A woman could, indeed, *redesign* the uniform itself to fit her natural inclinations.

And, for a time, women did. For a time, they even changed the concept of what beauty was to match their more natural desires. In short, the natural look became a fashion. Yet, as a fashion, it was as short-lived as other fashions.

Recently, Margaret S., the wine merchant who once cut her hair to within an inch of her scalp and threw away her bras and tight skirts, was having a plate of cheese and crackers after work in her condo in lower Manhattan. She'd been home about twenty minutes and hadn't had time yet to change from her work "uniform," the clothes she had worn that day as vice-president of the wine firm. She was wearing a Chanel-type suit, sheer stockings, moderately high heels, and a short but stylish haircut. Her eyeliner was prominent. Having given up on the natural look as well as the Twinkie look, she freely admitted she dresses for success. "You dress to suit your environment," she said.

This topic is a particularly fascinating one among women who once belonged to CR groups. Although most of the women still retain the initial insights about female appearance and identity they gained in their groups, they remain, on a day-to-day level, perplexed by the lingering emotional and political significance of their looks. Some see their looks as vital, in a practical way, to getting ahead. Others speak poignantly about the fear of losing theirs as they age. Although most women no longer look like Barbie, they admit to being somewhat confused about the difference between dressing to please others and dressing to please oneself. They remember the lessons they learned in CR, but these lessons somehow seem more applicable to another era. The women speak frequently, sometimes pointedly, sometimes in passing, of their weight, their hair, and their skin, and about how dissatisfied they are by their appearance. They wonder if they aren't still defined by male-dominated criteria—in the workplace and in the culture at large. They wonder if they haven't simply traded in one kind of mirror for another.

"I'm very, very careful about what I wear to work," says Mary W., a corporate lawyer in Manhattan. "I have a wardrobe consultant at Saks. I don't wear little bow ties, but I wear the equivalent of finely tailored suits. There are unwritten rules for everything in my business—how big the shoulder pads are, how short the skirts can be, how high the heels can be, how subtle the texturing of the stockings is. It's positively a uniform. If I showed up one day in a granny dress or, to take the other extreme, a black leather mini-skirt, I'd be ridiculed. I'd probably lose a lot of clout on the job, too."

Clearly, the timeless message of the Redstockings pamphlet is still applicable, even in the late 1980s. But the Redstockings pamphlet also implied that a woman could be replaced in a relationship if she didn't put on the "uniform" of sweetness— that "marshmallow and Twinkie" look of soft, vulnerable desirability. Is that message still applicable today?

In many confusing and contradictory ways it is. Although women suggested that they now had a choice to be "sweet" or not, they were mindful of the consequences if they chose not to be. Margaret S., for example, says she is sometimes troubled by what she perceives as her inability now to dress or comport herself for the sole purpose of attracting a man. Although she likes to appear attractive in a general sense (and does so), she no longer equates "attractiveness" with vulnerability. On the job and in her life, she is a strong, powerful woman—and her smart, chic, tailored appearance suggests this. But while she is pleased with her level of consciousness and the stripping away of vulnerability, she is aware of the risks entailed. Men, she says, still find a gooey surface more pleasing, at least initially, than one of strength. "I pretend less," she says. "My eyes don't blink. I don't know how to look adoring anymore. I've all but given up that fly-paper veneer. I've lost the body language of attracting a man."

The dilemma, of course, is paradoxical. As a strong woman and a strong feminist, Margaret isn't really interested in men who prefer sweetness to strength; yet without the "body language of attracting a man," as Margaret puts it, she says it is getting harder and harder to meet men in the first place.

The cultural image of what's attractive in a woman, which overtly or subtly influences both men and women in our society, appears not to have changed much in several important criteria from twenty or thirty years ago. To be sure the "Barbie" look, the "Natural" look and the "Twiggy" look are all passé, having given way in the mid-eighties to the muscled "athletic" look, and more recently to the bosomy "Madonna" look, but a recent perusal of TV and print media advertisements, in which women were featured, showed the following characteristics: Almost all of the women were thinner than the average woman, some of them extremely so. Most of the women pictured appeared to be between the ages of nineteen and twenty-five. A preponderance of the women were blond, and the majority had long hair. Almost all of them, except those in bathing suits, were wearing restrictive, confining, or sexy clothing—short skirts, cocktail dresses, suits, high heels, sheer stockings. All of them wore makeup, and some of them had on a great deal of makeup. Almost all of the women had manicured fingernails.

Although the styles had obviously changed, several important characteristics remained: The women's dress was restrictive and confining; in order to achieve the look they presented, it was evident that the women had had to spend a great deal of time preparing their makeup and hair; the end result of the look was that they appeared sexy and attractive to males; with the exception of their breasts, the women all appeared to be svelte.

Restrictive, confining, time-consuming, and sexy dress were all characteristics that women railed about in their CR groups. Twenty years ago, at the Miss America Contest in Atlantic City, the women who were protesting there said that they were "forced daily to compete for male approval, enslaved by ludicrous beauty standards that [they were] conditioned to take seriously and accept." Most interesting, however, is the fact that the look on current television and print ads continues to be as *unrealistic* today as it was then for well over 90 percent of American women. Even women who have made a conscious choice to reject the Madison Avenue depiction of beauty in our culture still find it difficult to resist the onslaught of media images of this portrayal and the judgments of those men and women who have not resisted the unrealistic model.

"This is the age of beauty," says Evelyn P., a forty-year-old accountant from Atlanta. "If you're not beautiful, you're invisible. Trust me. I'm not beautiful. I've been overweight all my life. I'm not blond. I can get all dressed up in my best outfit and walk into a store or restaurant, and absolutely no one will look at me. Or if they do, their eyes slide right by, as if they'd been looking at a lamp."

The fundamental desire to be wanted and loved and noticed causes women like Evelyn to try to make themselves into something they weren't meant to be. And never before have women had so many ways—and the medical technology—to alter their bodies: Face lifts, liposuction, breast augmentation and reductions, tummy tucks, wrinkle creams, colored contact lenses, and a vast array of hair and skin products have become almost common procedures and products on the American scene.

Being sucked into this vicious cycle of spending ever more money and time in the effort to alter one's body image is not a trivial issue, say concerned feminists. In an era when women already have more on their plates than they can manage, can they afford the time-consuming beauty routines that many women consider necessary to their self-esteem and sometimes vital in order to keep a job? More to the point, can women continue, without serious damage to themselves, to alter the very essence of who they are? Trying to make oneself over to fit an unrealistic image of womanhood is at best mood-altering. At worst, it can destroy one's health and spirit.

"Because she is forced to concentrate on the minutiae of her bodily parts, a woman is never free of self-consciousness," writes Susan Brownmiller in *Femininity*. "She is never quite satisfied, and never secure, for desperate, unending absorption in the drive for a perfect appearance—call it feminine vanity—is the ultimate restriction on freedom of mind."[9]

Although many women today do reject the Madison Avenue image of beauty—"I don't wear makeup; I have wash-

and-wear hair," says Jeannette F. "I can't be bothered wasting valuable time on a beauty regimen"—many others, feminist or not, are not immune from concern about the loss of their beauty in at least one arena—through aging.

"I think we all know that we're going to get older," says Celeste C., president of an interior design firm in Boston, "but we all think it will never happen to us. I'm aware that I move more slowly; I'm not as quick. I don't have the level of stamina that I used to have. Yes, I'm getting older. But I am much more aware of aging in terms of how it affects my appearance. We live in such a youth-oriented culture, and the world is not forgiving to people as they get older."

Celeste describes an experience she has been having lately. She walks by a mirror and looks at herself, and she thinks, 'Oh my God, that is what I look like now.' In her head, psychologically, she still thinks of herself as eighteen or even thirty. As she's approaching forty, the person she imagines and the person she sees in the mirror are different.

"When most women think about aging," she says, "it's not osteoporosis or arthritis they're thinking about. Who stays up at night wondering if their bones are going to get brittle? It's their faces and bodies they're worrying about."

The issue of aging, say women, is the last taboo. In the same way that for many years women did not share with each other the differences between expectation and reality regarding marriage or having children, there has been a conspiracy of silence about what it is like for a woman to grow old. "If women talked more about aging, if they shared more, there would be a greater sense of support, of camaraderie about it," says Celeste.

In their consciousness-raising groups, women had the opportunity to speak about aging if they wanted to: "What age do you consider to be 'old'?"; "What relationships do you have with women who are considerably older than you?"; "How do you feel about getting older?" But because most of the women who participated in CR in the early 1970s were in their twenties and early thirties, the issue of aging was not for them then the issue it is today. And today they are no longer meeting.

Edie G. belonged to a CR group in the early 1970s on Staten Island, New York, where she lived then. Today she is a forty-three-year-old court reporter living in Glenrock, New Jersey with her husband and two children. Edie looks younger than her years, nearly a decade younger because of her lithe figure, her smooth complexion, and her long, dark-blond hair. This is a matter of pride to Edie, who smiles when she is told she looks younger than she is. She confesses this is her main private worry—aging and the loss of her looks. "I will be devastated when I am no longer an attractive woman," she says candidly. "I wake up in the morning and I can't believe I'm forty-three. I can't really comprehend being that age. It's not that I'm in a deep depression over it, but it is on my mind a lot. Even though I will try to talk to myself, and tell myself I have to go on with my life and accomplish my goals, I haven't been able to accept it. I look for reactions in other people. I wonder, How many years do I have left to be attractive? I look at my face to see if I have any new lines. I listen to TV programs about face-lifts. It's always on my mind."

What bothers Edie most, she says, aside from any physical evidence of aging, is the way the men react to women in the law offices and courts where she works. "I watch the men and the way they look at women," she says. "It's the same as it always was. They look first at the bodies, then the faces. There is always the issue of attractiveness, of sex appeal, of youth. I hate to speak in generalities, and I'm sure there are men who make an effort not to think of women in these terms— and one thing that has been accomplished is that men aren't so blatant about it as they used to be—but it's there. I watch these older attorneys looking at the younger women. The men can entertain thoughts of going out with these women, whereas a middle-age woman isn't as likely to think she can go out with a younger man. And I know that consciously or unconsciously, I always feel in competition with younger women."

It may be that the lessons learned in CR years ago about body image were among those that seemed to "take" the least. The impulse to alter one's body image and appearance— whether because of perceived flaws or because of a fear of aging—seems to be as strong today as ever, if not more so. Questions about just who determines the criteria for female attractiveness, who sets the standards, are just as relevant today as they were a decade and a half ago. Although some individual women have made personal progress in this area— in freeing themselves from excessive, time-consuming worry about not being attractive enough or measuring up to some Madison Avenue standard—as a group, women appear not to have moved very far from the starting line. The notion of an acceptable "uniform" is still just as prevalent as ever. Indeed, because of the significantly larger number of women in the workplace—and because, as some observers suggest, both men and jobs are scarce for women in the late 1980s— it may be *more* prevalent than in 1972.

Can women, as isolated individuals, make much headway in understanding the reasons that cause a woman to alter her appearance so radically? Can they, on their own, come to terms with the reality of aging and what this means in a youth-oriented culture? Or are they missing out, by not sharing thoughts, feelings, and insights about being a woman today in the Age of Beauty?

SEVEN

Alone on the Mountain

Catherine is fixing herself a Weight Watchers pizza in the toaster oven in her kitchen. She hasn't cooked a big meal, she says, since her daughter went off to college.

She stands with her hands in the pockets of her jeans, leaning against the counter. Her head is cocked to the right, and a rueful smile plays about her lips as she recalls the most recent of her aborted relationships, a three-and-a-half week fling with a man named Tom.

At first, she says, she was attracted to Tom, whom she met one night when he asked for help at the bookstore, for all the usual wrong reasons: He was handsome, he was attentive, he was rich, he had a good job as a broker with a State Street firm in Boston, he had a wonderful apartment overlooking the harbor. . . . They saw each other three times in the first week. They went to lunch, to a movie, and for a long walk on Sunday all along the Charles River. As she got to know Tom, she found she liked him even more. He had a good sense of humor, he wasn't married, and his values seemed to be in the right place. He liked the fact that she owned a bookstore, he said.

He admired her dedication and her business acumen. He respected her life as a single parent and was moved by her stories of her struggles to make it on her own when her daughter was small.

Into the second week of their relationship, Catherine was beginning to wonder if something grand might be happening to her. For by then, they had been to bed together and she was able to add yet another attribute to her list: He was a good lover—"tender, considerate, and sexy."

"I was starting to fall for him in a bad way," she recalls. "You know what it's like. You can't think about anything else. Suddenly you're alive, revved up, in high gear. I was smiling all the time. A friend at work was kidding me like mad, and I was telling him to fuck off, but secretly I loved it. And then Tom would come to pick me up from work, and everything seemed rosy and glorious."

But Catherine had been there before. "There was this little voice telling me to be careful, telling me to watch out," she says. "I'd been burned. I'd let myself be deceived so many times before. But as each day went by, and as I was growing more and more fond of this man, that little voice was becoming fainter and fainter."

Until something happened in the third week to make Catherine perk up and listen to that interior voice a bit more intently. "He had theater tickets. He'd picked them up as a surprise. And so he kind of swept into the bookstore on a Friday night with a flourish—I suppose you could say like Prince Charming on his horse—and said, 'Drop what you're doing. There's a bottle of champagne chilling in my fridge. We're going to the theater.'

"I was really turned on," she says. "Who wouldn't be? But I was heartsick, too. I said, 'I can't drop what I'm doing. I'm in charge tonight, and we're going to have a reading. I have to stay here.' I didn't want to stay in the bookstore, of course, but I knew I had to. I'm the only one who can handle a reading. And it was an extremely busy night. I didn't even have time to argue the point with him. I

wanted just to be able to say to him, 'Look, I'm sorry. But you should have asked me first if I would be available tonight before you spent the money on the tickets. I like spontaneity just as much as you do, but I just can't walk out on my responsibilities like that.'

"He wasn't satisfied with a two-sentence answer, however. He wanted to talk it out, to persuade me. You have to try to picture what the scene was like—customers needing this, the author coming in the door wanting attention, my assistants confused over the seating—all the usual. And me dying because I really did want to go. Yet Tom just seemed oblivious to all of this. And then he got this sort of pout on his face and this little aggrieved tone in his voice, as if to say, 'Aren't I more important than your job?'

"I should have paid more attention to that little voice in the back of my head," she recalls, "but I thought, what the heck, he was disappointed, that's all. You don't drop someone over one misstep.

"But then he didn't call for about a week—a punishment, I suppose. Finally, he did call to invite me to go out to lunch. I felt pretty good about going—I really was attracted to him—but I could hear that something wasn't quite right in his voice. So I said to him, 'What is it, Tom? What's wrong? You don't sound yourself.' And he said, 'I've had a rough couple of days at work. I really need some high-class mothering.' "

She tilts her head back and looks at the ceiling. She shakes her head. "What can I tell you?" she says. "I've been there so many times, I know all the signs. He didn't want a woman or a friend or a lover—he wanted the classic female archetype. Someone who would drop what she was doing and swoon whenever he beckoned; someone whose commitment to her work would never take precedence over her commitment to her man; someone who would 'be there' when he needed TLC.

"So I saw him once or twice more," she says, "and that was that. He called one night and said he'd pick me up after work, and I said*

*thanks, but I was too tired. And there was this long pause. He knew.
He didn't call again."*

*Catherine wraps her arms around her chest and sighs. "I'll tell
you the truth," she says. "In the past four years, the only relationships
I've had that have lasted longer than two or three weeks were with
married men. They don't mind that I'm strong and self-reliant—in
fact, they like it. It makes their lives easier. I date married men,
because by the third or fourth date with a single man, I can see that
what he really wants is the same old stuff."*

*But Catherine says she often worries about where she's headed.
"Although I've reached a point in my life where I will not compromise
who I am simply to capture and hold a man," she says, "I sometimes
worry about being too self-sufficient.*

*"Each man I shake, each expectation that I shed, each step lighter
I get, and the higher I go in my evolution as a woman, the more
alone I am.*

"Do I want to be alone on the mountain?" she asks.

Men were always the topic—whether they were fathers, broth-
ers, husbands, lovers, or bosses, and whether they were spo-
ken of directly or indirectly, insofar as they had dominated
women's childhoods, schooling, relationships, marriages, and
experiences in the workplace. Of greatest urgency among all
this talk, however, was the nature of the relationships the
women had with boyfriends, lovers, and husbands. In their
CR groups, women spoke freely about their lovers and mates
and about men in general—pulling the veil of secretiveness
off their relationships and marriages and subjecting them to
examination and scrutiny. Personal problems such as sexual
incompatibility, dissatisfaction with traditional roles, money
worries, and a pervasive feeling of being worth less in a re-

lationship than a man was were aired and dissected. In some groups, relationships were vicariously experienced as women told of their ongoing sagas week by week—rather like a long-playing soap opera.

It was a time to examine both minute domestic detail as well as powerful movement rhetoric. Men, after all, said many women, were the enemy. This being so, how was it possible then to live with one? Could a woman love her master? Was intimacy possible between two unequals?

Anger toward men, fueled by personal experience and the collective testimony of the group, sometimes spilled over into the marriage. Or, vice versa, secret feelings of hostility in the marriage finally found expression in the group. The process was symbiotic, and very few relationships or marriages remained untouched by the consciousness-raising process. Either the relationships survived and grew stronger because of the insights the women were bringing home weekly—or they were unable to withstand the onslaught of the changing balance of power and dissolved.

One by one, women who had been taught the "myth" of being taken care of, or women who were used to taking second place in a marriage, began to experience the "click" of recognition. One woman's husband had total control of the money; she couldn't even get her own charge card. One woman's husband had never changed a diaper, cooked a meal, or washed a dish in his life, because, as he put it, his father never did, so why should he? One woman realized that if her husband were to walk out on her, she could not survive even two months financially. Another wife cried that her husband never took her seriously; he said she was "too emotional and hysterical." When a wife said she didn't feel like having sex, a husband grew abrasive, or worse, abusive, and started talking about "his needs." If she started talking about her needs, he rolled his eyes.

In their groups, women began to identify those needs—so long suppressed in the name of femininity. They wanted more intimacy with their men, they insisted; but intimacy between unequals, they realized, wasn't possible, any more than true intimacy was possible between a master and a slave. Likewise, shared power wasn't possible, they began to recognize, unless financial power was shared, too. If a woman remained economically dependent upon a man—could not, in fact, survive on her own without him—she could never really be his equal.

"We began by thinking of men as giants," says one woman of her group, "and then they fell."

But because the image of a powerless man was not particularly attractive (and not entirely practical, not to mention unrealistic), the image of the "evolved" lover or husband began to emerge. An "evolved" man, according to the ideal, did not think of women as worth less than men or himself. He believed that both women and men should have the right to work and maintain their own finances. He believed that because he shared the household he had as much responsibility to take care of the house as did a woman. He also believed that because his children were his children, too, he had the same responsibility as did his wife for their care, love, and hands-on maintenance. He took women seriously. He did not dismiss their opinions. He would not only hire women, he would work for one. He was committed to the nonsexist rearing of his children.

And with this creation of the ideal, evolved man came the exploration into different *alternative* ways of living as a woman. The ideal relationship, women said, would be an economic and intimate partnership of equals. Having achieved that, one could opt to enter into the institution of marriage for the sake of children, if one believed that children were better off within a stable marriage, or one could choose not to institutionalize the relationship, but rather simply to live together as equals, with or without children. Barring this ideal partnership and the absence of an evolved man, women could enter into more progressive kinds of adult "families"— communes of women with children who shared household chores, childrearing, and the fruits of their labor in the workplace. Or women could go it alone, a hitherto unthinkable option that many were finding more and more appealing. "If you didn't have a man, I was taught, you'd go to rack and ruin," says one woman. "This was the Noah's Ark theory of being, and when I was divorced, I was terrified. But then I discovered something incredibly important: I felt better out of the marriage than I did compromising myself just to keep a man. I learned that marriage wasn't going to be the solution for me."

For those women who participated in CR groups—and for millions of women who did not but who benefited from the messages emanating from CR—the quest to change the balance of power in an intimate relationship with a man, or to learn to feel comfortable living alone was the hardest and most painful of all the tasks women set for themselves. There were women, for example, who intuited right from the outset that the material being digested in CR was so threatening to their marriages and to the stability of their family life that they went home silent, prepared to mull over these issues, but not to act precipitously. After all, they reasoned, their husbands had married them in good faith, firmly rooted in traditional expectations. Was it fair to demand, in midstream, a fundamental overhauling of that initial bargain? "The group forced me to look at my values and to think about what was really important to me," says Carol M., an actress from Los Angeles. "I saw that it was possible to really screw up my marriage, because I was becoming awakened to a lot of things. A group of women sitting around do not always say great things about their marriages. So there was a little bit of a mental shake-up. Fortunately, I recovered. The marriage was my first priority."

Other women, enraged by their insights in CR, went home and assaulted lovers and husbands with new bits of information and exhaustive lists of demands. After an initial conflagration, compromises were made or relationships cracked apart at the seams. Men, with no similar place to go to raise their consciousness, either let themselves be nudged forward or remained bullishly steadfast in their devotion to the status quo. "My ex-husband and I were locked into a power struggle," says Annette S., now an administrator with a pharmaceutical firm in Manhattan. "The more I tried to speak out, the more he'd try to put me down. He didn't want to hear about my group, and when I'd talk about it, or try to change the way we were operating around the apartment, he'd come back at me by making fun of me and the whole Women's Movement. We got separated while I was in the group."

Younger women, barely out of school, or still in school, appeared to be single-minded about the type of man they knew they had to have, but often did not yet have relationships on which to try out these new ideas. Later, some discovered that a feminist perspective had a way of sabotaging relationships with men. Others, who thought of themselves as luckier, did find men willing to experiment with new ways of being a couple—and together they tried to forge nontraditional partnerships. "Mike and I share everything totally," says Lena R., a public high school science teacher from Portland, Oregon. "He cooks, I cook. He takes care of the kids, I take care of the kids. He doesn't like to vacuum, and I hate folding the laundry. I think he just reasoned that it was his house and his kids, too, so why shouldn't he do his share?"

Some women were committed to living alone; indeed, they celebrated their independence and freedom. Others found the single life unappealing, even frightening. They wanted a family, they said, and were still searching for the right mate. Still others drifted in and out of relationships much as they always had done, despite the basic training of CR—and sometimes because of it. Other needs, other longings, took precedence over their reason and intellect.

In talking to these same women fifteen years after CR, it becomes apparent that the struggle is as alive today as it ever was. Indeed, say the women, this is the area in which they feel they've made the least clear-cut progress. "I still make the same mistakes," says one woman. "It's an ongoing struggle."

"If anything, I feel as if we're backsliding," says another. "We've lost a lot of ground in these conservative times."

Another woman puts it this way: "CR has made my relationships with men much, much easier—I see things a lot more clearly than I used to, and I'm much clearer about who I am and what I want. But I'll tell you another thing: It's made my relationships with men a lot shorter."

Researchers tell us, nearly two decades later, that men are still more reluctant to express emotions, particularly those of sympathy, sadness, and distress, while women are still more inhibited when it comes to anger and sexuality.[10] Women, according to some recent surveys and polls, report nearly overwhelmingly a desire to make fundamental changes in their relationships. They say that they suffer from emotional and psychological harassment, that men don't listen to them, and that they wish for greater emotional and verbal closeness with the men in their lives.[11]

Clearly, the battle between the sexes remains a lively and complex one. But from the turmoil, experimentation, and upheaval of the consciousness-raising era, only two dominant choices have survived: to make a marriage of equals or to live a life of total independence. Gone is the appeal and even existence of female communes, and few women today (with the exception of those women approaching forty who envision themselves as single parents because they want a child but have found no suitable permanent mate) look forward to having a family outside of marriage. Women either think now in terms of making their marriages work, or they think about accepting the challenge of living alone.

Men work and women work. Women take care of children, and now men take care of children.

Do shared partnerships really exist today?

For some, yes.

"My husband does it all," says Maryellen W. of Seattle. "He takes care of the kids three mornings a week while I work. He rearranged his schedule when I had the baby so that he could help me out. He changes my daughter's diapers. He gives her a bath. He feeds her. He gets her dressed. Then he goes to work, and he talks to his co-workers, and he tells them about his morning, and they look at him like he was some strange species. 'My wife does all that,' they say."

Since the early 1970s, the character of the American father has changed dramatically from that of the traditional father of a generation ago. Primarily because so many mothers entered the work force, fathers found they had to pitch in or the family would fall apart. In doing so, they discovered an intrinsic love for the job. After all, the payoff was tremendous—an exploration of one's own nurturing instincts, from which their own fathers had been cut off, as well as a greater intimacy with one's children. And in addition to these personal payoffs, there was the new status accorded the hands-on father as well: He discovered he rather liked being seen in the nurturing role—at the park, at the supermarket, or taking the baby for a walk in the stroller.

So important has the concept of shared parenting become, in fact, that a few fathers have even stopped working for a period of time to stay home and allow their wives to pursue careers. Other fathers, albeit a minority, have negotiated job-sharing arrangements with their spouses or with other colleagues in order to play a larger part in child care. Still others are discovering that jobs that do not allow for time to be spent with their children simply have to be modified, despite the sacrifices. And these changes are not exclusively among the white middle class, either. Labor organizers report that paid parental child-care leave, for both sexes, is now a hot item on the bargaining table.

That more men participate in the rearing of children is indisputable. This revolution, however, has largely been confined to child care itself. It is still quite rare to find a dual-career or dual-wage family in which the father spends as much time at *all* the family's domestic chores in a given week as the working mother. Thus, while one aspect of shared partnerships appears, in large numbers of marriages, to be successful, many other aspects are not.

Statistically, men still make more money than do women, thus tipping the balance of power in their favor. And even when the wife makes more money than her mate, he often still retains the superior position. In 1986, the Boston University School of Social Work conducted a study of 651 employees of an unnamed Boston-based company. They discovered that women work twice as many hours on homemaking and child-care tasks as men. This was true *even if the woman's income was greater than the man's*. When children were sick, it was the woman who was most likely to stay home. Married female parents spent eighty-five hours per week combining work and family life; married male parents spent sixty-five hours.

Some observers who have pondered statistics such as these have suggested that the concept of the shared partnership is an evolving notion, by no means fully developed—an idea borne out by the comments of women today.

"My husband helps me a lot, he really does," says Irene L., of Needham, Massachusetts. "But he's a lawyer and works very long hours, whereas my schedule is lighter. Therefore it just makes sense for me to do the cooking and cleaning and whatever. I do sometimes mind on weekends, however, when we're both home, and I find that we sink back into the old patterns. I mean, why shouldn't he do the shopping and cook a dinner on a weekend?"

Although men have embraced childrearing, they still have a reluctance to perform household chores. Housework has always been a servant task—often dull, tedious, and repetitive. It delivers very few rewards, intrinsic or otherwise. Being a good vacuumer or a good dishwasher doesn't carry with it the panache of being a good father. And it has so long been associated with the powerless that to invest in it may suggest a relinquishing of one's own power within the family. Since those who have power rarely give it up, men have been slower to embrace domestic chores. Even if both partners in a marriage are sharing equally in childrearing, the working mother generally assumes the majority of household tasks.

These household tasks, in CR groups, were called "shitwork." Shitwork was defined as that kind of work, whether in the house or in the workplace, that is relegated to those individuals with the lowest status. Historically, this has been a painful issue for women primarily because shitwork has traditionally been a woman's domain, automatically conferring upon her the inferior "servant" position—either vis-à-vis her mate or her boss.

When women were in CR groups, they discussed the way in which they were expected to take on virtually all of the domestic chores—in particular the more onerous ones, such as cleaning out the toilet, taking care of the laundry, and doing the dishes. If a man did participate in domestic chores at all, it was most often in the rewarding and creative realms— such as cooking or taking the children to the park. Women often laughed among themselves at how grateful they were expected to appear when their mates took on a gourmet dish for the night, only to leave them with a kitchen that looked as if a bomb had struck.

Women went home from weekly CR meetings incensed, demanding that their husbands or lovers participate in shitwork. Sometimes men listened and tried to "lend a hand." Women went back to their meetings and told of subterfuge in the most willing of husbands. Men would do the task, *if told to do so*, but seemed incapable of seeing on their own that it ought to be done and taking responsibility for it. Men would (subversively, thought women) perform a task with good nature but with virtually no competence—and when women complained, would retort: "This is my idea of how the house should be cleaned; if you don't like it, then you do it." Women were then called "uptight" if they demanded a certain standard of tidiness, promptness with chores, or cleanliness. "My husband said, 'Lighten up,' just one too many times," says one woman who recalls, ten years after her divorce, that she deliberately walked out of the house for good, leaving her husband with a sink full of dirty dishes, a filthy bathroom, and no clean sheets.

Is the situation any better today? Among the women interviewed for this book, those who are newly married report that, yes, the marriages (often second marriages for many of the women) are built upon the premise of shared partnerships, and that, by and large, the domestic chores are split down the middle. Those women whose marriages are of longer duration, some dating back to the 1960s, have somewhat different reports: Men share domestic tasks considerably more than they used to, but women still take on the lion's share. And when men do participate in domestic tasks, it is most often a result of women entering the work force. In many households men *have* to pitch in—there isn't any choice. If the woman isn't there to start dinner, the man has to. Women are quick to point out, however, that many of the same obstacles to shared partnerships that they talked about in their CR groups still exist today. Men will participate in shitwork, if asked to do so, or when domestic chaos finally reaches a crisis, or when a woman looks obviously frazzled or begins to complain. The truly evolved man, they suggest, that man once envisioned by women in their groups, is still a rarefied species.

"You show me a marriage of truly equal partners," says one woman, "a marriage where all chores and domestic work are shared equally, a marriage where the male's interests don't, on balance, dominate, and I'm gonna go over and take a picture of it."

A large number of women who once participated in CR are now divorced and living alone. Statistics for this group nationwide do not exist, but among the women I interviewed, roughly a third fell into this category. Only a very small number of women had never been married, but this number would be expected to be larger for a younger population of women.

Among these women, two distinct and strong impressions emerged: By their own admission, the women truly enjoyed living alone—often surprising themselves with this realization; but they still felt it was not a fully acceptable choice in society at large.

"I would never remarry; I would *never* remarry," says Jeannette F. of Manhattan. "I love living alone. I love it. You go to a party and you don't like it, and you leave. You don't have to ask anybody's permission. When I meet a man, I just think, 'Would I rather be with this person or would I rather be by myself? Would I rather be doing exactly what I want to do, or do I have to conform to somebody else's wishes and thoughts?' I always choose me. I feel perfectly comfortable being this way. I love it."

"I'm happy," says Deirdre A., a filmmaker in Los Angeles. "I made a deliberate decision. Barring an ideal situation, I have a greater life alone. A rarefied life, I'll admit, but I'm alone by design. I love the work I do, I meet exciting people, I have deep emotional commitments to a variety of people. I'm not lonely—certainly no lonelier than I'd be in a relationship. I've proved this to myself many times. Recently I was living with a man. I found it asphyxiating. I didn't want all the compromises."

But Deirdre feels she is on the cutting edge, and that most people still think it's necessary to have a man. "Society doesn't permit you to be alone and feel okay about it," she says. "Women have not accepted the challenge of independence. The deal was to work it out within the concept of marriage. But there are all of us who live outside that structure. There are thousands upon thousands of women who are living their lives alone. If they would just allow it of themselves, they'd be happy. But they can't be, because they're still linked to this other concept of what's right."

Although there have been extraordinary women in the past who were able to carve out independent lives for themselves, living alone has almost always been for women a sign of failure. The image of the spinster in the American social pantheon has never been an attractive one—certainly not as attractive or as acceptable as the bachelor. Yet many women who once participated in CR say that they have chosen—"by design"—to live alone, even though living alone still carries with it the stigma of having failed. Having failed at a marriage. Having failed to be attractive enough to men. Having failed in some profound way to fulfill one's female destiny. For this reason, the joy of being independent and living alone often comes as a surprise to many women.

"It took me a long time to realize that I might be better off all alone," says Janet T. of Port Jefferson, New York. "I had to learn it the hard way. I don't think the younger women coming along after me will find it so difficult."

"It's sometimes hard to do," says Carol W., who works as a reading specialist in the public school system just outside of Santa Fe, New Mexico. "A lot of rewards have to come from your work. If your work isn't going well, then you're cast upon your own resources. But I wouldn't ever again try living with a man. I just know that I'm a happier person alone. I'd like to allow other women to hear this. There are certain barriers to the acceptance of living alone."

"Society's geared to getting you married," says Deirdre. "The concept of being independent and happy is a message that women don't usually hear. It's so against everything in the society, so much of a threat to the major institution in this society—the family. These are the currents in history that we're dealing with."

Many women say that they are living alone as a direct or indirect result of their participation in consciousness-raising groups. Being in the group and becoming free-thinking females either made it impossible to continue in a traditional marriage and thus led to divorce, and/or it made it impossible to live again with a man once that divorce had taken place. Thus some women are able to view their single status not as a failure on their part but on the part of men to measure up to their own standards.

While some observers have suggested that women who don't marry aren't asked, these discerning women know better: Men, they say, are not as evolved as women. With no men's movement to correspond to the Women's Movement, and with no place to go to raise their own consciousness, most men are still stuck in a more traditional era when it comes to goals and ideals in marriage. Thus, after the second or

third date, when it becomes apparent that a man is still looking for the traditional wife, the women lose interest.

"Men don't have the same value system as me," says one
woman. "The things I value about myself, men don't value.
I value my success, my intelligence, my accomplishments, my
commitment. But then I'll meet a guy and I'll find out that
what he really values is a woman's body or her ability to cook.
So I don't have relationships with these kinds of men. Why
would I? Why would they?"

"The men I meet are successful and are often attracted to
my independence," says another woman. "The problem is,
I'm not interested."

"My work takes tremendous amounts of energy," says Patty
R., an aerospace engineer from Seattle. "The energy required
in my job doesn't allow me to meet men."

These are the women who would seem to be happiest
"alone on the mountain"—a concept of the adult female life
quite alien to their childhood vision of womanhood, and quite
far removed from their own mothers' notions of how a woman
should live her life. But the climb to the top of the mountain,
despite many moments of satisfaction and happiness along
the way, is not without its difficulties. Indeed, because living
alone is still regarded by most Americans as a failure of sorts,
the journey is often fraught with barriers, obstacles, and frustrating backsliding.

"I sometimes worry about never having children," says one
woman who was divorced in her early twenties during her
CR group, and who has never, by choice, remarried. "And
sometimes I meet a man and fall in love, and I just want to
lie down on the floor and have him take care of me. You
don't always go forward in a straight line. Usually it's one
step forward, another backward. I'm pretty sure I'll always

live alone—I can't imagine being in a marriage now—but that doesn't mean that I want to be isolated. There's a big difference. I would like to belong to a women's group again. I do often wish I were in a CR group so that I could explore some of the issues that crop up when living alone. Most of them are small, like what to do at Christmastime, and some of them are big, like having and raising children. I remember vividly how good it felt in the group when you realized you were not the only one who had these problems, and I know these groups would be a tremendous support."

There are many who wonder if much can be accomplished, however, a second time around, without bringing men into the picture. Barbara B., a former coordinator of the Women's History Program at Sarah Lawrence College in Bronxville, New York, believes, along with many women who once participated in CR, that if a second wave of CR were to spring up, however haphazardly, it should, this time, include men.

"It would be difficult," she says, "and I don't think it should be done in couples, but what's most feared right now is that there is a lot of anger between men and women, and that without being released in a controlled setting, it will just get out of hand. In a group of women and men together, you might be able to find ways to communicate some of the problems, and you could take what you learned there back into your personal life. And you wouldn't necessarily have to forfeit that sense of solidarity that was so important for the first phase of CR, because there would be other women in the group, too."

In 1981, Betty Friedan promoted the idea of male-female cooperation to further the cause of feminism in her book *The Second Stage*. The book was regarded as highly controversial, however, since it seemed to suggest to many readers that a first stage had already been accomplished; there were many feminists who felt that this was far from true. Yet the notion of making a better stab at male-female *communication* at least, appears to be an idea whose time has finally come.

"You go to the bookstore," says Betsy W., the college art instructor from Somerville, Massachusetts, "and all the non-fiction books are about the same thing—men who can't properly love women and how women are supposed to cope with this. I think there are some areas in which we've made precious little progress—men having trouble with intimacy, men who can't express their emotions, men who still want to dominate women. Women can talk all they want among themselves, but unless they talk to men about this—on neutral ground—nothing's going to happen."

Other women also promote the notion of male-female communication in groups. "Our problems today are shared problems, not specifically female problems," says Patty C., the Congregational minister from Vermont. "It's not motherhood, per se, we need to talk about—it's shared parenting these days. It's not just women who should be lobbying for flex-time and part-time work at the office, it's men *and* women who need these changes. Men want child-care leaves, too. We've been operating in a vacuum long enough. We either work together or we'll sink."

EIGHT

Motherhood: A Bitter Debate

It is 8:06 on a Tuesday morning. Felicia is in a taxi headed south on Park Avenue, toward the financial district where she will wheel and deal, mostly on the telephone, all day. She has been up since six, playing with and dressing her son, and feeding him his breakfast. Although she looks impeccable, even eye-catching, in a gray silk dress and jacket, she says that she has learned to put herself together in eighteen minutes flat—and this includes a shower. The rest of the two morning hours are devoted to her two-year-old, who will, when Felicia is at work, stay at home with Maria, Felicia's housekeeper.

"I don't exercise. I don't read books. I don't watch TV. I don't eat out," says Felicia, enumerating on her fingers the lost pleasures of a distant era before Sandy was born. "I don't entertain. I don't see women friends. I don't have sex.

"I work and I'm a mother. That's it. I've cut it to the bone."

Yet for all her self-sacrifice and domestic efficiency, and despite her cool, well-groomed appearance, Felicia, thinking about time spent with her son (or, to be more precise, the time she doesn't spend with her son) looks, in moments like this, distraught.

"Last Saturday I took Sandy to the Museum of Natural History to see the dinosaurs," she says, "and I ran into a friend, an ex-colleague, from work. We had our babies at roughly the same time, but she didn't go back to work. She's been at home with her daughter for two years. And we got to talking—and she talked about her decision to stay home, and I talked about my juggling act, and right from the get-go I could feel these waves of disapproval emanating from her. She kept saying things like 'Oh, really?' And she was asking me these questions, like how many hours exactly was I away from Sandy. And although she was sure this wasn't true for my housekeeper, did I know about all the other housekeepers who just take the kids to the park and let the kids veg out while they sit on park benches and talk to their friends. And you could feel her disapproval—though she didn't say it in so many words. But it was there, in her tone, a kind of self-righteous, superior tone—as if to say, 'How could you leave your beautiful child for something as selfish, as ego-boosting as a career?'

"And, of course, this fed right into my guilt. Because I'm never certain that I'm doing the right thing. How can you ever be sure? And by the time I got out of the museum and onto the sidewalk, my hands were shaking so badly I could hardly get the stroller open."

In 1960, just seven years before the advent of consciousness-raising, and a year when Felicia herself was entering high school, only 15 percent of mothers of children under the age of five had paid work outside the home. Today two-thirds of the mothers of these young children leave their sons and daughters in the care of others and join the labor force. According to 1988 Census Bureau figures, the percentage of mothers with infants (babies under one year old) who return to the workplace before the year is out (and the majority of these do so by the end of three months) has crossed the 50 percent mark—making the working mother, says the Census Bureau, "the norm in America."

Indeed, it is not just the norm—it is a veritable boom. It is estimated by the U.S. Department of Labor that as we turn the corner into the 1990s, as many as 80 percent of all children in this country will be growing up in the homes of working mothers. In that decade, 80 percent of the women in the work force will be of childbearing age, and 90 percent of those will become pregnant. And as we approach the year 2000, two-thirds of the new entrants in the work force will be women!

Why this huge outpouring of women from the home into the workplace?

Historians argue that a number of economic factors contributed and is contributing to the working mother boom (see Chapter One) but most agree that equally important were the political, social, and psychological changes that followed in the wake of Betty Friedan's *The Feminine Mystique* in 1963. The Women's Movement, and in particular the grass-roots, consciousness-raising movement, encouraged women to become economically independent and to enter into male-dominated professions. As a result, women like Felicia see themselves both as breadwinners and as mothers. Never before have so many women pursued what they think of as careers. Many have social ties to the workplace (in the same way that men do) that often rival their ties at home. They think in terms of upward mobility, and they have career goals for which they strive. They see themselves as lifelong workers who will continue to work even when their families are grown.

The advent of the working mother is among the most significant changes in the American family in decades, along with the high divorce rate and the increase in the number of single-parent households. The launching of millions of women into jobs, careers, and professions may be the single biggest contribution of the Women's Movement—one of unparalleled benefit to these millions of women, but one fraught with many unforeseen difficulties and complications.

For at the same time that the Women's Movement, and in particular the CR movement, was giving women the workplace, it was also, in a painful paradox, giving them back their bodies and the experience of childbirth. Although the issue of motherhood itself was dealt with in CR in an ambivalent manner, the notion of a woman reclaiming her body and the childbearing experience from the male-dominated medical profession was a powerful one that CR groups explored and made possible. Equally powerful, however, was the notion of leaving the home and going out into the workplace. While both experiences are integral to a woman's life, their simultaneous occurrence in a society not yet ready to accept her wholeheartedly at the workplace can cause her to feel torn between two opposing forces. Indeed, as we turn the corner into 1990, these two opposing forces are causing millions of women to ask of themselves and others hard questions— questions to which we do not yet have all the answers.

Diane R. and Lauren P. are both forty-one, and both live in the Boston area. Diane is director of admissions for a junior college just outside the city; Lauren is the co-owner of a travel agency near Fenway Park. Each of the women has one child, a daughter. Diane's daughter is nineteen, entering her sophomore year at the University of Michigan. Lauren's daughter is four years old. Each belonged to a CR group in the early 1970s, though not to the same one.

Diane's daughter was born when she was a senior in college.

She had left school the beginning of that year and was living with her husband in a small apartment in the Back Bay area of Boston. It was 1968. Because most of her friends were busy with studies, extracurricular activities, and the heady politics of that eventful spring, Diane felt alone and isolated in her pregnancy. Although she went regularly to see her doctor, she did not attend either alone or with her husband a single childbirth course. Indeed, she did not even know any such courses existed. She did not read any books on pregnancy and birth and bought for herself only Dr. Spock's *Baby and Child Care* to have on hand after the baby was born.

Diane's contractions began on a late May evening. She went directly to the hospital. There, her husband was instructed to leave her in the care of the labor and delivery nurses. Diane didn't see him again for forty-one hours. Diane was given an enema and "prepped"—her pubic hair was shaved. She was horrified by these events, but it didn't occur to her to protest. Who would ever question a hospital procedure and a doctor's authority? she says now of that era. Something terrible might happen either to her or to the baby, she thought then.

To speed up a sluggish labor, Diane was given Pitocin—a drug that increases the strength and frequency of contractions. To cope with the pain, the nurse gave her first Demerol, then scopolamine, which produced in Diane a "twilight sleep." The drug, however, had the adverse effect of making Diane feel out of control. When she would come to, during the worst of the contractions, she would begin to cry and moan as she came awake. Worse, the scopolamine seemed to counteract the Pitocin and to slow down the labor. After more than thirty-six hours—which she spent entirely with strangers—the doctor "took" the baby using a high-forceps delivery. Diane was anesthetized during the delivery and remembers nothing about it at all. Indeed, she did not even see her baby until eight hours later.

Diane was not encouraged to breast-feed her infant. She never heard the word *bonding* used in conjunction with a mother and a child. In fact, she says, she had a great deal of difficulty with parenting during the infant and toddler years. Her peers were in graduate school or were starting jobs and new marriages. For most of the time, she says, she felt baffled.

Lauren's daughter, by contrast, was born in the birthing room of her local hospital—an inviting room with a double bed and curtains on the windows. Lauren's husband was present for the entire labor and delivery. He was, in fact, an active participant (coaching Lauren to breathe properly; massaging the small of her back; assisting, in his hospital gown, in the delivery) and had been so since the couple had first discovered Lauren was pregnant. Lauren, during the course of her pregnancy, had attended Lamaze classes with her husband and had visited a birthing center to investigate the possibility of having the birth outside the hospital. But because of her tendency toward high blood pressure, Lauren and her husband chose to have a natural labor and delivery, though in a hospital setting in case the worst happened. During her pregnancy, she was given amniocentesis to determine if the fetus had any detectable genetic defects (Lauren was over thirty-five), and she had a sonogram. Her labor was difficult but average in length for a first baby (thirteen hours), and because she was able, with her husband as cheerleader, to keep up with the breathing methods she'd been taught in childbirth classes, she made it through the labor without drugs. She refused, and was allowed to refuse, an enema, the "prep," an internal fetal monitor, and an IV drip. Until the last hour, she spent most of the labor walking around the room, and sitting in a chair. When her daughter was born, and the baby had been cleaned and examined (a brief procedure which took place in the birthing room), the nurse dimmed the lights and all of the hospital personnel left the room. The new family was left alone to be together, and Lauren breast-fed her baby for the first time.

Two women, the same age, but separated in this critical milestone by a revolution. Diane had her baby before CR. Lauren had her baby after CR.

Childbirth in America was, in the space of a decade, revolutionized. Partly this revolution was the result of advanced technology, but more significantly, it was the result of the desire of women to reclaim for themselves their own bodies and the childbirth experience—a desire fostered in consciousness-raising groups. In CR, women asked themselves why they should be excluded from the decision-making process when it came to the birth of their own children. After all, women for centuries had been birthing babies without intervention and without having to be put to sleep. Why couldn't they, too, be awake and alert? Was all this intervention necessary? Why should women be excluded (literally, when a drape was used) from observing a gynecologist's examination of their own bodies? Why had they never protested when an obstetrician or a gynecologist had treated them condescendingly or had refused to answer their questions?

This massive act of reclamation on the part of hundreds of thousands of women—symbolized and in large part fostered by the publication of *Our Bodies, Ourselves* in 1969 by the Boston Women's Health Book Collective (the title alone telling the whole story)—brought about on the part of women a new awareness or "consciousness" about the reproductive system, childbirth, and childrearing during the infant years.

A conspiracy of silence was broken as women took control of their bodies (some aggressively so as they experimented in their CR groups with gynecological self-examinations) and as they began to question the old traditional theories of child-rearing. Alternative methods of birthing and of raising children began to proliferate. Women became active and alert participants in the births of their children. They sought childbirth training, had natural deliveries, believed in the concept of early bonding and breast-fed their babies. They haunted bookstores and developed massive libraries on the new, more progressive, nonsexist theories of childrearing. In short, CR encouraged pregnant women and new mothers to become more intensely *involved*, more intensely *conscious* during the birth and nurturing experience.

Paradoxically, however, this emphasis on being in control of one's own body and of one's childbirth has had the effect of strengthening the bonds between mother and infant *at the very time in our history when women are expected to leave their infants and go back into the work force.* Thus two powerful forces emanating from the Women's Movement—that of being more in tune with one's female body and it's natural instincts and desires, and that of taking one's rightful place in the job market—appear to have clashed head-on.

Women today are outspoken about the emotional, economic, and practical conflicts that plague them as a result of the collision of these two powerful forces. Never before have women been expected to take on so much responsibility for educating themselves about the "right" way to guide and rear their children. And never before have they been encouraged to enter and stay in the work force as they are today. While the benefits to women of entering and remaining in the work force are indisputable, the problems can appear to be nearly overwhelming: How do women work and care for children simultaneously—particularly in a country so lacking in child-care resources or in flexible alternatives at the workplace?

Again and again, women who were once in CR groups and who are now working mothers speak of guilt. It is a topic, they say, that was not addressed in their groups, primarily because so few mothers then *were* working outside the home—and also because many of the women who participated in CR did not yet have families. The issue of working and caring for children at the same time hovered at the edges of their thinking, but did not claim center stage. Other issues then—getting *out* of the house, maintaining equal partnerships with men, discovering one's own sexuality—felt more pressing. But today, say these working mothers, guilt would be a number-one topic.

Guilt, which implies knowledge of wrongdoing may have deep social or psychological roots. But guilt may also be caused by external pressures as well. In this case, the guilt that today's working mothers feel is caused by both internal and external factors but has more to do with *fear* of wrong-doing than remorse for it.

As we have heard in a previous chapter, the women who joined CR groups were, for the most part, raised in traditional homes. Dads went out to work, but mothers stayed home. Dads earned money, mothers washed the floor. Dads had status in the outside world, moms did not. As daughters in these homes, women learned that this was the way of the world. If you were a girl, you intuited, whether you particularly liked it or not, the job description of your mother would eventually be your own. You had better get married and have children. You had better be a good wife and mother. And your destiny would be fulfilled primarily in this role.

The women, in their CR groups, changed that job description. They learned they had choices. Taking advantage of an explosion of opportunities and realizing the need to be economically independent, they went out into the job market and pushed hard at the edges of woman's place in the work force. Those who were married already and had children hunted for people to take care of their children while they went off to work for the first time. Those women who were not yet married, or married with no children yet, waited to have families. Between 1972 and 1982, the rate of first births for women in their thirties rose 50 percent; the rate of first births for women in their late thirties rose 83 percent. By the time these women had their babies, they were fully ensconced in the workplace. Most had plans to return.

Yet returning to work after the birth of a child can be painful—fraught with stress and domestic tension. Many women remain isolated during this critical moment in their lives and are plagued with anxiety. Because almost none of them have had working mothers, they often feel themselves to be veering off from the proper way of being a mother. They worry about whether or not they are harming their children by leaving them in the care of others. After all, they themselves were not left in daycare centers or with housekeepers. They had full-time mothers in the home.

And if this internal strife were not enough, most working mothers today find themselves confronted with enormous practical problems to solve as well. Moreover, many find themselves in inhospitable working environments that still operate on the principal that for every working parent on the job, there is another parent at home taking care of the children. That this is absolutely no longer the case seems to be seeping only very slowly into the corporate consciousness.

More than one hundred other countries have better national daycare policies than we do. There are nine times as many parents seeking childcare slots as there are positions available for there children. Childcare leave is still not universally available to all parents who need it. Sick childcare leave remains an almost radical concept. On-site daycare centers are a rarity. Only a small minority of corporations offer working parents flexible schedules.

Worse, working mothers are isolated—cut off from support systems by the very nature of their daily tasks. "I'm never alone, and yet I feel alone all the time," says Margaret L., the mother of two girls, ages five and three, and a financial comptroller for a bank in St. Louis. "I'm never alone because there are always people around me, everyone wanting a piece of me—my boss, my colleagues, my children, my husband. And yet I feel all alone because I never have anyone to talk to about this thing that I'm doing. I'm busy all the time. I race through my life. I don't have friends anymore. I have people I chat with at work and all, and once in a great while, we'll have a couple over to dinner. But I have no one really to talk to. Sometimes, when I'm feeling overwhelmed, I think to myself: Where, *where* is there someone to talk to about all this?"

Mary V., who is now thirty-eight, belonged to a consciousness-raising group in Manhattan in 1972. Today she is a magazine editor. She has one daughter who is six. "When I first went back to work after having Betsy, I kept thinking: Why isn't there anybody to tell me how to do it? I just felt so lost. I felt lonely and helpless and as if I was always having to pave the way. I was constantly having to break down barriers. There was no reassurance out there. There was no one saying to me: 'This is the right way to do it.' "

•

The fear that one is not doing "the right thing" by trying to remain in the workplace while one has young children is not merely self-imposed. For many women the guilt is made worse by a group of individuals working mothers never imagined would be antagonistic toward them: other women. These other women are those who have chosen to remain at home with their young children. Some have left prestigious and lucrative jobs. Some have sacrificed a higher standard of living to be home with their kids. Others have felt more comfortable in the home. Whatever the reasons for their remaining at home, at-home mothers often feel strongly about the choices they have made. So strongly, in fact, that the entire working-mother debate has had the effect of polarizing women into two different camps: the working mother camp, and the at-home mother camp. In this often acrimonious debate, each side tends to be defensive about its stand. Perhaps no other subject can spark such passion as the decisions a woman has made about how to raise her children.

For their part, working mothers feel that the at-home mothers deliberately misinterpret their motives for working and point the finger at them for not being good mothers and for not caring enough about their children. They say that they have been accused of attempting the impossible (wanting to be "superwomen"), of being selfish and self-obsessed, and of "trying to do it all," as though women were greedier than men.

On the other side, at-home mothers often speak of feeling devalued, of being dismissed, of not having any status in the world at large, and of being taken advantage of by working mothers.

For many women, the mutual antagonism has caught them

off-guard, stunned them into an awareness that women are today divided on this issue. It is the first time that women have had to think in terms of a them-and-us situation in which the "them" is female.

"My daughter attends a kindergarten in which most of the children have mothers at home," says Eileen J., who lives in upper-middle-class suburb in New Jersey. "Most of these mothers are affluent enough to have a choice to stay home or not. I don't. I have to work. And both my daughter and myself have been discriminated against because I work. We invite other children over to play, and the other mothers won't let their children come when they hear that there will be a housekeeper here. So then they don't invite my daughter over to play at their houses. They think I'm working just for my ego. I can't tell you how upsetting this is to me. I've never felt such antiwoman feeling before."

Passions run deep on both sides, with working mothers taking the brunt of the fallout. From the at-home mothers, the comments range from the mildly concerned to the outraged. "There is something so special about making a home," says Alexandra T. of Newton, Massachusetts. "But people who only work don't have the time to do that. It's not that they don't want to impart these values to their children, it's that they only get fifteen minutes with their kids. I know it's important to be a liberated woman, but what will happen if we give up on this moral imperative to raise our children as civilized people with connections in the world?"

"I can always go back to a job," says Wendy L., a former hospital nutritionist in Cleveland. "I won't always have this child to raise."

And from one at-home mother outside Chicago: "I am just sick and tired of all these working mothers trying to justify their actions. Is there any job more important than raising a helpless, defenseless little baby?"

The gulf between working mothers and at-home mothers has had a number of serious consequences. For the first time in years, women are at odds with each other. Indeed, some women feel acutely hostile toward other women and know that this hostility is returned. Where once women experienced kinship with other women, today they are divided. For some working mothers, this has had the effect of making them ashamed of their desire to work, causing them to hide behind the excuse of "having to work," and to downplay many of the reasons for working they once advocated in their CR groups. Thus the debate threatens to undermine freedom of choice for large numbers of women.

In addition, because of the split, women are not united in the endeavor to improve childcare and working conditions for working parents in America. At-home mothers, believing that women should remain at home to rear young children, feel no compunction to be advocate for better daycare: Indeed, some, feeding on alarmist media reports, vilify daycare institutions. At a time when women in this country need each other more than they ever have, in order to effect critical legislation that will help all families in America, they are, instead, isolated and bitterly divided.

In 1972, the push was to get women out of the home.

"In our group," says Laurel R., "we were all housewives, and we all had children. It was a rule in the group that we could talk about anything *except* our children. It was felt at the time that we hid behind our children, that we used talk about them as an excuse not to talk about ourselves."

"I didn't have children at the time," says Abigail R. of Cambridge, Massachusetts, "but several of the women did. And they would say how hard it was, how frustrating it was to be confined to the home, to be a housewife. And I came away from that group knowing I didn't want children for a very, very long time."

"There was a feeling," says Kate W. of Lebanon, New Hampshire, "that we were all foundering in some way—but the women who were at home with kids, they were really the ones who were lost. I always felt that they were the ones who had the most work to do."

Some groups (primarily those composed of younger, unmarried women in a university setting) never discussed motherhood at all; being a parent still seemed years away, irrelevant to their immediate concerns. Other groups came to the subject because several of the women in the group were mothers themselves and were beginning to chafe at the strictures of the role. Still other groups focused intently on the issue: Was it possible to be an emancipated woman if your chief occupation in life was changing diapers and wiping crayon scribbles off the walls? In groups that followed a set format, women asked themselves the following questions: "How does, or would, being a mother affect your self-image? Does being a mother live up to your expectations? Is being a mother different from being a father? If you live with someone, do you share childcare responsibilities? Do you consider childcare equal in status to paid work? What are some of the myths of motherhood?"

The Women's Movement, promoting the notion of *choice*, encouraged women to choose to do something other than that occupation which had been thrust upon them and for which they had been groomed all their lives. In an effort to embrace a wider variety of roles, old ways of being were cast aside. Women, so long resigned to lives without choice, were eager to tackle other endeavors that made use of more talents than nurturing. In the early years of any movement, revolution is necessary to achieve new goals. In this particular revolution, motherhood, as one's sole occupation, came in for sharp attack. In an effort to flee the bonds of motherhood, motherhood itself had to be devalued. Women whose investments increasingly took them away from the home began to place less and less emphasis on the home environment. They were led to believe, either by themselves or by others, that bearing children was not real success. And it would be a long time before motherhood itself would begin to seem appealing again—a choice in itself.

How, then, to explain this fact—that the single most significant thread to emerge in my conversations with the women interviewed for this book is the unqualified pride they have taken in their mothering?

Though they were proud of their career progress and though their successes in the outside world had increased their self-esteem, nearly all, when questioned, said they had done their best work as mothers. This was true of working mothers and of at-home mothers, whether these mothers saw themselves at home for only a short period of time or until their children were grown.

Despite the push to get *out* of the home, then, the heart remained there. One doesn't have to look very far for an explanation for this: The warmth and passion of the mother-child bond endures political theory, bad press, and even impassioned rhetoric.

Of equal importance, however, is that the women today confine themselves, when talking of pride, to motherhood itself; they do not give themselves high marks for domestic housewifery, or even for being spouses. Indeed, when identifying themselves, they speak of being workers and mothers—rarely "wives." Stripped of its associations with housewifery, motherhood is felt by those women who have children to be not a limiting experience, but rather, an enriching one.

It is clear, however, that despite the joy in their motherhood, women today face many contradictions and practical dilemmas. The notion of shared parenting, the idea of the female as the primary parent, the bitterness that divides women, and the backlash against working mothers all need to be explored. Women, acknowledging the deep pleasure that comes from being a mother, need to find new ways to merge the two experiences of mothering and working, rather than seeing their choices as "either/or." And ultimately, because a revolution in the home demands a revolution in the workplace, women need to investigate a new way of going to work in America.

But women are again, in their own words, isolated. They are isolated by the burden of trying to combine working and mothering in a society that has not made itself ready for them. And they are isolated because trying to do both jobs without benefit of necessary support systems often consumes all of a woman's energy and time. Thus, women today find themselves at a remove from a network of other women who have similar problems.

"I don't have time to meet other mothers in the park," says Michelle J., a dance therapist from San Francisco. "I don't meet too many other mothers in the course of my work. So I'm going it alone.

"It would be a hell of a lot easier," she adds, "if I had someone to talk to."

NINE

The Threat

It was dark, a March night, the first year the group met. They'd been talking about shitwork, a lively topic, full of passion, despite the ostensible dreariness of the subject: Who cleans the oven in a marriage? Who scrubs out the tub? Who cooks the meals night after night after night . . . ? And they'd forgotten the time, as they'd often done.

It was late, past midnight, and Maryanne was scurrying along the street. J.J. had walked her as far as her own building, with Maryanne's in sight. The two women had been talking energetically, full of bravado, so Maryanne was feeling confident, not suspicious, not afraid. Walking fast, as they'd taught each other to do late at night, looking purposeful.

Then she reached her door. She took out her key and breathed a sigh of relief. There was always something comforting about having made it home when it was dark, about letting the door slam shut behind you, with your own apartment only three short flights up. Her *two roommates would doubtless be asleep by now. They all had classes in the morning.*

But the door didn't slam shut. Her brain registered the silence immediately, even before she saw the foot in the door. She turned. She opened her mouth to say, "What?" but there was the knife, the glint of steel, and no sound came out. He was white; his skin was bad; he had dark hair. He advanced and she backed up. He seemed to know the building, pushing her along the corridor till they reached the dark place under the stairwell where mothers kept the strollers and the children's bikes.

Her mind reeled, stopped, shut down. Women talked about strategy, but now there was none. He had a knife. The tip was inches from her throat, then hovering in front of her face. She was afraid for her eyes. She wanted to shield her eyes, but she didn't dare bring her hands to her face.

He told her to lie down, but before she could obey, he pushed her roughly against the wall and down onto the dirty concrete floor. He fell upon her, but he kept the knife at her throat. He had her skirt up; she felt pain—his fingernails scraping her abdomen as he pulled at her underpants. He had her sweater up. He was biting her. There was white heat in her head, behind her eyes. She kept her head back, her throat arched. He was pounding her into the concrete. Please God, she intoned silently, Please God.

The point of the knife was in the soft spot under her chin. It was poking her too hard, piercing the skin. His head was bent, buried in her shoulder. He didn't know what he was doing. "You're hurting me," she screamed finally.

He pulled the knife away. He reared up off of her. He stood up. He kicked her hard in the hip with his boot to make her roll over and away.

She heard the door slam. There was blood running down her neck, and though she could feel the wetness, she couldn't move. . . .

"I just kept saying, 'Thank you, God,' 'Thank you, God,' because he hadn't killed me."

Maryanne is sitting on the sofa of her small house just outside Cleveland. She is only three weeks away from her due date and is having difficulty, as she tells her story, finding a comfortable position in which to sit. She has told the story calmly, though with some gestures—her hands hovering over her eyes, touching the soft spot under her chin where there is still a scar, crossing at one point over her breasts.

"I lay there for a long time," she says. "My hip hurt badly, and I didn't know if it was broken or not. But then after maybe twenty minutes or so, I began to shake violently, and I started to freeze. I knew I had to get up the stairs. One of the strangest things is that I knew I didn't want to wake anybody up. I didn't want anyone to see me like this.

"I finally was able to stand. I got myself to the bottom of the stairs and started up. But there was no strength in my legs. Absolutely none. My legs were like jelly, just trembling. So I literally had to pull myself up to the third floor with my arms.

"When I got inside my apartment, I went right into the bathroom. I bandaged the cut under my chin and got into the shower. I took a shower for a very, very long time. I didn't want to get out because I didn't know what I was going to do next. I really didn't want to do anything. I just wanted to lie down and have it all go away. I didn't want to talk about it. I didn't want to call the police. I remember thinking to myself that it was true what they said about the shame. But having anticipated it didn't make any difference. The shame was deep and overwhelming. His marks were all over me. I was horrified. My hip was swelling. It wasn't broken, just badly bruised. Once when I was a child, about nine or ten years old, I'd been walking along

a street in my neighborhood when a man called me over to his car because he needed directions. And when I got to the car and looked in the window, I could see he was naked and he was touching himself. I just walked away as fast as I could. I never told anyone. I'd been ashamed then, too."

Maryanne's plaid sofa dominates her tiny living room. All of the furniture matches, as if it had been bought at one go. There are framed needlepoint sayings on the wall. One reads: "You can never be too thin or too rich." Before she sat down on the sofa, Maryanne pointed to the saying, indicated her enormous belly, and laughed.

Her house is brand new, part of a development of other brand-new houses. The development is called Water's Edge, but it is unclear exactly where the water is. Or the trees. The newly formed landscape of this pristine suburban development is almost entirely devoid of natural landmarks. Maryanne, in another nod to the needlepoint bromide, has explained that this is a starter house, the best that she and her husband could afford at the moment.

"I didn't tell anyone at all about the rape for about three or four weeks," she says. "When people asked me about the bandage under my chin, I always made a joke and said, 'I cut myself shaving.' Then one night, in the group, we were talking about something entirely different—abortion, I think. And it was my turn. And before I even knew what was happening, the story was coming out. I was crying, and the story was coming out. And then everyone was holding me, and getting me a glass of wine, and some Kleenex, and I remember the tremendous relief of getting it out of me.

"The women said I had to go to the police. And they said they would go with me. It was an extraordinary thing. Not one of us knew where the police station was, but we called them and asked, and we all got in taxis and went there. And the women walked in with me, supporting me, like a small army. Actually, it was kind of comical

when I think back on it—that part, anyway. Ten or eleven of us walking in en masse. I remember the policeman on duty looked stricken. I think he thought we were a demonstration.

"I suppose I got a fair shake, primarily because the other women were staring daggers at the police the entire time. I wasn't humiliated, as you sometimes hear that other women are. But there wasn't much of a case. Too much time had elapsed for there to be any kind of a hot trail. I couldn't give enough precise details. I hadn't noticed any identifying marks or any jewelry or anything. I certainly didn't know the man, as women sometimes do. The police were nice to me, but you could tell they thought it was hopeless. And it was. They never caught the guy—or if they eventually did, they didn't relate it to my case. They did say, however, that he had probably been following J.J. and me for a couple of blocks. And his knowledge of the stairwell seemed to indicate that he might be from the neighborhood."

Maryanne says it took her a long time to get over the rape. The marks lasted for months, and while they did she would not entertain the thought of having another relationship with a man. In fact, it took her almost two years before she could go to bed with a man again. She says she couldn't have an orgasm until almost a year after that. "The wounds of a rape go very deep," she says.

But, in time, the psychological wounds did begin to heal for Maryanne. Four years later, she found herself in Oregon, where she was doing graduate work. Although she was able to view the experience without cringing, the rape wasn't entirely resolved in her mind. There was more work to do, and she began to think about giving to other women what had been given to her in her CR group.

"I had seen in my CR group how valuable a peer-support group was and how good it felt," she says. "And I remembered my feeling of being relieved when I was able to speak about what had happened to me. All these feelings motivated me to be able to do that for other women, too. I began by setting up peer-support groups for rape *victims. Since 1980 I've been more or less continuously involved with victims of sexual violence. Mostly I've organized groups in the cities and towns in which I've lived, usually under the auspices of some larger welfare organization or NOW.*

"We generally meet in the evenings," she says. "When the women first come to the groups, you can see that they feel frightened and isolated and alone. Almost all of them think that if only there was something they'd done differently, they wouldn't have been raped. But when the women have been to a meeting or two, and they've compared notes, they find that they have all shared that same feeling. They're not alone. And the abuse hasn't been of their making. It's a validating experience. It helps the women to broaden their perspective and to heal."

Maryanne leans back on the sofa and lays her hands gently on her belly. "You cannot imagine," she says, "how many women out there have been victims of sexual violence. You cannot imagine how many unsuspecting women have been raped by the men they thought they trusted—teachers, fathers, doctors, psychiatrists. The numbers are staggering. The violence is staggering."

In CR groups that relied on a format, rape as a topic came up for group discussion regardless of whether anyone at the meeting had actually been raped or not. "Have you ever been raped?" the format asked. "By a stranger, a husband, a friend or by someone you knew? Did you feel you provoked it in any way? Did you call the police?"

The numbers of women who had actually been raped by strangers were relatively small in comparison to the numbers of women who met in CR groups, as is true for the general population. But virtually all of the women were deeply familiar with the threat of male violence, sexual or otherwise. It was a menace that hovered at the edges of their lives—in catcalls, in sexual harassment at school or at work, in illicit and sexual touching by fathers, doctors, and teachers, in angry slaps by husbands. The women had known about it since childhood when their mothers had told them to be wary of strange men, and it had continued into their adult lives as they learned to tread cautiously in the cities and on dark streets. It was a given. It was a piece of information that never went away, that made women cautious in a way that men didn't have to be, that made women fearful in a way men didn't have to be.

"Why was this so?" asked the women in their CR groups.

While many women at first thought the subject of rape remote, they soon, through the principle of commonality, began to have insight into the ways they had been affected by the threat of male violence. Almost all of the women could remember incidents, however large or small, in which they themselves had been accosted and had felt threatened: a man exposing himself in the woods; a hand on a thigh in a movie theater; a man following you on the street. The talk made women angry and motivated them to learn ways to protect themselves. Lessons in self-defense were part of some CR groups meetings.

The women also began to have insight into the roots of sexism: One gender sought domination over another, even when it took physical intimidation to do so. In 1975, Susan Brownmiller published her remarkable book, *Against Our Will*, further raising the consciousness of thousands of women:

To a woman the definition of rape is fairly simple. A sexual invasion of the body by force, an incursion into the private, personal inner space without consent—in short, an internal assault from one of several avenues and by one of several methods—constitutes a deliberate violation of emotional, physical and rational integrity and is a hostile, degrading act of violence that deserves the name of rape.

And while a majority of women had not actually been raped by strangers, many of them began to perceive that they had in fact been raped by lovers and husbands whenever they had been forced to have sex when they hadn't wanted to, or 'against their will.'

"It occurred to me that there were times in my marriage that I was having sex when I hadn't wanted it," says Carol B. of Fort Wayne, Indiana. "No, it wasn't even so much that I had *actively* not wanted sex at the time: It was never up to me. Because I needed my husband's protection and care, I couldn't even allow myself to think about whether I wanted sex or not. So in the group I began to articulate the fact that I often did feel violated. I felt violated because I had no choice. And I had no choice in sexual matters because I was powerless. I had two young children, I had no income, and I could not walk out."

Other women began to have similar insights. Elizabeth V., now the owner of a garden nursery in Rhode Island, recalls her husband asking her to engage in sexual activities she was uncomfortable with: wearing S&M lingerie and going to pornographic movies. He rented a camera once and pressured Elizabeth to make their own. Elizabeth says she understands that these activities are fine if both partners want to do them. The problem was, she just wasn't comfortable. She'd try them and wouldn't want to do them again. Her husband would then become angry and insulting. All other women like these things, he would say. What was wrong with her? He would put so much pressure on her, by relentlessly criticizing her, that she would give in. And she'd hate herself for doing it.

"I'd feel as if I'd been violated," she says. "I've never been able to talk about sex comfortably, but I finally did in my CR group because I was frightened and didn't know anymore if I was normal or not. Maybe he was right; maybe I was too repressed and there was something wrong with me. And I realized, hearing the other women speak, that they, too, though sometimes for different reasons, often felt like they were being violated. And I realized my feelings were valid. It was a very powerful vindication for me."

To many women, such a sexual violation often felt like abusive behavior. For others, refusing a man his sexual desires led directly to physical violence. More than one woman in her CR group made this connection between sex and abusive behavior. "I had three kids under the age of seven," says Monica A., now a forty-four-year-old travel agent on Long Island. "I was exhausted, wiped out, snowed under, however you want to put it, I was a basket case most of the time. My husband would want sex at night. It was my duty, he said. He actually said that. It was part of the *contract*. So I'd do it just to get it over with. Or I'd say I had a headache or I was too tired, which was the truth. And he wouldn't say anything at first. But then if I refused again the next night, you could see the anger building up. First it would be the silent treatment, then he would start becoming hostile, then, if it got really bad, there'd be a big fight, and maybe he'd smack me. So what was the message? I had to do sex when he wanted it, even if I was exhausted and hated it, or there'd be hell to pay."

In the formats that the women followed in the CR groups,

there were, apart from questions about rape, surprisingly few questions about violence. Today no format would omit the topic of domestic violence—not necessarily because there is more domestic violence today than there was in 1972 (although *reported* incidences are way up), but because there is more awareness of this issue than there was then.

"Domestic violence was on the fringes of our thinking," says Ivana G., a librarian from San Diego. "We'd talk around the issue, but no one in the group ever admitted she'd been hit, though I know that it was true of at least two of the women, who told me privately. It's happened to me. It's happened to a lot of women I know. Maybe it starts with a simple push during a fight, and that turns into a little shoving match. Then because his machismo has been injured, he gets a little out of line and suddenly you're on the floor. A friend of mine was having a fight with her husband and shouting at him to leave and they got close to the door, and suddenly he swung around and hurled *her* out the door and locked it. It was January, and she only had a sweater on, and she was freezing. He finally let her in because the kids were screaming."

One of the most positive outgrowths of the CR movement is the proliferation of shelters and peer-support groups for battered women, as well as for rape victims. The powerful dynamic of women together, women supporting women, and women finding strength in commonality that sprang from CR led feminists and feminist organizations to channel this process into support groups for victimized women. Except in very remote rural areas, today one can find shelters and support groups for rape victims and battered women in nearly every county in the country. Although these groups serve an issue-specific population of women, and tend not to attract

as many middle-class women as they do women of the working class and underclass, such groups are rapidly moving into
the mainstream of many suburban areas.

Women today insist it would not be enough, however, to
focus only on physical violence—as important as that would
be. Emotional violence, too, would be a large topic. Women
who run shelters for battered women say that helping a
woman to free herself of physical battering is only half the
problem. When battered women come in to the shelters, their
self-esteem is at an all-time low. Often it's not the physical
beatings or slaps that have made them feel this way—it's been
the constant chipping away at their self-esteem by the men
who have been controlling them. The battered women have
yielded up control of their lives to men, and the men, often
because they, too, have little self-esteem, have taken it out on
the women. The women come in believing they're no good,
that they're responsible, that they're ugly. Such a dismal self-
image is difficult to break free of. It's easier, say social workers,
to get the women to say no to the physical beatings. They,
at least, are tangible.

Many experts in this area also believe that domestic violence
is contagious. Man beats wife; wife beats kids. As with wife-
battering, reports of child abuse today are also tremendously
on the rise. From 1976 to 1984, reports of child abuse in this
country increased 156 percent. Child abuse is rising by 9
percent a year, and two million cases of bruises, broken bones,
and burns are reported to the authorities annually (many
cases go unreported). Battering, according to some experts
is a *power* issue; and it has been suggested that men are vic-
timizing women at an ever-increasing rate because they're
more afraid now of losing power. Likewise, women who are

abused by men often choose to assert what little power they have left on the powerless—their children.

"It's bad," says Fran G., who works in a battered women's shelter in upstate New York. "Child abuse would be a big topic in CR today. Some of the women who have been beaten, whether physically or emotionally, no longer know how to control themselves. Inside, they're enraged and depressed and they take it out on their children. For some, it feels like the only outlet they have. I had one woman here who was not allowed ever to raise her voice in the house when her husband was home. He couldn't tolerate it. If she did raise her voice in anger, he'd beat her. So what happened? As soon as he left for work, all the rage would come out and she'd scream at the kids. She knew what was happening and it made her sick, but she couldn't control it. Here, in the shelter and in the groups, we deal with the issue of child abuse, too. You have to."

The legacy of the consciousness-raising movement in the area of violence to women is double-edged. On the positive side, the example of CR led directly to the formulation and promotion of hundreds of shelters and peer-support groups for battered women. And because of the new awareness and insights about victims of rape and how they have traditionally been treated by society and the criminal justice system, rape victims are not harassed as consistently as they were fifteen years ago. Progressive legal recourse for rape victims and rape counseling have also proliferated in the last decade.

On the negative side, however, CR failed to grapple extensively enough with the subject of domestic violence, including wife battering, emotional violence, and child abuse.

These issues, in 1972, were thought not to affect the large majority of middle-class women; wife-beating, whether emotional or physical, was thought to be largely confined to the working class and underclass. But today, with the subject more at the forefront of our collective consciousness, many of the women who used to be in CR have been forced to look at the subject. What are the causes of emotional abuse in a relationship? they ask themselves. What does a woman protect by hiding it, or ignoring it until it's too late? How does that legacy get passed on to her children? Is economic independence always the answer?

In their CR groups, women talked about rape by strangers and by lovers and husbands. They shared tales of sexual violence and gained insights into the causes of this behavior in men, and the roots of their own shame. Many of these women were forever freed from the traditional humiliation of rape; and some even learned effective self-defense techniques. But none of the women was freed from the *threat* of violence, sexual or otherwise. The knowledge that a deranged or angry man can at any time make a woman his victim is still part of the given of being female in America—just as large numbers of women have been living for years with wife-battering as a given. The "threat" is as real, as frightening and as inhibiting as it was fifteen years ago. No mother today lets her daughter walk city streets (or even suburban streets) without years of admonitions about speaking to strangers or staying away from isolated areas. While mothers of sons teach their boys lessons in staying away from strangers, too, the threat to boys wanes as the boy grows into a teen-ager and then into a man. For a woman, it is never over.

"We come back to that old adage that 'Anatomy is destiny,' " says Fran G. "Women have had a lot of difficulty with that one, but it's hard, in this area anyway, to deny. A woman and a man get into a fight, they're not equal partners. At any time, he can physically overpower her. It's only when he *agrees* to be equal partners that she can feel some kind of safety. Most men unconsciously 'agree' because they're civilized and that's how they've been raised. But if you think about it, he still has all the power. It's his decision to agree or not. And at any time, if he gets riled enough, he can decide not to agree anymore and break the rules. I think a lot of women unconsciously live under this threat and are deeply affected by it."

TEN

Women Exploiting Women

J.J.'s boys, Harry and Jasper, tear through the living room on their way to the kitchen in search of vital items: the pail that goes with the shovel, a rubber football, Harry's catcher's mitt, Jasper's other sneaker. The boy's father, J.J.'s husband Harold, stands at the door of their townhouse just off Capitol Hill, in a pose of benign and sleepy patience. It's his morning on duty, and he has been up since six getting the boys fed and dressed and keeping them entertained until it was time to go to the park, a ritual they engage in every Saturday morning.

J.J., in her bathrobe, is enjoying the spectacle enormously. It's her morning off. It's part of the deal she and Harold have worked out between them in order to stay sane with two full-time careers and two boys under the age of six. One day on the weekend he gets up with the boys and spends the morning until lunch with them. On the other day, she does the same. Thus each of them gets at least one morning alone—to sleep, to think, to read the paper, or to attend to some important errand that is best done without two little boys in tow.

Such was not the case when J.J. was growing up in the Roxbury section of Boston. One of six children, only three of whom had the same father, J.J. lived in a house full of adult women—her own mother, her mother's mother, and several aunts (her mother's sisters). Never at any time was there a father to take the kids to the park. There was, however, a biological father, whom J.J. did see from a distance from time to time. His name was Arthur, and he was a dealer. J.J.'s mother, had, on pain of a brutal beating, forbidden J.J. to go within a hundred feet of the man. During her entire childhood, J.J. never spoke to her father, and to this day she doesn't even know if he knew she was his daughter.

But J.J. was smart. Extraordinarily so. An early reader despite the dearth of books in her house, J.J. found the library one day on the way to the grocery store for her mother, and created for herself there a place of refuge from an apartment too full of children and women. The librarian, charmed by J.J.'s singular attachment to the dingy, run-down structure, pointed this early passion out to J.J.'s principal at her elementary school, and the story stuck with her from grade to grade, from teacher to teacher. Always, the teachers found J.J. exceptional, the one on whom to pin their hopes. It was in that library, in fact, that J.J. developed her love for classical music, the librarian having pointed out to J.J. the collection of records for lending over by the back wall. But having no record player at home— and more to the point, knowing that no one there would tolerate Beethoven or Brahms—J.J. would not take them out. So the librarian, an older black woman J.J. now refers to fondly as Mrs. Myra, brought her own turntable from home and let J.J. listen quietly to records in the supply closet—a gesture for which J.J. has always been eternally grateful.

Singled out as she was, J.J., in that era of Black Power and tokenism, found doors opened to her that might have been shut five or six years earlier. A door opened at Boston University and with it a scholarship to attend college there. From B.U., with a degree in political science, she made her way to New York, where she took up her graduate studies at N.Y.U. It was then that she met the group.

"You love that story, right?" says J.J. laughing. "It makes me sound like Abe Lincoln."

But the story, says J.J., is no more remarkable than the stories of anyone like herself who finally made it through high school, out of the ghetto and into university.

"You scratch the surface of most of us middle-class black women and you're going to find we're first generation or at best second generation out of the ghetto or off the farm. Our ties to our families are deep, and we never forget where we came from, and where most of them are still at."

So clear is this memory, in fact, that it is J.J. alone of all the other women in that Greenwich Village CR group, who brings up what is perhaps one of the most troubling aspects of the legacy of the Women's Movement—that of women exploiting women. "When we all talk about solidarity among women, and how we don't have that solidarity any more, we don't mean, and have never meant, solidarity among all women," says J.J. "Certain women were never included. Women's Liberation was never intended for women of the underclass. Well, maybe on paper it was, but not in reality. For the most part, solidarity among women refers to women of the middle class, maybe some white women of the working class. That's it. Black women had their own thing going. Those of them who were political at all were in Black Power. But most of them were just trying to survive. And today!"—J.J. hoots—"today, what a joke! There's no such thing as solidarity among women today. It's the opposite. You've got women exploiting women, there's no way to whitewash that fact."

Before the advent of the Women's Movement in the late 1960s, some few white women of the upper-middle-class elite employed other women to work in their homes—as nannies for their children, as cooks, as housekeepers. But, by and large, white middle-class women tended to their own domestic chores. Cleaning your own house was, after all, the job of the middle-class housewife—a job description that did as much to spur the Women's Movement as any political rhetoric. The notion of rich women employing poor women to work for them always had about it unpleasant class and racial overtones, and was occasionally decried, but it was, because it was primarily confined to elite women, removed from mainstream thinking. Today, however, women who employ women are part of the mainstream.

"And it's a nasty situation, if you ask me," says J.J.

J.J. is referring to the large number of middle-class women, women who have careers and children, women who call themselves feminists, who employ black, Hispanic, white, and foreign women of the working class and underclass in low-paying jobs to tend to their child-care and domestic chores so that the middle class can profit from and enjoy the fruits of the Women's Movement.

"I can give you some examples," says J.J. "In my own family in Boston, my mother, bless her soul, who's nearly sixty-five now, travels on a bus all the way out to Dedham, where she watches two pre-schoolers for a working couple. He's a dentist and she works in insurance. So my mother gets up at six in order to be there at seven forty-five when they leave for work. And she can't leave their house until five forty-five at night when the mother gets home. So my own mother isn't in the house until six-thirty or after. That's a hell of a long day for a sixty-five-year-old woman. And you know what she's paid? Two hundred dollars a week. That works out to four dollars an hour—ten thousand dollars a year. No pension. No health insurance. No job security. No paid vacations. I tell her she'd do better at McDonald's, but she won't leave. She says they need her." J.J. grimaces. "I can just imagine the song and dance they give her."

The situation that J.J. describes is among the most troubling aspects of the legacy of CR and the Women's Movement, one that feminists wince at and have been unable to resolve. In the absence of universally available, good-quality child care, women who have taken advantage of the opportunities made possible by the Women's Movement and who have also desired to have families, have found that the only way to do both simultaneously is to employ other women to care for their children and to clean their homes. How-to books for working mothers today in fact advocate this solution: Hire others to shop for you, clean for you, take care of your kids, mow your lawn, and do your laundry, the books say. But they neglect to mention exactly who these domestic laborers are supposed to be.

"The United States has no daycare policy for working mothers," says J.J., "so what are working mothers to do? You can't really blame them, though I think they must, somewhere down deep, feel some guilt when they see how badly paid these workers are. But you ask any working mother, and she'll tell you she's desperate. There aren't enough child-care workers for her to worry about whether or not she's exploiting anybody.

"I find this issue very disturbing," adds J.J. "It was one thing when you had an elite conservative few exploiting other women. It's quite different when you have a large majority of supposedly liberated, progressive, feminist *women exploiting other women—because they think it's their due, their right. Something's gotten awfully twisted around here. It's a nasty kind of hypocrisy. It's as though we're saying: 'Okay, I made it, so liberation is for me. But you didn't make it, so liberation isn't for you.' It's as though the fruits of liberation were only for a certain class of women, who are stuffing themselves while the others are starving."*

Yet J.J. herself sees no immediate way out of this dilemma.

"So," she says, "here goes the big confession. 'How does she *go to*

work?' you're asking yourself. Well, I have someone working for me, just like that couple in Dedham have my mother working for them. I've got a Hispanic woman. Want to hear the terrible story? She's a single parent with two kids. Her own mother watches her kids while she's here with mine. I tell her to bring her kids with her, but she says four is too much to watch. Who could blame her? So I pay her what I think is a decent, generous amount, but that amount doesn't begin to compare with what I make, and she thinks it's a great salary. She'd never give up this job. How could she afford to? She's trapped in this job. But think of it. She never sees her kids. She's seeing my kids. I tell you, I wake up in the middle of the night sometimes knowing I'm going to be punished for this. I mean, at least I see the situation. I'm politically aware of how bad it is. But I can't fire her. This woman desperately needs the money and is grateful to me for the job. Yet I'm the one enjoying the fruits of Women's Liberation, and she's nowhere. She's never going to be anywhere. Maybe if she saves her money, her kids will make it someday. But she doesn't even know what Women's Liberation is."

It was a dilemma no one foresaw in CR. No one talked about it. No one could imagine it. The obstacles to getting out of the house, making a lifelong commitment to work and becoming economically independent seemed so overwhelming that no one thought to wonder who was going to take care of the kids and the domestic chores. Daycare did not turn out to be the answer for the majority as it was hoped it might be. Some women, concerned about a flurry of bad publicity that daycare was receiving, became wary of putting their children in institutions. The government did not pick up the ball, as others thought it might when it became clear how many women were entering the work force. And corporations, always reluctant to embrace social change, have been remark-ably slow to subsidize child care for its male and female workers. Yet women have entered the work force in droves.

Perhaps no one anticipated the huge outpouring of women from the home to the workplace. Perhaps women thought the lesser challenge of figuring out the domestic routine would sort itself out. But whatever the reasons, the job was done backwards, leaving hundreds of thousands of women disenfranchised, if you will, from the Women's Movement. It's as if the Women's Movement had built a dazzlingly beau-tiful house and had forgotten to think about the foundation. Today that foundation, eclectic and unstable as it is, is the labor of the millions of exploited women in this country.

The exploitation of women by women takes many forms: the hiring of full-time, live-in, child-caretakers and house-keepers who have only one day or evening off; full-time baby-sitters who work from seven in the morning until seven at night for low wages; illegal aliens willing to work long hours at hard chores for pitiful wages; neighborhood mothers with no marketable skills who take in children in their homes for as little as a dollar an hour while other, more affluent women in the neighborhood go off to work; poorly paid daycare workers; women who clean houses and shop for working women; and relatives—mothers, grandmothers, sisters—working for little or no wages at all. Nearly every woman interviewed for this book who had once belonged to a CR group and who was now or who had been trying to manage both children and a career simultaneously had employed an-other woman to tend to her children and/or her domestic chores. Not all of them, however, were aware of the moral and political dilemmas involved. Many seemed relieved merely to have found any kind of good child care.

"My child-care situation has been the pits," says Jennifer M., a financial comptroller with a large bank in Manhattan. "My daughter, Annie, is four now, and by last count I've had six caretakers since she was born. I know this is a terrible situation. All the books say it is. But there just wasn't anything I could do about it. The first woman I hired, a nanny, I had to dismiss because she was very controlling and wouldn't care for the child the way I had asked her to. Then I hired a woman from Salvador, a political exile, but she left suddenly, and we never heard from her again. Then I hired an *au pair* from Ireland, but she had a boyfriend, and was unreliable. The stories go on and on and on. My husband and I have always been against the idea of daycare, so I wasn't able to hand my daughter to an institution. And I couldn't quit my job because we needed the money. It's just been a nightmare."

Arlene J., who lives near Rochester, New York, has felt herself to be luckier, but seems to have little consciousness of the rights of the women she employs. Arlene is a pediatrican in a neighboring town; her husband is a contractor. The couple have a three-year-old daughter. "We have a wonderful, wonderful woman who lives with us," says Arlene. "She's from Haiti. I'm not going to get into whether or not she's here illegally. She has one day a week off, usually Sunday. And she has a boyfriend, whom she sees then. She stays there with him on Sunday nights. But she's always back here right on the dot of seven on Monday mornings. She's totally reliable. My daughter thinks of her as a second mother."

Other women have tried a variety of different types of child care in hopes of finding that magic combination (magic for them, that is): good care for little money. Still other women have learned to employ women workers to ease domestic and marital tensions. Pat R. sells advertising space for a small newspaper just outside Seattle. She says she and her husband were going "totally crazy" from chores. The house was a disaster, and the yard looked abandoned. They'd come home from work, and it was all they could do to get supper on the table and the children into the tub. Pat and her husband fought constantly about who should be vacuuming and who should be cleaning the bathrooms. But then they solved the problem. "And I don't know why we didn't think of this sooner," says Pat. "I hired someone to come in twice a week while we're not here to clean the house, do the laundry, and get some things started for supper. And he hired a lawn service that comes once a week in season and takes care of the yard. It's been a miracle. My husband and I no longer fight, and our house is clean. It's taken a lot of stress out of the marriage."

The exploitation of women by women is not confined to the home, however. For several reasons—primarily the devaluation of women's work or work having to do with children in this society—the job of daycare worker remains an underpaid position. Some workers receive wages of less than $200 a week, even though they are expected to put in full-time hours. Yet few of the working mothers in this country can afford to fret over the underlying politics. Indeed, the reverse is often true—working mothers are usually relieved when they find daycare centers that can offer a maximum number of hours of good-quality care for the least amount of money. That the workers are most often other women, many of them with their own children, is a political fact that must be glossed over by other more affluent women if they are able to go to work at all. It is a situation that has been called by some a national scandal.

"I try to take a special interest in the women who are working at the daycare center," says Frances I., a public high-school teacher who puts her preschool son in daycare nearby during the hours of eight in the morning to four in the afternoon while she herself is working. "I think most of the mothers do. We often talk about how lucky we are to have found such a good place. And I'd like to see them make more money, I really would. I know they are underpaid. When I compare what I get for teaching children all day and what they get for teaching children all day—and that's what they're doing; if you are with children, you're teaching them—there's no comparison. I'd never work for what they get. At the same time, however, I feel powerless. I know we all do. We've got too much on our plates as it is—working, trying to keep a family together, trying to do some chores at home. How can I take on the fight to get child-care workers better pay? I can't."

No one suggests that the exploitation of women by women is a deliberate and vicious attempt to subjugate some women at the expense of others. Many women are unaware that the system from which they benefit might be exploitative of other women, and they bristle when the idea is presented to them. Yet the facts are hard to deny. In a country that has seen a rapid and nearly overwhelming influx of women into the work force and has not kept pace with its social services, primarily child care, the exploitation of women by women is difficult to avoid.

Nor is the problem necessarily solved when children reach school age. In suburbs all across the country, women with children at home appear to be dividing into two ranks: those who work outside the home and those who work inside the home. Although some of these women may originally have belonged to the other camp (working mothers who chose to stay home with their children for a time; at-home mothers who find they must enter the work force because of economic necessity), they tend to feel passionately about the choices they have made, and they see themselves as having a particular identity based on those choices. Because of the deep investment they have made in these choices, they often view the "other camp" with suspicion or disdain. This tends to be especially true for the at-home mothers, women who feel they are bucking the tide, women who feel they have sacrificed prestige, money, and status to give of themselves to their children. They often speak of the working mothers with alarm, and more strongly, with irritation and anger. And nowhere is the split between the two groups more evident than at the schoolyard. This is their battleground; this is where they meet—or, more to the point, don't meet.

"I'm carrying the load for these working mothers," says Debbie S., a former nurse who hasn't worked outside the home since she gave birth to her first child, now in second grade. "Me and a couple of other women. There's a class trip, we're the mothers who go. The kids want a Brownie troop, I have to start it because there's no one else. The School Fair in May, I run that, because there's no one else to do it. I'm secretary of the PTA. My whole time is spent down here at the school. I stand here waiting for my daughter, and I see these other kids, getting on buses to go to after-school programs, or they have their baby-sitters standing here, teenagers, waiting to take them home. We had a snowstorm and they called off school, and I had to take four kids home because they couldn't reach the mothers at work. The working mothers have just given up the whole ballgame and have just assumed that we'll pick up the slack. I resent it. I really do. And then I go and do all this work, *for their kids*, and I never get a thanks. In fact, I meet these other mothers sometimes on weekends in the supermarket, they hardly give me the time of day. Working mothers look down on us. They'll tell you they don't. Or they're too busy to think about it. But they look down on us, there's no getting around that."

The anger is explosive. It simmers just below the surface. On a recent television talk show in Minneapolis, the show's producers decided to pit four working mothers against four at-home mothers on-camera. A studio audience, composed of women of both camps from this midwestern city and its suburbs, was there to watch the proceedings and add their comments, much like the Phil Donahue format. The show was astonishing. No sooner had the host introduced the participants than chaos erupted, the host barely able to contain the fireworks. The working mothers maintained, with all the passion and fervor they could muster, that they had just as much right as men to work, that some of them needed to for economic reasons, that they had talents they had a right to explore, that their children were well cared for, that their children were growing up with progressive views about men and women, that their husbands shared child care with them, that they had committed themselves to lifelong work, and that if they gave it up for a period of time, they might lose all that they had worked for. The at-home mothers were scornful of the working mothers. They said the working mothers cared more about success and money than they did about their kids; they cited juvenile delinquency, the high rate of drug use among teen-agers, latchkey children; and last, but not least, the exploitation of at-home mothers by working mothers. One by one, the at-home mothers told their angry stories: The neighborhood children had to play at their houses because the homes of the working mothers were empty; mothers, like Debbie, complained they had had to take on a larger than fair share of the work load at the school; working mothers regarded them, they said, as cheap labor when it came to baby-sitting; playdates were not reciprocated because the working mothers were too busy. At times, the women could not contain themselves. Both sides often tried to outshout the other. The studio audience, pretty evenly divided, resembled a ringside audience at a boxing match.

What was remarkable was not necessarily the arguments themselves—both sides had irrefutable and articulate points to make—it was the passion behind the arguments. Watching this show, it was impossible not to draw the conclusion that there exists in America today a deep and sharp division among women. And no small cause of that split is that one group feels exploited and/or dismissed by the other.

Women feel exploited by other women in the arena of child care, but exploitation of women by women exists in a more subtle form in the workplace as well. The corporate work ethic is antithetical to women's solidarity. It goes against the grain of collective action, and fosters the idea of individual achievement. It's every man for himself—or, in this case, every woman for herself. When women got their chance to scramble up the ladder, say some of the women in business, they did it just the way the men did it—over the bodies of other women if they had to. Do women, they ask, who are in management positions treat the secretarial pool any differently than men do? Are they particularly sensitive to the issues that affect the masses of women in corporate America who are much further down the ladder?

The issue of maternity leave is an example of how women are often maneuvered into watching out for themselves, but not others. A woman lawyer or investment broker becomes pregnant. She goes to her boss. She's built up a lot of credit. He doesn't want to lose her. So he tells her that *for her* because she's such a valued employee, he'll make an exception to the rule: He'll give her, say, six months instead of the usual four in maternity leave. With full pay, with her job back. She's unbelievably grateful. Who could blame her? So then the boss says to her, 'But listen, don't broadcast this around the office. I'm doing this for you because you're a valued employee, but I don't plan on doing it for every woman who walks in here.' And he means it. If ten minutes later, the woman's secretary were to walk in and request the same privilege, the boss would very likely just shake his head and say his hands were tied, the policy was already written and he couldn't change it.

Such a policy, say women in business, co-opts women with power. It divides women into the haves and the have-nots, in terms of both clout *and* money. Women who might have the power to make change are making individual, private decisions instead and letting the women without power in the corporate system fend for themselves. It has made the women without power—the secretaries, the middle management—resentful and angry.

In many professions, women have begun "networks"—groups of professional women in upper management who can share practical information about their work, and who can help each other by referring clients much in the same manner men have made use of the "old boy network." Although these female networks are among the few remaining ways for women to be together, they remain today a very limited apparatus created by and for an elite group of women. Being invited to join a professional network is almost a confirmation of power, an invitation into the select ranks of one's field. The overwhelming majority of women workers do not belong to such select ranks, nor will they ever.

The issue is an ugly one—one with disturbing moral overtones—but one that needs attention nevertheless. In the early 1970s, women learned that important social change was not possible unless women were united. Today women are divided: in the domestic arena between the working women and the at-home women; in the corporate arena between the upper management and the rank-and-file. The divisions were created not deliberately, but in the confusion that accompanies any rapid social change. It was a dilemma that could not be foreseen, but now, as it is just beginning to be recognized, it is one that must be grappled with.

ELEVEN

The Fairy Godmother: The Power of the Collective

Jane is sitting on her couch in her apartment in Manhattan's Green-wich Village. As she was on the night of the reunion, she is tucked into a corner, her legs curled up under her. Even at fifty-five, she still favors the same style of clothing (or "nonstyle" of clothing, as she puts it) as she did twenty years ago: a large droopy sweater, a denim skirt, and boots. Her hair, steely gray, is pulled back into a severe bun, and though she is a plain woman, her eyes are beautiful—a vivid, alert, cornflower blue.

By her own account, she has not had an easy life. She feels herself to be a woman who was raised in one era, with one set of expectations, but who discovered, in another era, a different notion of what it meant to be a woman. Caught as she has been between the two, often irreconcilable, ideals—the traditional and the more emancipated—she has lived a life of struggle and compromise, feeling her way, bucking the more rigid ideas of her husband and her upbringing. She says that she has suffered, and one senses that this is not a word she uses lightly. She says that she has not had an altogether happy marriage, that it has been "rocky," and beset with power struggles. She knows that she has sacrificed herself ("an old-fashioned word," she says) for her family, and she sometimes has deep regrets at not having made more of herself, at not having pursued her art the way she once imagined she might. "I gave of myself fully for my children," she says, proud of that selflessness; yet she will also say, in the next breath, "I sometimes think of myself as having really missed the boat."

It was the Women's Movement, and specifically her CR group, she says, that gave her consciousness and "upset the applecart." Yet she harbors no ill feelings toward either. Indeed, she is passionate in her gratitude toward her CR group, an irony she addresses.

"It's possible my life would have been easier if I'd never heard of the Women's Movement," she says, "but I was asleep, dead inside, before I joined the group. The group woke me up, made me start asking questions. Maybe I'll never have all the answers, and maybe the questions can cause you a lot of heartache, but if you're a woman in this society, and you don't know how to ask the questions, I think you're done for."

I ask Jane to tell me what it felt like to be in the CR group. She smiles. The response is immediate, almost startling. This is a question she can answer, wants to answer.

"As an entity, I loved it," she says with evident enthusiasm. "Even though there were individuals whom I didn't care for as much as I did others, and even though, from time to time, there were uncomfortable feelings that surfaced, as an entity—as a collective entity—*it was wonderful. It was wonderful because it was collective, because it was an* us. *Not a* you-and-me. *The* us *was the message. It was the most important thing. We understood that we were all in this together, and that was what made it work."*

She takes a sip from a can of Diet Pepsi and looks out the window onto Washington Place, recalling feelings from fifteen years ago. "I used to try to explain to my husband what it felt like to be in the group, and I remember at first I used to say to him that the group was 'mother.' But I came to realize that 'mother' wasn't really the right image. There was always time to spill your guts if you needed to, and there was among us a kind of bottom-line trust, but this was not a group of pushover women. The group did not just give you carte blanche approval. If there was garbage, you came to see the garbage. The group as an entity was stronger, tougher than just mother. It was more tuned in to the real world—not protecting us from it, but giving us the nerve to go out there and be part of it.

"So then I realized that the analogy I was searching for was something stronger: Instead of being 'mother,' the group was everything I thought a 'fairy godmother' should be. Not the fairy godmother with the pink tulle and the wand"—she laughs—"but the fairy godmother who clues you in to how things really are. She's caring, but objective. In literature, the fairy godmother is effective and competent. She makes things happen. She's androgynous—unattached and unconnected. The mother is too intimate, too close, not objective. But the fairy godmother has the distance of the female god and protector. You know that the fairy godmother's vision is real."

A decade and a half after the fact, women recall their time spent in consciousness-raising groups with a passion and nostalgia that is often surprising. It is impossible not to hear in their voices, not to see in their faces, the profound impact this collective experience has had on their psyches—producing, in turn, strong feelings of gratitude, strong memories of solidarity, and often wistful longings for its return in their lives. It is reminiscent of the way women will talk of an early love affair or of childbirth, the intensity of the event rekindled in the recollections.

One evening, in a suburb outside of Boston, I asked a group of nine women who had once belonged to the same consciousness-raising group in the early 1970s to say the first word that came to mind when they thought about being in a CR group. The words they used, in succession, were *close, safe, warmth, love, perspective, intimate, supportive, stable.* The last woman said *holds.* It was an odd word, an odd usage. I asked her to explain what she meant. "The group held us," she said. "It held me when I was having a hard time and it held me when I was having a high time. When I think about the CR group, I think about being held, even though I don't think anyone ever actually touched me."

It was pertinent that all of the characteristics the nine women described were ones dependent upon and borne out of a collective experience. The words *warmth, love, close, intimate,* and *holds* suggest shared feelings; the words *safe, perspective, supportive,* and *stable* indicate community. Interestingly, no one said, *self-esteem* or *career opportunity.* Instead, they focused on the collective rather than the personal, and it was in the memory of the collective that their passion surfaced.

"We weren't depressed at meetings; we were really very, very happy to be with each other," says Edie G., of her own group on Staten Island in 1973. "We felt our isolation disappear. That was the wonderful part of the group, and we just felt very much in tune with each other. We were sorry to see it disband."

"For me, on the deepest level," says Connie F., of a group she belonged to in Seattle, "when I think about CR, I think about a feeling of connection to other people. I had an awareness that I was not alone. I think the wish to belong and to be valued never goes away."

"It was a flowering of affection," says Ramona B., from Southfield, Michigan, who once belonged to a CR group at

Berkeley. "I was brought up in a world in which women were competitive with each other. And in the group, I learned how to love women."

Other women describe their groups as "extended families"; still others speak of "unconditional solidarity." "Husbands came and went," says one woman with a sigh, "but the group was always there."

This sense of the stability and the nonjudgmental support of the collective is among the strongest threads to emerge when women speak of their CR experience. It is not, strictly speaking, the "political through the personal" that the architects of consciousness-raising intended as its underpinnings. Yet for most groups, the sharing of personal histories forged a collective epiphany that in the broadest sense is a political one. For the women came to realize that it was only in this forged collective that personal progress and personal insights were possible. In a corollary to the architects' original tenet, one could accurately say, "The collective *enables* the personal." It was the collective endeavor that paved the way for the personal journey—even though, ironically, the women forged the collective experience by speaking of their personal histories first. Thus, for many, the personal and the collective worked together in a kind of symbiosis, enabling women to discover themselves only by discovering each other.

"I would have had a lot more pain in my life if I hadn't had the support of the group," says Laurel R., the financial administrator in Manhattan. "I wouldn't have had women behind me with their hands on my back saying, 'It's okay. You can take the next step and we'll be there to catch you if you fall. We've done it, so try this or try that.' We used to applaud if a woman was able to do something she hadn't been able to before. We'd just get these big grins on our faces and clap our hands spontaneously, not because one *should* applaud, but because we just felt like it.

"I would hate to think of who I would be today without that experience," she continues. "Being in the group allowed me personally to know what life was like not just in my own little part of the world, but for other people. I could, in essence, expand my risk-taking, expand my choices, paint my picture bigger. The exposure was to a much broader base of life—the panoramic view versus the one little still shot."

Individual progress was enhanced by the safety net of the collective. One woman from Maine recalls a moment in her consciousness-raising group when she suddenly and painfully woke up from what she describes as a long sleep from the self. In the midst of a group discussion, she remembered being an adolescent girl and standing upon an outcropping of rocks near her home, looking out to sea. She had felt then, with the bravado of childhood, that everything was possible, that "the world was in my teacup," that wonderful things were going to happen to her. But then she had married while she was in college and had had four children in quick succession, burying that thrilling sense of self. "I realized during that one evening in the group that I had not taken my adult life seriously. I had not paid any attention to where it was going, and I had lost all of that sense of wonder about myself or the future. And what happened that night is that I went through a wave of remembrance and sadness, and then one of tremendous anger. It was both an inward and an outward anger: the first at myself for neglecting to ask myself the serious questions this group was now asking itself; and the second was social anger at a system that had allowed me no longer to take myself seriously. That realization was very empowering—but it really began with those women. We had to struggle to give ourselves back to each other. It wasn't me giving me the license to take myself seriously again. It was the group."

With the safety net of the collective, making personal progress often meant a shedding of an old, confining skin. Jeannette F. says that for her, the impact of CR was immediate. "I was in the process of getting a divorce, and right away I began to strip away the old ideas about myself and acquire new ones. I remember saying to my lawyer I didn't need alimony—I could work and make my own living. I remember thinking that I could start my own business. I had never worked, but I kept thinking, 'I can do that.' When I think about starting the business, it's very linked with feminism in my mind. I quit cooking gourmet meals. I went camping for the first time in my life. I stopped going to the beauty parlor once a week. I mean, if you can't wash your own hair, what are you?"

Again and again, women speak of this sense of empowerment gained from the CR experience. In their groups, the shared insights and testimonies gathered together into a collective nugget, the power of which was immeasurably greater than the sum of the individual parts. Most, in the early 1970s, called the experience "sisterhood"; Jane has called it the "fairy godmother." This semantic labeling, and the attention paid to the words the women use to describe their CR experience, is significant. For it tells us what CR was not: It was not psychoanalysis, and it was not group therapy.

From the outset, the architects of CR saw the potential pitfall in confusing the consciousness-raising group with that of the therapeutic group or the encounter group. Irene Peslikis, a founding member of Redstockings, enumerated, in an essay written in 1969, what she called "Resistances to Consciousness." Among these was the notion that women's liberation was therapy.

> This, whether or not you belong to the organization, implies that you and others can find individual solutions to problems, for this is the function of therapy. Furthermore the statement expresses anti-woman sentiment by implying that when women get together to study and analyze their own experience, it means they are sick, but when Chinese peasants or Guatemalan guerillas get together and use the identical method, they are revolutionary.[12]

It was easy for those resistant to or unfamiliar with CR to confuse it with group therapy, for, from a distance, CR and group therapy appeared to be similar. In both cases, a number of individuals went into a room, sat in a circle, and shared their personal experiences. And theoretically, in both cases, the individuals went there for the purpose of improving their lot.

But there, the similarities end.

Implicit in the group-therapy experience is the idea that those who participate are ill in some measure. Exposure within the group is intended to make the *individual* well. The forging of a collective is never a goal. The group dynamic is intended to resolve personal and private dilemmas—not political or societal ones. In group therapy, the conflict must be dealt with on the deepest psychic level, and it is not the intention of group therapy to see society as to blame for one's problems.

CR was quite different. Women were not ill, said its architects. Wellness was not the point, because women already were well—it was the society that was ill. Solutions, therefore, could not be individual. Rather, the collective was the point. The "click" was the point. The commonality was the point. Solutions existed, but they were not psychic ones, they were political ones.

Judith S., an actress in Manhattan, has been in both group therapy and in a CR group. She describes the difference between the two experiences this way: "In a consciousness-raising group, you get to blame outside forces," she says. "In your own therapeutic work, it's not terribly useful constantly to blame outside forces. It's more of an internal process. Therapy ignores your place in time, your culture. You talk about your particular parents, your particular history, your childhood, your various traumas. In consciousness-raising, the group is much more aware of the moment, the present reality in which we live."

Although CR was not intended to be group therapy, not everyone who participated knew that nor felt that. Nor did all CR groups function in the manner for which they were designed. Some CR groups became quasi-group-therapy encounters, straying from the political agenda to the psychic. Although the urge to solve one's childhood or marital dilemmas (or to break through one's angst) within a group structure was powerful, most women whose groups strayed into this area speak of their groups "degenerating" at this point, of wandering off into an alien and risky territory not completely understood. And with this "degeneration" into the purely psychic often came a flaunting of the rules of CR. When the group began to feel more like a group-therapy experience, women felt freer to criticize each other, to speak of feelings of personal animosity within the group, to analyze relationships among the women present, to lend advice and offer personal support for daily dilemmas.

Even today, when recalling their participation in CR, a few women confuse the CR experience with the therapeutic experience. Some did both simultaneously and now cannot accurately remember what took place in which group. Some speak of "catharsis" in the CR groups, a term more appropriate to the group-therapy experience. Other women, though they remember clearly the differences between CR and their own therapy, are not clear as to which "helped" more. Some groups, which formed on their own without an umbrella organization and without a format, merged the two experiences in a haphazard manner, not entirely understanding the differences between the two. And still other groups deliberately turned to the therapeutic encounter when they felt the CR agenda had run its course. Laurel R. of Manhattan recalls that at one point her group invited a psychologist (a woman) to enter the group and to run meetings. The psychologist charged each woman a fee—a new wrinkle for the already two-year-old group. At first, no one protested, but later, when the psychologist lead the group into the territory of anger, friction and tension began to surface in the group and eventually led to the group's demise. After a hiatus, the group made its way back together again . . . this time without the shrink.

The architects of CR were anxious to distance the CR experience from group therapy for another reason as well. As soon as CR began to develop, it was clear that its critics were numerous. The phenomenon, after all, was a revolutionary one—one which, fairly directly, had come from the Communists of China. Those invested in the status quo—primarily men, and to a large extent the establishment media—were quick to dismiss CR, derisively labeling it no more than a "hen party." There was an implicit suggestion made as well of nefarious lesbian activities within these groups. How convenient, then, for these critics was the notion of psychotherapy. For centuries, women who had protested their oppression had been labeled "sick," "crazy," "mad," and "witches." More recently, they'd been called "depressed" and "emotionally unstable." Even many of the women themselves who joined CR did so thinking they were ill in some way. By putting CR into the category of therapy, those who were threatened by CR were attempting to remove it from the much more explosive and dangerous political realm.

The CR experience was a seminal one for those who participated in it, and in their memories, these women retain an intense nostalgic regard for the CR group phenomenon. Most say today they feel they would have become entirely different persons without it. Some say it saved their lives.

Hearing the women speak with such feeling, I was often plagued with an image that would not go away, an image at once poor and excellent. For what the women most reminded me of, as I sat in their living rooms or their kitchens or their offices, watching their faces and listening to their stories, was men who have gone to war—an incongruous analogy given the nature of their recollections. But the image persisted. To be more precise, the image was really of boys who in battle grew up to be men because they saw things and heard things and did things that forever changed them.

In the common rhetoric of the day, the women enlisted in a war against sexism. The banner they struggled under was called "feminism," and the battles they fought were for self-respect, strength as a collective of women, and political awareness of those forces that united them. Once a week, they shared thoughts, feelings, fears, and intimacies with more abandon than at any time before or since. Like a company of soldiers whose naked selves are exposed on the battlefield and who become dependent upon each other for survival, the women, in their groups, gave of themselves totally and were bonded together in the process. And if they had scars to show for their struggles, they also had their medals. They called themselves feminists and were easy with the label.

But as with soldiers who have returned to peacetime, who they are now impinges on who they used to be. Like veterans who meet years afterward in an American Legion Hall to recapture a fading valor, but who worry in their daily lives about meeting mortgage payments, ending troubled marriages, and growing older, the women, too, know that the experience that once united them is more alive in recollection and in memory than it is in the present.

The medals and the labels are growing dusty. The war cannot be said to be over, but the fervor of the initial battles has waned. . . .

TWELVE

Four Million Albatrosses: Feminism Today

Sandi is on the phone with a federal judge. In the space of the three-minute call, he manages to call her "honey" four times. Each time he calls her "honey" Sandi rolls her eyes and mouths the word across the desk. When she hangs up, she is shaking her head, but more with bemusement than with any real distaste.

"Sure, I could say to the judge, 'Hey, listen pea-brain, I'm not your honey,' but he's a sweet old guy, and what harm does it do? And anyway, that's not what feminism means to me."

Which leaves the door wide open for the next question: What does it mean to her then if it doesn't mean protesting the demeaning diminutive?

"What does it mean to be a feminist?" she asks rhetorically, repeating the question, her arms spread over her desk. She shakes her head again, this time as a gesture of astonishment, of mock disbelief that anyone should need to ask her the question at all.

"It means everything in my life!" she exclaims. "There is nothing it doesn't mean. It means total equality of opportunity, no matter

where I am, no matter what society I am in. But it also means equality in my own head—in the heads of all women. Feminism is a state of mind as much as it is the creation of opportunity."

Then she thinks a minute.

"But we're still not there yet," she says, lowering her arms, reality for the moment overtaking her exuberance. "I see women a generation behind me, women right out of college. And they're still carrying around a lot of that old baggage. Maybe they're not carrying twelve million albatrosses like we did, and their burden isn't as heavy. But are they free yet? No—they're still carrying four million albatrosses."

Although much has been said about the death of feminism, the dormancy of feminism, and how we are now living in a "post-feminist society" (as if feminism were somehow behind us), it is ludicrous to think that feminism is not very much with us as we turn the corner into the 1990s. The texture of life, for most of us, would be radically different if that phenomenon known as the feminist movement had not taken place when it did. Catherine would not own her own bookstore. Sandi would not be a lawyer. Felicia would not be making $160,000 a year. J.J. would not be sharing parenting with Harold. Maryanne would not be working with rape victims. Indeed, the rape victims would have no place to go.

Without feminism, the contributions of these women to society might have been buried beneath the minutiae of a million housewifely tasks. Some of the women might never have developed a complete sense of their own sexuality. Almost certainly, all of them would have lived a life of foreshortened horizons and of shut doors.

Imagining life today without feminism is difficult to do, a kind of proof that many of the changes begun in the late 1960s and early 1970s are now an integral part of our daily

existence. Already two generations of American women have
come of age in an era when women's rights in many arenas
are now almost taken for granted. Women's talents and
skills—at the workplace, in government, and in the arts—are
now recognized and genuinely sought with greater frequency
and consistency than ever before.

Yet the lifeblood of feminism today is no longer in a *collective* movement of women joined together for a common
cause. Rather, it exists in the very *personal* interaction each
feminist woman has with her world—her mate, her family,
her bosses, her colleagues. As a political issue, feminism has
yielded its intensity to other issues—so much so, in fact, that
women coming of age today, though they have benefited
from the efforts of the preceding generation, particularly in
the area of career opportunities, now largely regard the
Women's Movement as historical and have turned away from
a collective focus. For other women, women like Catherine
or Sandi, who did witness or participate in the movement,
feminism is a value system to which they still subscribe, but
one in which they have largely relinquished any active role
they might previously have played. To be sure, there are some
committed women today who *do* actively work for the movement, but their numbers are significantly smaller than they
were fifteen years ago.

Because of this waning of activist fervor and because the
Women's Movement is not at the forefront of women's consciousness today, some confusion exists about what exactly
feminism really means. In my reporting, I almost always
asked a woman, as the interview progressed, whether or not
she considered herself a feminist today. Or, how did she define feminism? Or, what did it mean to her to be a feminist
now? How did that differ from being a feminist in 1972? What

emerged from these interviews was this: Feminism today, like beauty, is very much in the eye of the beholder.

Given that all of the women who were asked this question did once belong to consciousness-raising groups—in which most actively sought to educate themselves about this political concept called feminism—their responses were wide-ranging, contradictory, and sometimes even baffling. Almost immediately it became apparent that no one clear definition would emerge. Often, confronted with the question, they tossed the ball back to me: What did *I* mean by feminism? Although I returned these volleys, ostensibly in the name of objective journalism, I began to wonder if I *could* answer the question, if a universally apt definition was even possible today. For the smorgasbord of definitions women gave to the word *feminism* seemed to suggest that during a decade in which radical rhetoric and social activism had been generally unwelcome and largely absent, women had been shaping and molding their own personalized visions of feminism to suit their private realities.

Most surprising, however, were the women who had once belonged to CR groups who now rejected the term entirely (some referring to it as the "F-word"). These were the women who had once embraced the political theory but now seemed to be turning away from it, either creating their own words for what they believed in, or attributing to feminism unattractive, distasteful, or too-radical-for-them associations.

And then there were the women who chose to define feminism by what it was not—or rather, by what it hadn't yet accomplished. They were able to describe feminism, and thus identify themselves as feminists, only by measuring the success of feminism to date.

To wit:

———

"Is feminism marching and picketing, learning karate, giving up makeup, and letting the hair grow on my legs and under my arms? Then, I'm not a feminist."

"Feminism means that the power of the world is shared. That our views are respected. I've taken on quite a bit of male coloring at my job, but there are basic things about being a woman that no amount of coloring covers—caring about people. Establishing a balance between work and home. Women have a complexity and depth that men don't have. If we had a feminist president, education would be a priority. Health would be a priority. Old people wouldn't be shunted off to die."

"Has feminism made my life perfect in that I'm always comfortable with what I'm thinking and feeling? No. Has feminism improved where I was? Yes. My life is ninety-five percent better because of feminism."

"Yeah, I have to consider myself a feminist. Feminists are people who aren't brutal. I want to scream when I see a man mistreating a woman. I saw a man trying to shove a woman into a car. It made my blood boil. But when I read about women's issues, I get bored. I'm not particularly interested in women's groups anymore. I'm more of an artist. I don't go out there to marches, because it's too hard. You have to give over your life to that. I've given my life to dance."

"If feminism enables women to feel entitled to develop themselves in all areas, that's a positive thing. But in my view, we still have a long way to go until we resolve the obstacles in the way. I don't believe that women are respected. They are still devalued and held in contempt. I know there is a handful of women who are successful, but basically the old attitudes are still very much in place. We don't value the things women have to give as much as we value the things men have to give. Feminism isn't about getting out there and becoming a doctor or a lawyer. It's about putting a value on all kinds of roles."

"I've never stopped being a feminist, but it's all on a personal basis. It's in my life, in my relationships, in how I advise or counsel my daughters or my son, my girl friends, anybody I know. I admire those women who are still very active. It amazes me that they are so strong on all the issues, but I'm glad they are doing it because I'm not. I'm, you know, doing it my own way."

"It strikes me that except for a few things like equal pay for certain jobs, we are back where we started. I work all day. I bring home a paycheck. So why do I have to do all the work at home as well?"

"A lot of women have trouble with the word *feminist*. They think it means you're a man-hater or a dyke or a troublemaker. I meet women who *are* feminists in the way they live, but they will not admit to being feminist. They say, 'No, I'm not. I don't want that label.' "

"The way I see it, only a few elite women are better off. The vast majority of women are really suffering because there is no decent child care for them. Because they don't get the promotions when they have to take time out for their children. These are feminist issues because women and children are tied together."

"I've never been militant in a way that's abrasive, but in terms of being a mother, I think I do make an effort to make my daughter aware of all the different possibilities in life. I often find myself in conversations with her about what it was like twenty years ago, or one hundred years ago, and about how people used to think that women couldn't do so many things, and isn't it nice now that women can do whatever they want. I think she has a good sense of females having power. Of females being very competent."

"I don't go around saying 'I'm a feminist.' If anybody asks me if I am a feminist I will say *yes*."

"I don't know what it means to say the word feminism these days."

"The situation of women cannot be radically changed until capitalism is done away with. I think any ideology that wants to become serious politically has to project a society that is good for everybody, not just part of the society. But I do think that the special oppressions of women must be heard and must be understood."

"I'm reluctant to take on labels. I don't like the word. I don't like separating women's issues from human issues."

"That's the word with the capital *F* which means that you have to go and do something about it. You have to be in touch with all the people who think as you do and you have to take positions and get involved with women's political caucuses. And I've always stayed very far away from all that."

"On campus, if you're a feminist, you're a lesbian."

"Being a feminist means helping women achieve all that they can and not allowing those rights to be taken for granted."

211

"Now I feel so strongly about being a feminist, it's just hard for me to believe that I was this nonthinking person for so many years of my life."

"A feminist is someone who cares about what happens to women in today's society."

"I am not a feminist, and yet I believe in all the feminist causes. I have marched with groups and have contributed money to campaigns. But I consider myself a *humanist* because I think that a lot of men have been treated unfairly. I think that a lot of women have become insensitive to men because of the Women's Movement."

"It's a real big world out there. And if we were going to measure the feminists against those who don't perceive themselves as feminists, I think the feminists would be in a very small minority."

"Most people bristle at the word *feminist*. It conjures up all sorts of aggressive and abrasive images to them. Do you know how many women will say to me, 'I'm not a feminist, but . . .' And then they'll go on to say every single thing that makes them clearly a feminist."

"*Feminism* has become a dirty word. I consider myself to be a middle-of-the-road, middle-class feminist. Yet I know that I am part of a minuscule minority just because I believe women should not be worth less than men."

"There's tremendous hostility to the word *feminist*, because the issue is power. Those who have it don't want to give it up."

"I call myself a feminist and not a humanist, because we have to raise women up to the level of men."

"I'm a feminist, but I'm not going to fall all over myself trying to prove it to the world. I don't like being called a girl. I prefer being called a woman. But I'm not going to stop eating in a restaurant because they call the bathroom the ladies' room. And yeah, I don't like it when somebody says, 'I now pronounce you man and wife.' But I'm not going to stalk out of the wedding ceremony when I hear it."

Feminism, right from the inception of the Women's Liberation Movement, has always been a tricky political theory—fraught with hidden land mines, particularly as the theory expanded to encompass a large number of more complicated issues. If you are a feminist, for example, does that mean you consider men the enemy or do you think men and women have to work together to solve "the woman problem," as it has been called by some? If you are a feminist, do you eschew all forms of artifice in your appearance and dress, so as not to capitulate to the sexist image of females in this society, or do mini-skirts have nothing to do with raising women's salaries? Trickier yet, might a feminist use a certain style of dress to get what she wants in the business world so that she can move as far ahead as she can? If you are a feminist, does that mean you'll brook no guff from any man who stands in your way—or do you have to do it for other women, too? Can you be a feminist and never in your life have performed one political act for another woman? Can you be a feminist and not even consider *yourself* political?

Even in its early days, when the Women's Movement was in its prime, there was dissension in the ranks as to what the political theory of feminism was all about. No wonder then that today's women have such disparate notions about what it means to be a feminist. Yet today's smorgasbord of definitions of feminism does reveal certain pertinent clues about what women are thinking and feeling.

Especially prominent is the suggestion, as Sandi has said, "We're still not there yet," implying that feminism has been an evolution, not a revolution, in our culture. The central snag is power. It is still not shared equally by men and women, nor is it shared equally among the classes. Some speak of a disenfranchised group of women for whom the Women's Movement still seems to have little impact. Yet, although a few women feel that precious little has changed in twenty years, most are comfortable with the idea that while life is not perfect for women, it is considerably better than it was before feminism's widespread infiltration into the culture.

Also quite apparent among the women is a distaste for labels. Some women even reject the label *feminist* altogether in favor of *humanist*, a term that implies a way of life rather than a struggle, and—more to the point—is genderless. (Interestingly, the term *humanist* was, even in the early days of the Women's Movement, preferred by some of its leaders.)

The definitions the women give to feminism—and their attempts to place themselves inside or outside of this political theory—also indicate that activism is largely dead. In its place, women have taken to feminism "in their own way." A number see themselves as role models for their children; others feel their feminist deportment at the workplace is a form of activism. Indeed, many would go so far as to raise the consciousness of the people they come into immediate contact with in their personal lives, but they have no desire to go farther than that.

214

Implied, but not always stated in their definitions, is a sense, too, of operating in a vacuum. Because of this, a number of women who describe themselves as feminists say they feel they belong to a minority—"a minuscule minority," according to one. It would seem then that although many women to-day—and virtually all of the women interviewed for this book—are living lives richly dependent upon the fruits of feminism (they enjoy jobs, rights, and salaries that would not have existed without it), they still feel that feminism is not part of mainstream thinking.

■

Daphne is fixing herself a supper of sorts in the cramped corner kitchen of her one-room apartment that might pass, in real estate ads, for a "studio." It is on a nearly deserted street, too west of SoHo to be considered fashionable. Along one wall of the room is a faded rose-colored sofa, which appears to be Daphne's bed as well. Dishes crowd the sink, and Daphne offers a quick apology for the untidiness of her apartment. It is hard, she says, to keep things neat in such a small place. Indeed, many of her belongings appear to be placed around and stuffed onto the shelves of a wide maple bookcase on spindly legs. It is impossible not to think of the contrast between this room, which resembles nothing so much as a transient student's apartment from the sixties, with Felicia's spacious, impeccably decorated apartment just a mile or two north of here. Two women, from the same CR group, whose lives panned out so very differently. . . .

Daphne has just returned home from the art gallery where she works part time. She is famished, she says, as she fixes herself a plate of cheese and raw vegetables. And then finally, she moves gracefully into an overstuffed armchair across from the sofa and is ready to talk about one of her favorite subjects—politics. It's a subject that has never been far from her thoughts, even if it no longer dictates her actions.

"We've all forgotten this now, but originally, in '68 and '69, the

215

movement was a political one—very, very radical, in fact," she says, giving her hair a toss. "When women protested the Miss America pageant, that was a very radical action at the time. We've forgotten many of the tenets of the Women's Movement—marriage as slavery, communal child-raising. Some women were even talking about over-throwing the government. The Women's Movement at heart was a revolutionary movement, one that terrified a lot of people at the time. Think of it—we were trying to overhaul the entire essence of woman and family in this country. There's no aspect of life—none—that wouldn't have been deeply affected by this if it had occurred."

Daphne nibbles on a stalk of celery and takes a sip of mineral water. She keeps a bottle of white wine in her refrigerator for guests, she says, explaining in an easy, straightforward manner that she herself never drinks because she is a recovering alcoholic. "CR itself was revolutionary when it began," she continues, "and its original intention was strictly political. . . . Well, it depends on how you define political. I think it allowed women to change their personal lives, but it didn't really harness all that tremendous revolutionary energy it was supposed to. It certainly didn't in our group. Maybe Jane goes on marches. J.J.'s involved in mainstream politics now. And I know Maryanne did some work with rape crisis centers a while back. But the rest? Catherine? No. Felicia? No. Sandi? No. Me? Not anymore.

"We took what we learned and invested it in our personal lives."

Daphne puts the plate of food down on the floor and slips off her shoes. She crosses her legs under a long gray-green skirt and lifts her hair off the back of her neck.

"When I think about the remnants of the Women's Movement now," she says, "the main thing I think about is how very far women have journeyed from those radical roots. You wouldn't find one woman in fifty today who would remember what it was really like in

the beginning—maybe one in a hundred. I think we scared ourselves.
We allowed a veil to pass over our eyes, to change our vision . . .
to tone it down.

"But in doing so, we lost something very valuable," she says.
"There's no joy anymore. There doesn't seem to be the celebration of
women there used to be."

As with the word *feminism* (and beauty), the success or failure
of CR's basic tenet also appears to be in the eye of the beholder. If political success is defined as a broad-based change
in the perceptions and thinking patterns of a large number
of people, then CR was a political hit. If it is defined, however,
as a translation of those perceptions and thinking patterns
into actions that will benefit other individuals, then CR begins
to sink on the charts.

From its inception, CR was meant to be a political movement—not vastly different from radical cells in Communist
China, where by speaking about "pains," one could come to
understand their political causes. This political intent was
directly stated in the first paragraph of the CR format promoted by the New York Radical Feminists—a format that
became the blueprint for CR nationwide.

> One of the purposes of consciousness-raising is to make us
> aware of the societal pressures that oppress women. Some
> women use the awareness gained from consciousness-raising
> solely in their personal lives without becoming active in the
> Women's Movement. This is a valid purpose of consciousness-
> raising. It is hoped, however, that consciousness-raising will
> help to radicalize us, as women, to participate in whatever
> action is necessary to change our society.

Other statements went even farther. In an essay entitled, "The Personal is Political," by Carol Hanisch, reprinted in *Notes from the Second Year* (1970), the author, who had been involved in two consiousness-raising groups, wrote:[12]

> So the reason I participate in these meetings is not to solve any personal problem. One of the first things we discover in these groups is that personal problems are political problems. There are no personal solutions at this time. There is only collective action for a collective solution. I went, and I continue to go to these meetings because I have gotten a political understanding which all my reading, all my "political discussions," all my "political action," all my four-odd years in the movement never gave me. . . . I believe at this point, and maybe for a long time to come, that these analytical sessions are a form of political action. . . .

And Robin Morgan, editor of *Sisterhood Is Powerful: An Anthology of Writings from the Women's Liberation Movement* (1970), wrote in her introduction: "Women's Liberation is the first radical movement to base its politics—in fact, create its politics—out of concrete personal experience. . . ."

As CR spread, however, and left the tidy confines of the radical groups that had spawned it (the New York Radical Feminists, the Redstockings), it began, like a child, to take on a personality and a shape similar to but different from its parents. The original architects had underestimated the tremendous thirst that women would have to be able to speak, finally, in a safe place, about their lives. This slaking of that thirst, and the sense of relief that followed quickly in its wake, was so powerful that for hundreds of thousands of women it became the dominant focus of CR—not the political investigation of sexism per se, but the heartfelt, almost obsessive outpouring of private stories and secrets. And with it came the tremendous realization that one was not alone. So potent was this outlet that CR became, for so many women, as necessary as a fix. They did not think of themselves as political visionaries. They thought of themselves as women who had come home.

Not surprisingly then, women who once belonged to CR groups have widely differing views on the political nature of their CR experience:

"Our group was very different, nonpolitical," says Arlene S. of Pomona, New York. "Other groups seemed to have a harshness to them. The message was you had to move forward, you had to deal with issues. There was a sense of confrontation and judgment. Our group, I feel, accomplished so much more, but in a different way. We just talked about ourselves, and it was very warm."

"We perpetuate sexism until we become conscious of the part that we play," says Phyllis F. of New City, New York. "That's what women's groups were meant to do because they were really well thought out. They were actually political groups. They really got me. You know, if you said politics to me back then, I would have left the room. I came from the dead 1950s, and I didn't know from radical politics. But in the group, they just said, well, the personal is political. Just work on yourself, that's politics. Okay, I could deal with that. And you know, it works. Not immediately that minute, maybe, but over time. There are battered women's shelters and rape crisis services across the state of New York that did not exist in the early 1970s. These came out of CR."

"It was a time of tremendous turmoil," says Frances H. of San Francisco. "And I think the turmoil may have preceded our understanding of what was really going on. It was like being a little boat on a rocky sea, and you think it's your fault that you are rocking the boat. But in fact you are on this tremendously disturbed social ocean. So that's how I think of CR now. We were this little boat battering around, having our conversations, but, now, as I look back, in fact, I see a much larger panorama."

"When I first joined consciousness-raising," remembers Abby T. of Braintree, Massachusetts, "I was aware of its being part of large political ferment. There were the civil rights movement, the assassinations, the antiwar stuff, the SDS organizations on campus. The Women's Movement just seemed to flow out of all this, and so right from the beginning I thought of it as political."

"At the end of each session," recalls says Jeannette F. of Manhattan, "we would do what was called 'summing up.' We were supposed to think about what had been said that night and see where the common threads were. That was when we would have our political insights."

"The politics happened," says Miriam W. of St. Paul, Minneapolis, "when you realized that your problems were not of your own making."

Some women never entertained the word *politics* during the entire time they spent in CR. Other women came to understand that they were participating in a political movement only in the broadest sense: It was politics, they were told, simply to recognize that some problems for women could not be solved on an individual basis. For yet another group of women in CR, the talk translated into action: They went out from their living rooms and into the public arena and actively worked to change laws or to improve women's lives. And finally, for a fourth group, the CR experience was merely one part of an ongoing education in the radical politics of the Women's Liberation Movement.

The beauty of CR—and the foundation of its success—was that it did not demand obedience to leftist dogma. Seeking to politicize large numbers of mainstream women, the architects of CR understood that you could not promote this politicization too strongly or you would scare off most women. By stating openly that it was okay to use CR "solely in their personal lives," its creators opened the doors to hundreds of thousands of women who might otherwise have turned away. In the initial and explanatory paragraphs of CR formats, the drafters said to women: Take this experience and do with it what you will. Be active or not. Be political or not. That is your choice.

Hearing the women define what they think feminism is today, and yet having heard so recently about what it felt like to be in CR fifteen years ago, two contradictory facts emerge:

Consciousness-raising, with its weeks, and even years, of meetings, remains alive in the memories and feelings of women today. Women speak of CR "changing my life," and of "saving my life." For some women, CR has about it a feeling of "Glory Days."

Yet feminism today, for many of these same women, appears to have lost its vitality.

How is it that CR can have meant so much to these women, yet many of them disassociate themselves from feminism today? This paradox leads one to wonder, did CR take? In other words, once having gotten your consciousness raised, did it stay there?

"Once I have awareness of an issue," says Margaret S. of

New York, "and I've practiced it the right way instead of the wrong way, I can rely on it. But there aren't just four issues. There are dozens. I think I've conquered the biggest ones. If a man is putting me down, I have no problem standing up and walking out. If a man is promoted over me, I have no problem speaking my mind. Fifty or sixty percent of what could happen in life, I'm fine with it. I don't have to think about it, and it doesn't hurt. But every day something new crops up. Either I have no awareness of it, or it pops up in such a different guise that I'm sideswiped."

"Consciousness-raising was a fantastic personal experience," says Wendy R. of Minneapolis. "I'm not as closed a person as I once was, but I don't have the need to share that I did then. Or rather, I sometimes feel the need, but I'm just too busy. Or maybe I'm just too lazy. CR is a lot of work. You don't get your consciousness raised for nothing. I'm putting that hard work into my business now."

Wendy says she sometimes feels embarrassed that she's no longer active in the Women's Movement. "I think about the pornography issue or the failure of ERA, it makes me angry. So I could go on marches, but I don't. When I'm not working, I'm a couch potato. I'm no longer political. If anything, I'm a capitalist. I'm also more conservative. You have to be to succeed these days."

But if activism didn't take for Wendy over the long haul, certain aspects of CR did. She finds it relatively easy to talk about herself, for example—her foibles and her successes— and laments that other women she knows, younger women who did not have the benefit of CR, have remained so closed. Another aspect of CR that took for her is sex. Her consciousness got raised about sex, she says, and stayed there.

But it didn't necessarily make relationships with men any

easier. "You take two steps forward and one step backward," she says. "Feminism doesn't all of a sudden make you a totally different person. Part of me can be very strong and assertive when it comes to men; and part of me is still that sixteen-year-old girl sitting around waiting for the phone to ring."

Like Wendy, other women say that certain aspects of CR took better than the rest. Almost without exception, for example, they have a greater ease in talking about themselves as women and a greater fluency about women's issues. And without question, they say, CR increased their sense of self-esteem and contributed to a growing feeling of being able to be independent. They are more knowledgeable about sex, a knowledge that doesn't go away, they insist. Nearly all of them got their consciousness raised to a point where they were able to commit themselves to a life of work. And nearly all say they have gone much farther with jobs and careers than they ever imagined before CR. In addition, because of this, nearly all are economically independent and they continue to believe in the value of being so, another lesson that has remained with them.

Health consciousness also took. They say they are more knowledgeable about female health matters and believe they have certain inalienable rights both within and vis-à-vis the medical establishment.

And finally, these women have an awareness of what sexism is and how it operates. They talk about the importance of raising their children with nonsexist attitudes.

Somewhat murkier are the issues that didn't seem to "take" quite as well:

In becoming more assertive and redefining what it means to be a woman, many women wonder if they haven't become too much like men.

As a result of this, they wonder if women's issues and those areas of life pertaining to women (such as child care) haven't continued to be devalued.

Many women are still struggling with unequal partnerships in marriage.

Many say they are still doing the "shitwork."

Many say that being a feminist makes meeting men harder.

Many women feel keen competition again with other women. They also speak of antiwoman feeling from other women.

They say they are exhausted from the demands of trying simultaneously to keep a home and a job—and they see no clear way out.

They see the sexual liberation of women (and men) being sharply curtailed by the public health tragedy of AIDs and other sexually transmitted diseases. They feel confused and frightened, and are unclear as to how to behave in certain circumstances.

Many who are lesbians, or who politically support lesbians, feel that antilesbian sentiment is as strong as it ever was— some say even stronger.

Many say the lessons about body image didn't stick. Many are as obsessed about their own physical flaws as they were before CR.

Many are now newly obsessed with aging.

Many feel that the role of homemaker and mother has never been made a viable or an attractive choice by the Women's Movement.

Most are troubled by the lack of universally available, good-quality child care for all women who need it.

Many are troubled by what appears to be a rise in the number of reports of wife-battering and child abuse.

Many women are concerned about a growing tendency on the part of one class of women to exploit another.

And finally, many are fearful that the gains made by women—the right of a woman to terminate a pregnancy in the first trimester, for example—will be allowed to slip away.

Clearly, the women seem to be saying, while CR allowed women to make the transition from one era into another, and changed them fundamentally as persons, it could not and did not completely conquer sexism.

THIRTEEN

Women Together,
Women Alone

It seems unlikely that we will see again, in the near future, a revolutionary women's movement of the same caliber and pitch as that of the early 1970s. By their own admission, women are too busy, too fraught, to be able to channel their energies into such an intense political cause. Yet there is no denying that there *is* something afoot in the land—a mood of restlessness and uneasiness. There's a feeling of unfinished business, of strings left dangling, of complex issues yet to tackle and resolve.

Women no longer meet in consciousness-raising groups. Women rarely meet in groups at all. One of the ironies of the Women's Movement is that in preparing the ground for greater career opportunities for women, it sowed the seeds of its own demise. It's a matter of simple physics. Women who combine career and family life simply don't have any time left to devote to feminism or CR or activist issues. Energies are channeled not outward toward public issues, but inward toward success in the workplace and toward children and husbands at home. Anything that's left over goes for personal restoration.

"My involvement with women's groups ended when I went to work and then got into law school," says Leslye S., a lawyer in Pearl River, New York. "I was working full time during the day and going to law school every night, so at that point, I had to stop going to any kind of meetings. I bowed out of my feminist commitments; I could no longer attend a group. I just didn't have the time."

Edie G. of Glenrock, New Jersey, also feels that women's endeavors elsewhere have made gathering together with other women almost impossible: "At this stage, everybody is so busy just trying to fit everything in that we really don't have that kind of time," she says.

And yet these same women are acutely aware of their isolation, and they worry about it.

"I was sitting on a bench at the Museum of Modern Art talking with a friend, a woman friend," says Edie, "and we were getting into why husbands in general don't satisfy all women's needs. And we'd heard all the usual statistics about how men are unable to communicate, but somehow we felt that wasn't all of it. There was something else. We were exploring this issue, and I felt we were really on the brink of something, when one of the kids came up and said he wanted to go to have some lunch, and our conversation was just cut off. It was such a terrible feeling just being totally cut off. We both felt so frustrated. My friend said that if she had more thoughts on the subject, she would write me a letter, but it wasn't the same. You've lost the moment. You've lost the dynamic. And that's what I feel is missing from my life—the chance to explore these kinds of issues."

Other women, too, speak of isolation, using the vocabulary of loneliness.

"I don't really talk to anyone anymore," says Betsy W., a college art instructor from Somerville, Massachusetts. "In my department, the women are so competitive and hostile, it's like stepping into a time warp."

"I think women are lonely," says Frances H., of San Francisco. "They don't have each other any more, and they've been so conditioned to believing that having a man is the answer that when they don't have one or when it's not working out, which is usually the case, they feel unbearably lonely. I feel it myself all the time. There's this sense of no one to talk to. You have your children, and you love them, but it's not the same. There are so many things you can't tell your children. . . ."

"I miss being able to be open and honest with women friends," says Patricia E., an environmental planner from Washington, D.C. Patricia, who once belonged to a CR group for three years, from 1971 to 1974, and who characterizes her group as having been "highly successful," is now a single parent—the mother of two preteens. "I feel isolated with this issue of middle age. I'm alone in my house with my two boys, or I'm at work, swamped with projects, and at neither place do I really have anybody I can talk to about how you get through middle age with only old age staring you in the face. Most of the women in my old CR group are scattered all over the country, and there are really only two of them who live at all nearby. But we almost never get together. We send Christmas cards and the like, but that closeness is gone."

For some women, marriage has taken care of the isolation ("I don't miss my group," says Lauren L., a dancer in Manhattan. "My husband has taken the place of it"), while for other women, newly divorced or never married, the isolation is extremely painful ("It's agony, *agony*, being alone," says Eileen R. of Cambridge, Massachusetts. "I just hate having no one to talk to, no one to turn to").

For most women, however, the desire to gather together with other women speaks more to a sense of missing an important dimension in life rather than to missing a lifeline. "I find I have a real need to have female friends," says Joyce H., a social worker from Boulder, Colorado. "Like the old Chinese saying, we live in interesting times—especially for women. Most of us have experienced a revolution in our lives. I don't think you can sort this all out on your own. We began all this in groups, and I think we need those groups again to get our bearings."

Women have been meeting in groups throughout history—not just in "interesting times." Consciousness-raising was not an aberration, but rather a continuation of a natural tendency in women to gather together for a shared purpose. While the origins of CR were in large part political—stemming from leftist self-critical sessions—they also were one more link in a long chain of women's groups formed for the purpose of sharing work, thoughts, feelings, hints, tips, practical information, and sometimes simply gossip. The old quilting bees, sewing circles, and social work organizations of earlier centuries are the most vivid and dramatic examples of women gathering together in groups, but the progression can also be seen in more recent times in the book clubs, bridge clubs, social clubs, women's auxiliary groups, and park-bench mothers groups of the 1950s and early 1960s.

In this current period of isolation, which has now spanned more than a decade, many women speak of needing somewhere to go to talk with other women. Specifically, women want support for the endeavors of their daily lives. If the first wave of consciousness-raising was about having choices, say the women, then the second wave should be about making those choices work. For choice without knowledge, without information, without consciousness, the women once learned, is not really choice.

In the wake of the first wave of CR groups, feminism has been integrated and personalized. What is now needed, women insist, is a new, more empowered, collective response to the problems that confront women today.

"Women discovered they didn't have to be alone," says Gail G. of New City, New York, "that they could share problems. It worked for ten years. Now we have different problems and different issues. The kids are grown and off to college. We need to come together again."

In small, tentative ways, women *are* coming together again. Rockland County, a collection of formerly rural and now-suburban towns thirty miles north of Manhattan along the west bank of the Hudson River, once boasted a large feminist population. Whether this was because Betty Friedan lived in Rockland (in the village of Grandview) or because of the diligence of a number of tireless, though lesser-known, feminist organizers is not clear. But Rockland once had a thriving NOW chapter and dozens of consciousness-raising groups.

In Rockland County, today, as of this writing, NOW no longer exists and hasn't for some time. Yet recently something happened in the county that made it clear that, after a decade-long hiatus, feminist preoccupations were very much in women's minds.

In October 1987, the Volunteer Counseling Service of

Rockland County sponsored, with the help of a nebulous group loosely referred to as "the women's community" in Rockland, a women's conference called "It's Time!" There hadn't been a similar conference in the county in eight years, and prior to that, attendance at that type of conference was typically 150 to 200 women. On October 25, 1987, however, more than 500 women jammed the corridors, hallways, and rooms of the Quality Inn Tappan Zee in Nyack. They had come ostensibly to attend workshops on various subjects of importance to women ("My Body, Myself"; "Women of Age"; "Mothers and Daughters"; etcetera) but before the women even got to their workshops, it was evident that something else, something electric, was in the air. It began as a small question threading its way through the clusters of women, and then became the rallying cry of the entire conference: "Where are our women's groups?" the women asked each other. "We need to meet again," they shouted.

Phyllis F. and Gail G., who were among the organizers of the conference and who are still with the Volunteer Counseling Service, were amazed at the strength of the feeling that emerged, but today are not entirely surprised that women feel the need to come together again.

"I think there are many younger women out there who have not had the benefits of CR," says Gail. "And there is another group of older women who are feeling very lonely. Women say to me, 'Why did I let it fall behind me?' "

"I have the sense that there are many women who were in CR groups way back in the early 1970s," adds Phyllis, "but who have gone on with their lives and have become busy with their careers and life changes and relationship transitions and therefore haven't had time to meet with other women. And they are missing it. A number of them have said to me: 'It's been an absence in my life.' For that group of women, women just entering their forties, there are a lot of changes. They're trying to negotiate those life changes, which always feels better to do in a group.

"We learned, in groups," she continues, "that there is no need to go through all of this without the kind of support and care and connection that we found through the Women's Movement. But in the course of having so many other stresses and commitments and responsibilities, some of us have forgotten that basic training. But no matter how many other responsibilities we have, not taking the time to talk to other women ends up dissipating our energies. When you put the time in, it increases your energy to do all the other stuff better."

Women are coming together again elsewhere, too. In Westfield, New Jersey, a group of working mothers meets on a regular basis. In addition to the sharing of practical information and support, they also tackle, often with the help of outside speakers, broader issues of concern to them. Indeed, most women's groups self-formed over the past decade have been concerned either with issues of motherhood or of work: They are mothers' groups that may initially have been formed as play groups for children; or they are networking organizations within corporations or within professions. In both cases, mutual support as well as the sharing of information about how to *negotiate* the business of their lives—whether that be toilet-training toddlers or recruiting clients—is the initial foundation of such gatherings.

After CR petered out on a widespread scale in the mid-1970s, it was still offered through the auspices of NOW. Rather than the open-ended CR meetings of the eary 1970s, however, this phase of CR was considerably more organized.

Women signed up for ten-week courses, which "facilitators" directed and ran. A different topic, selected by the facilitators, was discussed at each meeting. It is, in fact, still theoretically possible to participate in this program, though the numbers of participants since 1980 has been extremely small, and in most areas of the country, nonexistent.

Still, some groups, formed in the early 1970s, never stopped meeting—or if they did, for a brief haitus only. I found one group in Pomona, New York; one on Long Island; one in Newton, Massachusetts; one in Minneapolis. As their participants own lives have evolved, the issues that surface in these groups' discussions have evolved. Visiting such groups and hearing the women speak about what troubles them today suggests issues that would probably surface in other groups if women were to reconvene again.

Aging would be high on the list. "We talk about aging a lot," says Nancy T., a concert pianist from St. Paul. "It is certainly among the things I think about when I wake up on any given day. All her life a woman is concerned with her appearance. Talking about it makes you aware of how much other women suffer, too, when they age. Talking about it gives you the tools to deal with it. You can't resist aging. You can't continue to look twenty-five when you're ninety. What you have to do is challenge the values of society that make aging so painful and unacceptable."

Other women, in other ongoing groups, agree that aging is a high priority among them. "I just went through a real period of mourning over turning forty," says one woman from Newton. "I talk about that a lot in the group—it's a real outpouring of what I am losing. My kids are older, I don't have babies anymore. I don't call attention to myself the way I used to. And it helps a lot to be in the group. Nobody was naïve enough to try to convince me that life begins at forty, but people said there are a lot of good things, and they talked about what those things are."

On the homefront, two issues that did not surface in the original wave of CR groups, but which do come up in ongoing groups today, are the dilemma of the "sandwich" generation and the problems of raising teen-age children.

"Here I am smack in the middle," says Jeannette F., who belongs to an ongoing group on Long Island. "My mother had this accident—she fell off a stepladder and really hurt herself. She lives with a housekeeper during the weekdays, but has no one on weekends. So I have stayed there all weekend. And it's really hard for me, really hard for me to take care of my mother. I want to be somewhere else. Then my daughter says, 'Can you baby-sit?' And my mother says, 'When are you coming back?' And I feel—'What about me?' I want to go to my health club, I want to go to my movie course.

"Being stuck in the middle of the sandwich is a woman's issue," she continues, "because women are still the caretakers. How many sons do you see staying at home with aging parents?"

Laurel R., whose ongoing CR group meets just twice a year now, says a big issue for her is the raising of teen-age children—something that didn't surface fifteen years ago because none of the members of her group had teen-agers then. "I was not prepared for a seventeen-year-old and what happens when they decide to spread their wings. We were having some really tough problems with our seventeen-year-old, creating a tremendous emotional upheaval for me. This was an issue that some of the other women were going through, too, and it helped to be able to talk to them about it."

The dilemma of being able to stay on the job and still raise children often surfaces as the most urgent issue in ongoing groups. But rivalry among women and antiwomen feeling also comes up frequently in discussion. Says one woman, "I mean, it's hard enough competing with men, but now we have to deal with competing with each other."

And for all of the ongoing groups, the old frayed, careworn, and yet well-loved issues continue to crop up: "What do we talk about?" asks one woman rhetorically. "Oh, the usual— careers and marriage and men and sex."

While the reconvening of women's groups would be a welcome source of support for the turning-forty and the post-forty generation, say women who once participated in CR, it would be vital for a younger generation of women, few of whom have ever had the benefit of CR or of the collective support of other women.

"I definitely think there's something important missing in the lives of the younger women coming along today," says Amy B., an account executive with an advertising firm in New York. "There's a lot expected of the younger women, and they don't have connections with each other. I see them, I work with them. They are very busy doing what men used to do, but what's been lost is a sense of themselves as women. It can't be easy for them. Women are expected to be super-women, but I feel sorry for them, because there's nobody there to give them a gentle hand on the back, saying, 'It's okay, you don't have to do it all. We understand.' There's no message for them other than, 'You are expected to move ahead.' "

Women who are in their late twenties today are the first generation of women whose education was significantly influenced by the feminist movement. Many went to formerly all-male colleges, and doors they never knew had once been shut were open for them. Being a woman in the culture has been for them a completely different experience than it has been for women just ten years older. As a result, many of these younger women fail to see the relevance of feminist thinking in their lives.

Recently, a feminist lawyer from Boston organized women at her firm to get together to have luncheons so that she could pass on information and share strategies of a practical nature. When the luncheons were confined to this agenda, they were successful. After a time, however, the woman lawyer added other more subtle issues to the agenda: She began to bring up the topic of how the old boys always seemed to get the interesting work and how the women in the firm were expected to fit into a traditional model.

"The response from the younger women," says the lawyer, "was you know: We don't have a problem. We're here, aren't we? All we have to do is work hard. . . . It wasn't that they were willfully blind or that they were hostile to women. It was that they didn't get it yet. The doors had always been open for them. But then you talk to them when they hit thirty, when the career and family issues come up, or when they've achieved a certain level at work and they hit that first door that doesn't magically open for them, and they're lost. They don't have the mechanics or the apparatus to confront lovers and husbands and bosses. They've had no practice. They don't have a support system to help them make changes."

Barbara B., former coordinator of the Women's History Program at Sarah Lawrence College, says: "I think it would be great for younger women to have some experience with CR. I see women in their early thirties who don't like their personal lives right now. They're involved in happy relationships, but they don't feel like they are equal. They're still responsible for the house and children, no matter how much help they get. And they don't have any way to confront those problems directly. It's not really the 'problem that has no name,' as it was in Betty Friedan's day. Women today have enough of a vocabulary and understanding of what they should be able to expect in the world to know what the problem is, but what they need is a way to communicate those concerns more directly."

Will there be a second wave of CR? It is, of course, impossible to say. The hyphenate itself, never a felicitous one even in its heyday (for can one's consciousness be properly said to be raised, or is it rather *expanded*? And is it consciousness we mean, or *awareness, insight, intelligence*?) seems quaintly reminiscent of a bygone era and not entirely relevant today.

Yet there is something in the air, a mood, a feeling. Women were once together, and they liked it. Much was accomplished.

Today women are alone, and they don't like it. Whether a group is called "consciousness-raising II," "networking," "working-mothers groups," "at-home mothers groups," or "women and men together," women are gathering again—slowly, tentatively, unclear perhaps about the agenda or the membership or the process, but united in the recognition of one irrefutable fact:

Much remains to be accomplished.

■

A blustery, raw March evening. Near the corner of Marlborough and Dartmouth, third floor. Seven o'clock.

Catherine is sitting on a daybed in her apartment, her back against the wall, her knees pulled up to her chest with her arms wrapped around them. She rests her forehead for a moment on top of her knees, and then looks up. Beside her on the daybed is a letter—a handwritten letter on heavy gray bond with an engraved letterhead. Catherine picks up the letter, holds it in her hand, and then puts it back on the bed. Her face is drawn, paler than usual. She sighs deeply and holds her head with her hands.

The letter is from Felicia, she explains. It was waiting for her when she got in. It contains bad news.

The bad news is that Jane has breast cancer. Felicia has seen Jane in the hospital and, according to the letter, Jane has weathered the operation all right, but is feeling depressed and shaky. Jane hadn't planned on telling Felicia about her illness, but Felicia found out when she called her house a few days ago to arrange a lunch date— a very belated lunch date tentatively made at the reunion in September—and Richard, Jane's husband, told her that Jane had just had a double mastectomy and was recovering from surgery. She'd been battling breast cancer for two years, starting first with radiation therapy and then, nine months ago, with a lumpectomy. When she had the reunion at her apartment, she had already had two procedures and yet didn't tell a single one of the women there about either of them. She had kept it to herself, Richard said, because she'd been so frightened.

The letter contains other news, too, of a happier nature. Maryanne had her baby just before Christmas—a boy—and is just now returning to work on a part-time schedule. Maryanne called Felicia, not only to tell her her good news, but also to ask her advice about returning to work with an infant. And Daphne has reopened her court battle to get joint custody of her son, with a decent hope of winning this time. Felicia was able to put Daphne on to a sharp lawyer, and because Daphne is working full time at the gallery now and has just moved into a bigger apartment, her chances are better.

Good news and terrifying news.

"*I feel devastated about Jane on so many levels,*" *says Catherine,* "*my head is reeling. When I think about it, I am afraid for her. She's the first one of us to have to face something like this. I can imagine her fear, how bad it's been for her. And to lose her breasts—this important part of our body. To be afraid that you won't see your children entirely grown. To be afraid of dying . . .*

"*And then almost immediately, I think about myself,*" *she says candidly.* "*There's this sense of its being my turn next.*

"*When I think about the future,*" *she says,* "*sometimes I'm so frightened. If you ask me what I really believe, I have to tell you that I think there's a lot of pain ahead. There are so many unknowns out there for me, for any woman alone. Aging. Menopause. Loss of beauty. Loss of sexual attractiveness. Having your children leave you. And maybe somewhere down the line, God forbid, an illness like Jane's.*

"*I ask myself: Do I have the courage to go through this alone? Can I make it on my own? I don't mean economically. I'm not afraid of that. I mean emotionally. It's hard to face these issues all by yourself. I try not to let these thoughts rule my life, but when you hear about something like this*"—*she gestures to the letter*—"*it brings it all right to the front of your mind.*

"*And I say to myself, 'Who will I turn to for support if I get breast cancer?'*"

She picks up the letter and holds it in front of her.

"*I sometimes have a hankering to be with other women again,*" *she says.* "*I'd like to talk with a group of women who live alone, who are like me, about all these issues. I know it would help. If we'd had our old group back on a regular basis, Jane would have told us all about the cancer; she wouldn't have had to go through this alone. I remember vividly how powerful that kind of support is—for whatever it is you're going through or want to do. I remember how powerful a message you get of 'You're okay.' "*

She folds the letter very carefully into a square and puts it on a side table. She takes a long breath and lets it out slowly. "But," she says, "that's not my reality right now."

Reality, in the form of a noisy bustle at the front door, intrudes upon her thoughts. A shout from the hallway.

"Hi, Mom. Don't panic. It's just me."

Before Catherine can even rise from the sofa, a tall, blond young woman is in the doorway, smiling broadly, enjoying the effect her surprise visit is having on her mother. Beaming, Catherine leaps up and embraces her daughter. The resemblance is striking—in the shape of the face; in the alert, intelligent eyes; in the lovely, erect posture.

"I had a class at the museum," Elizabeth explains, "and I thought I'd pop over and see me old Mum before I have to go back to Cambridge." She is shedding a backpack and denim jacket as she talks. She lets both fall onto the floor. "This course is wicked hard, but I love it," she says. "We're doing Renaissance now. I'm not staying to supper, but I'm starved. What have you got for a snack?"

And again, before Catherine can even answer, Elizabeth has vanished from the doorway, off to the kitchen to rummage through the fridge. Catherine stands in the center of the room, looking through the door as if at a vivid afterimage of her daughter. She smiles, laughs, shakes her head, as though bewildered.

She turns, then gestures toward the empty doorway. "It's all hers now, isn't it?" she says.

■

AFTERWORD

Blueprint for a Second Wave

The process of consciousness-raising was most successful when women followed an agenda. The formats used in the early 1970s initially were products of the Redstockings, the New York Radical Feminists, and the National Organization for Women. Later groups amended and edited these early blueprints to suit the needs of their members. Although some CR groups did meet without published formats, they often gravitated naturally to the topics and rules included in those formats.

This format is intended for women today. It is partially based on those elements of consciousness-raising that were most successful in the early 1970s, and acknowledges an enormous debt to the initial architects of consciousness-raising—individuals who shrewdly and brilliantly designed a process that would change the lives of so many. But the focus of this format is on topics that concern women as they turn the corner into the 1990s. During my interviews, I asked women what issues they would like to tackle if CR groups were to reconvene again today. This format is the collective answer to that question.

As a blueprint for a new kind of consciousness-raising, it is intended for women in groups, but it need not be limited either to women or to groups. Because it has been suggested that today's issues and problems cannot be resolved without the full participation of men, men need not be excluded from this process. Nor is it absolutely necessary to form or join a group. Individual women who are unable to find a group, might benefit from reading some of the questions and mulling them over.

Although it was stated in some of the original formats that an optimal size for a group is eight to twelve women, in practice many successful groups consisted of as few as three women or as many as fifteen. (Keep in mind that the larger the group, the less time each individual woman will have to speak.) Groups may be formed in neighborhoods, at places of work, or among acquaintances. Because jobs, work relationships, and personal or social friendships might be threatened by the intimate testimony of the women, or because women may feel inhibited from speaking the truth if they think social friendships or their jobs will be in jeopardy, confidentiality is a prerequisite of any group.

Some of the women who use this format will have participated in consciousness-raising already. Others will not. Those who have never had such an experience may wish to refer to the format used in the early 1970s (see Appendix) and include some of the topics in it. Others, who have already explored most of the issues in the earlier format, may wish to move directly to this one.

One of the purposes of consciousness-raising is to make

women aware of the societal pressures that oppress them. Some women will use the awareness gained from CR solely in their personal lives without taking action that would benefit other women, and this is a valid purpose of CR. Other women, however, may be moved to participate in whatever action they feel is necessary to raise the collective consciousness of their local school systems, their communities, and their places of work.

Women today often feel competitive with other women and isolated from them. Therefore, it is also a purpose of CR to break down these barriers and encourage open, honest communication among women. And it may be, for some groups, a purpose of CR to break down barriers and encourage open, honest communication between women and men.

PROCEDURES

Select a topic. A topic is usually selected at the previous meeting so that those who wish to may have time to consider it. The suggested list of topics that follows is meant as a guideline and not as a questionnaire. Refer to the list when you need to, and include what you like. Sometimes you may even wish to spend an entire meeting on a single aspect of a topic. The format is designed to ease strangers into the CR process by talking about less threatening topics first ("Childhood Expectations") before moving into more difficult areas.

Go around in a circle. In the past, women who participated in CR found that sitting in a circle created a kind of "free space" that had previously been unavailable to them. Each women is allowed to speak as long as she likes or needs to without fear of interruption. By proceeding in a circle, women who are more reticent, therefore, will have the same opportunity to speak as more dominant women. The circle configuration also helps women listen to each other and may break down feelings of competitiveness.

Don't interrupt. It is important not to interrupt another's testimony, except to ask a specific informational question or clarify a point. If someone's experience reminds you of one of yours, you might take notes so that you remember what it is you wish to say when it is your turn. Everyone will get a chance to speak.

Never challenge anyone else's experience. Although what one individual woman says may not seem true for you, allow her to speak her mind. Criticizing another's testimony may inhibit her from speaking honestly. Without honesty, there is little value in the consciousness-raising experience.

Avoid the temptation to promote one woman to the position of leadership. In the early years of CR, those groups that were the most successful were those that were leaderless. It is not necessary to have a leader for a CR group. (Some CR groups, under the auspices of NOW, do use facilitators.) Decisions that are made (where to meet, when to meet, what to talk about) can be made collectively. Groups that were dominated by leaders—either formally or informally—tended to be beset by resentments and personality conflicts. In consciousness-raising, each woman is equally important. What she has to say is just as valid as what anyone else in the group has to say.

Sum up. After all of the women have related their personal experiences with the topic, the group may try to find the common element and see what conclusions can be drawn. At this point anyone may speak, and it is not necessary to go around in a circle. It is during this process that certain collective actions may become clear to the women present.

SUGGESTED TOPICS FOR
CONSCIOUSNESS-RAISING

It is helpful at the first meeting for each woman to discuss briefly her reason for wanting to be part of a consciousness-raising group and what she expects to get from the group.

Childhood Expectations

1. Did you grow up in a home in which your mother worked inside the house (in the traditional homemaker role), and your father worked outside the home (as a breadwinner)? How did you regard your mother's life? Your father's life? Who seemed to have the more exciting role? Who seemed to have the superior role?

2. In your childhood home, who performed the household chores? Your mother exclusively? Did both parents share these chores?

3. Did you think, when you were a child, that the roles your parents had were the proper roles of men and women in society? Did you ever envision yourself as a mother? As a worker? What did you want to be when you grew up? What did you think it was going to be like to be a woman?

4. In your family, were you treated differently from boys? How about by other adults—at school or at church?

5. What toys did you have? What games did you play? What activities were encouraged? Discouraged?

6. What were your parents' attitudes toward your education? Did you feel they had the same attitude for girls as they did for boys? What were your parents' academic expectations of you?

7. What were your teachers'/guidance counselors' expec-

tations of you? Did you feel they had different expectations of female and male students?

8. Were you ever led to believe, as a female child, that you would be taken care of by a man? Were you ever told that you would have to be economically responsible for yourself when you grew up?

9. What sorts of futures did your girl friends envision for themselves? Your boyfriends?

10. Were you ever discouraged from taking a certain course in school?

11. Did you ever feel that boys were better than girls?

12. Did you grow up believing that women and girls were worth less than men and boys?

13. Were you ever taught that certain ways of dressing or of behaving were "unfeminine" and therefore unacceptable?

14. If your mother stayed at home, and did not work outside the home in a paying job, how did you feel about that? How do you think she felt about that? What if your mother *didn't* stay home?

15. When you were a child, were you ambitious? Did you want to be successful?

16. Did you believe that one man, and one man only, would be right for you?

Female in America

1. Are you living a life as an adult woman similar to the one you envisioned for yourself as a child? If it is different than what you envisioned, what accounts for that difference?

2. As an adult female now, do you feel your childhood expectations were realistic? Which ones were? Which weren't?

Were any of them actually destructive? Were you adequately prepared for the life you are now living?

3. If you wanted to give advice to young girls in America today, what would that advice be?

4. Do you feel dependent upon a man? Economically? Emotionally?

5. Do you believe that one man, and one man only, is right for you?

6. Are you comfortable being in charge of a group? Being assertive? Expressing anger in public? In private?

7. What does it mean to be feminine to you? Masculine? Androgynous? Which do you feel most of the time? How do you think others view you in terms of these three characteristics?

8. Are you ever accused of being too abrasive? Too hard? Too masculine? Too tough? Who makes these accusations? How do you feel if someone characterizes you that way?

9. Do you find that the same qualities that help you to succeed at the workplace are appropriate in the home? Do you ever feel that you have to switch roles? Or switch personas? Is the transition difficult?

10. Do you feel valued as a woman—at work? In the home? Where do you feel the most valued? Where do you feel the most comfortable?

11. Do you feel that women today have a more difficult life than men today? Why or why not?

12. Do you enjoy the company of other women more? Or of men more? Why?

13. Do you feel that traditionally feminine activities have been devalued? Does that bother you or not?

14. Do you feel that you have a better life than your mother did? Describe why or why not.

---

15. Do you wish you had been born male rather than female? If so, why?

16. If you were a man, would certain endeavors, tasks, or behaviors have been easier for you? Which? Would certain activities have been more difficult? Which?

17. Do you feel competitive with other women? Why?

18. Do you feel isolated from other women? Why?

19. Do you ever experience antiwoman feelings? From men? From women?

20. When people ask you what you do, what do you answer? How do you feel about that question and your response?

21. Do you ever wish that someone would come along and take care of you?

22. Are you being taken care of now? How do you feel about that?

23. Do you believe that men and women are equal? Do you believe that there are essential and fundamental differences between men and women? What are these?

Sex

1. Do you have time for sex?

2. If you have one primary sexual partner (a spouse, a long-term lover), are you comfortable sexually with him (or her)? Are you assertive or passive? Are you able to express your needs? Are you comfortable saying *no* to sex if you don't feel like it? Does one person dominate the other in sexual matters? Who? What does it feel like?

3. When you grew up, did you receive an adequate education in sexual matters? Do you feel that you are fully informed now? Is there something you would like to know more about?

4. Do you think men have different sexual needs from women? What are they?

5. Do your sexual needs fluctuate? What causes them to fluctuate?

6. Is it necessary for you to establish emotional intimacy with a partner before engaging in sex?

7. Are you personally afraid of sexually transmitted diseases such as AIDS or herpes? Has the fear of these diseases changed your lifestyle or sexual habits in any way?

8. If you are single, do you think about this issue when you meet someone new?

9. Does the threat of AIDS make marriage more attractive to you?

10. Does being cautious affect how you feel about your sexuality?

11. Do you feel sexually attractive to men? Why or why not? Do you care?

12. Do you have enough information about contraceptives? Do you use them? What method? How do you feel about the methods you have used? Do you use contraception or does your partner? Are you satisfied with this arrangement?

13. Are you sexually threatened by other women? By women at work? By your own daughter?

14. Do you feel that as a woman ages, she loses her sexual attractiveness? Do you feel that as a woman ages, she loses her sexual desire?

15. Is sex an important priority in your life?

16. Have you ever felt sexually attracted to another woman?

17. If you are not a lesbian, how do you react when you meet a woman whom you know is a lesbian?

18. Have you ever had an abortion? Describe your experience. How did you feel about it? Would you ever have another

one? If your own daughter told you that she wanted an abortion, how would you counsel her?

Women in the Workplace

1. Where do you work? What do you do? What are you paid for what you do?

2. Are you paid the same as a man would be if he had your job?

3. Could a man have your job? Why or why not?

4. Do you believe that work inside the home (homemaker) is as valuable as work outside the home (in the labor force)? Why or why not?

5. How did you end up in the job or the career that you are in? Do you like it? Is this what you want to be doing? Is this what you envisioned doing when you were a girl?

6. Do you consider yourself ambitious?

7. Where would you like to see yourself in five years' time? Ten years' time? Twenty years' time?

8. What things do you get at the workplace that are not available to you elsewhere?

9. Are you more comfortable at work or at home?

10. Do you think success is important? Very important?

11. What are the aspects of your work that give you the most pleasure? What are the aspects of your work that are the most distasteful?

12. If you were a man, would you be farther along in your career? If you were a man, would you be making more money?

13. Do you ever feel competitive with other women? Describe the situations that make you feel competitive.

14. Do you ever feel competitive with other men? Describe the situations.

15. Who are the bosses in your area of work? Men or women?

16. Are there any jobs in your field of expertise from which women appear to be shut out? In your line of work, is it possible for women to rise to the top?

17. Do you think that there are such characteristics as feminine values and masculine values at the workplace? Explain what these might be.

18. Do you ever feel compelled to adopt a masculine mode of behaving, speaking, or dressing at your workplace? How do you feel about that?

19. At your place of work, do you gravitate more toward other women or men?

20. Are you the boss of other women? Of men? Are you comfortable in this role? What do you like about it? What, if anything, do you dislike? Do other women take you seriously? Do men take you seriously?

21. Do the people at the very top echelons of your workplace or career value women as highly as men?

22. Have you ever experienced any condescension toward yourself on the job because you are a woman? Have you ever failed to get a job because you were a woman?

23. Have you ever experienced sexual harassment on the job? What took place? What was the outcome? How did you feel about it? Did it affect your job performance in any way?

24. Would you like to change the nature of your work, or your schedule in any way? Why?

25. Does your job leave you adequate time for a personal life? For your spouse? Lover? Children? Yourself? If not, how do you feel about that?

26. How would you rate your work in terms of priorities? Is it very important to your self-esteem?

27. Are you entirely self-supporting? Do you wish you were?

28. Do you employ other women? Do you treat them differently than men? In what way?

29. Is your workplace progressive in its thinking about the dual-career family? Does it offer on-site daycare? Daycare subsidies? Flexible benefits packages? Adequate paid child-care leave? Sick child-care leave? Job-sharing? Flex-time schedules? Part-time work? Which of the benefits listed above would you like to see at your place of employment?

30. If you left your job to have a baby, what sort of leave would you take? Would you be able to return to work on a modified schedule? Would you want to?

31. If you employed another woman, and she had a baby, what kind of flexibility would you be prepared to offer her?

32. Is part-time work possible in your field? Why or why not?

33. How are working mothers regarded by the management of your place of employment? Are they discriminated against in terms of salary increases or promotions? Would you give a promotion to a working mother? Why or why not?

34. Does your partner (mate, spouse, lover) work, too? Who makes more money? Who works longer hours? Whose job takes precedence? Who is considered to have the better job?

35. Would your partner take time off if you had a child? Would he ask his boss for parental child-care leave? For part-time work? For flexible scheduling? Why or why not?

36. If you both work full-time, who takes care of your home?

37. How does your partner feel about your working? Your success? Do you ever feel competition between you? Does your work life harm your marriage in any way? Does it make it better?

Body Image

1. How do you feel about your body? Do you have aspects about your physical appearance that you don't like? What are they? What do you do about them?

2. Do you dress to please men or women or yourself? Are you able to distinguish? Where do you think your standards for what's attractive in a woman come from?

3. How do you feel about the image of women presented on television? In advertisements?

4. Do you behave differently around women than you do around men? If so, what are some of these different behaviors?

5. What steps do you take to change your appearance on a daily basis from what it naturally would be? Makeup? Hair coloring?

6. How long does it take you each morning to be presentable to the world? How do you feel about spending this time? Does your mate, spouse, lover spend the same amount of time?

7. Is there a specific or unstated dress code at your place of work? What is it? How do you feel about it?

8. Have you ever consciously dressed for "success"? What did you do? How did you feel about it?

9. Is your general style of dress restrictive, confining, or time-consuming?

10. Do you exercise? What do you do and how often? Do you do this for your health or for your appearance?

11. How old are you? How do you feel about this age? What age do you consider to be "old"? How do you feel about getting older? Have you noticed any changes in your body?

12. Are there things about getting older that you would like

to know more about? Menopause, for instance? Do women who are older than you ever speak to you about what it is like to be their age?

13. Do you ever feel that you are losing your sexual attractiveness? Your physical attractiveness? How do you feel about this?

Relationships

1. What is your concept of the ideal marriage or relationship? Where did that ideal come from? Have you ever had a relationship that achieved that ideal or came close to it?

2. Do you believe that marriage should be a partnership of equals?

FOR THOSE CURRENTLY INVOLVED IN A RELATIONSHIP:

1. Why did you get married or enter into this long-term relationship?

2. If you are in a long-term relationship, but not married, do you plan to get married? Why?

3. If you are married, does it live up to your expectations?

4. How does being married affect your self-image?

5. Who does which chores in your relationship? Who does the more onerous chores, such as cleaning the bathrooms, cleaning up after a meal, and washing the floors?

6. Do you believe that a relationship of two equal partners is possible between a man and a woman? Why or why not? Do you know anyone who has this kind of relationship?

7. In your relationship, who makes the most money? Does that fact overtly or subtly affect who has the most power in the relationship?

8. In your marriage, do you feel that you have as much

power as your mate? Are there areas in your relationship in which you consciously give up power in order to have a more harmonious relationship?

9. Have you and your mate achieved the kind of intimacy you would wish for? If not, what is keeping you from achieving that?

10. Are you more comfortable in a relationship than out of it? What do you think you sacrifice in order to remain in a relationship?

11. Are you frightened by the idea of living alone?

12. If you were one day to live alone, could you support yourself?

FOR WOMEN NOT CURRENTLY INVOLVED IN A RELATIONSHIP:

1. Are you living alone by choice or by circumstance?

2. Are you comfortable living alone? How does living alone affect your self-image?

3. Do you feel pressured by your family or society to get married?

4. Have you been married before? If so, would you rather be married again, or do you prefer living alone?

5. What aspects of living alone are difficult for you?

6. What aspects of living alone are easier for you than living with another person?

7. If you have been married before, what aspects of marriage do you miss? What aspects of marriage are you glad to be free of?

8. Are you frightened by the prospect of living alone forever? If so, what is the source of that fear?

9. How do other people around you feel about the fact that

you are living alone? Your mother, for instance? Your
friends?

10. Do you date men? If so, what qualities in a man do you
look for? Do you date men with the idea of forming a long-
term relationship, or to have lovers and friends?

11. Do you meet men with the same values and ideals as
yourself?

12. If you are independent, are men threatened by that independence, or attracted to it?

13. Do you feel there is a stigma attached to living alone?
Do you think other people regard it as a failure on your part?
What kind of a failure? How do you feel about this?

DIVORCE

1. Have you ever been divorced? How did you feel about
it?

2. Does being a "divorcee" affect your self-image?

3. What is the marital status of most of your friends?

4. If you have been divorced, why did you stay married as
long as you did?

5. What are the most difficult aspects of being divorced?

Motherhood

1. If you are a mother, how does being a mother affect your
self-image?

2. How would you feel if you couldn't have children?

3. How did having children change your life?

4. Does being a mother live up to your expectations?

5. Is being a mother different from being a father?

6. If you live with someone, do you share child-care responsibilities? If so, is it because of an agreement, because

one person nags the other, or because both feel equally responsible?

7. Do you consider mothering, or child care, equal in status to paid work?

8. Do you believe that boys are intrinsically different from girls? If so, what are some of these differences? Do you believe there are certain activities that are inappropriate for girls? For boys? How would you feel if you found your son playing with a doll?

9. Do you enjoy being a mother?

10. What aspects of being a mother are frustrating to you?

11. Does being a mother ever make you angry? Why?

FOR MOTHERS WHO WORK
OUTSIDE THE HOME:

1. Were you working when you became pregnant? If so, did you return to your job after the baby was born? How much time did you take off? How did you feel about that? Did you want more time, or was it enough? Did you return to full-time work?

2. What benefits does your place of work offer to working mothers? What kind of child-care leave or child-care facilities does it have? Does your company offer any flexibility in its work schedules? How do you feel about your company's policies regarding family issues? Have you ever tried to change those policies? What happened?

3. How much time do you get to spend with your child/children? Is this amount of time satisfactory to you?

4. Do you ever feel guilty being a mother and working at the same time? What is the source of this guilt, do you think?

5. What kind of family did you grow up in? Did your own

mother work? How does she feel about the fact that you work? Do other people ever cause you to feel guilty about your decision to work?

6. Do you and your mate, if one is present, share child-care responsibilities? Are they shared equally? Who stays home with the child if the child is sick?

7. What child-care arrangements have you made? Are these arrangements adequate? Does the issue of child care ever cause you anxiety? Are there any forms of child care that you would not use for your child? What are those?

8. Why do you work? Do you believe that working mothers should leave their children in the care of others only if they *have* to work to make ends meet?

9. Have you ever been made to feel uncomfortable in the company of women who stay home with their children? What happened?

10. How do you feel about at-home mothers? Do their lives seem less interesting than yours, or do you envy them?

11. If you could make changes in your life as a working mother, what would those changes be?

12. Have you ever actively lobbied at your place of work, in your community, or within your school system to make changes that would benefit working mothers and/or the children of working mothers?

13. What changes in society as a whole do you think are necessary to accommodate the large numbers of children growing up in the home of dual-career families?

14. Is your life more stressful than you would like? What is the source of that stress?

15. Do you believe that you are harming your children in any way because you work?

16. Do you believe that your children benefit in any way—

besides the purely economic—from the fact that you are a working mother?

17. As a working mother, do you, or have you ever felt, isolated?

FOR AT-HOME MOTHERS:

1. Were you working before you had children? Why did you leave the work force to be with your children? Do you believe that you are a better mother for having left the work force?

2. What sacrifices have you made to stay home with your children?

3. How do you regard working mothers?

4. How do you feel about the different kinds of child care? Would you ever get your own child some child care? Why or why not?

5. How does being an at-home mother affect your self-image? When people ask you what you do, what do you say?

6. Do you ever feel that working mothers look down upon you? Do you ever feel angry toward or resentful of working mothers?

7. Do you believe that working mothers are harming their children? If so, in what way?

8. How does your mate feel about the fact that you stay home with the children?

9. Do you ever imagine yourself reentering the work force? When?

10. Do you believe that the female should be the primary parent?

11. Are most of your friends at-home mothers or working mothers?

FOR SINGLE PARENTS:

1. Are you a single parent by choice or by circumstance?

2. How does being a single parent affect your self-image?

3. If you are a single parent by choice, why did you choose to have a child without a mate? How did other people around you—your parents, for instance—feel about your decision? Did people try to talk you out of it? Did you receive any support?

4. Do you think single parents have special difficulties that other parents do not have? What are these?

5. As a single parent, do you ever feel isolated?

6. If you could make changes in your life, what would they be?

7. What changes in society, at the workplace, or within your school system would make your life easier?

Violence

1. Have you ever been raped? By a stranger, a husband, a friend? What happened? Did you feel you provoked it in any way? Did you call the police? What was the outcome?

2. Are you ever harassed on the street or at your place of work by men? What do you do in those situations?

3. Have you ever been coerced into having sex? Have you ever felt pressured to have sex with someone when you didn't want to? Do you feel pressured to have sex with your mate? What form of pressure does he exert? What happens if you refuse?

4. Does the fear of violence cause you to live your life differently than you would if you did not have this fear? What precautions do you normally take?

5. Have you ever experienced physical violence in a rela-

tionship? What happened? What was the outcome? Does it happen regularly? What causes it? Have you ever sought help for this?

6. Have you ever experienced emotional violence in a relationship? How would you define emotional violence? What happened? What was the outcome? Do you consider yourself now to be a victim of emotional violence? What causes it? Have you ever sought help for this?

7. Have you ever been violent toward anyone else? Toward your children? What form did the violence take? Have you ever sought help for this?

Women Exploiting Women

1. Do you employ other women to help perform some of your domestic chores—whether it be cleaning or child care? What do these women do? How much do you pay them? Do you consider them adequately paid? Have you ever felt guilty about the amount of money you have paid other women who help you perform domestic chores? Have you ever treated these women badly?

2. Why do you employ the women that you do? Do these women have families? Who takes care of their children?

3. Have you ever known any other women who treated their domestic employees poorly?

4. Would you ever consider employing a man to clean your house or take care of your children? Why or why not? Have you ever met a man or heard of one who worked in this capacity?

5. Do you consider the work that your cleaning woman does is less valuable than the work you do? What about the woman who takes care of your children? If you consider the work

equally as valuable, would you pay the caretaker or cleaner the same wages you yourself make? Why or why not?

6. Do you employ women to work for you in the workplace? Do you treat them any differently than men? Do you pay them differently than men?

7. Do you yourself work for another woman in a domestic situation? As a cleaning person or to take care of children? How do you feel about this job? How does having this job affect your self-image?

8. Are you adequately paid?

9. Do you have children yourself? Who takes care of your children?

10. Have you ever been treated badly by a woman employer? What happened? What was the outcome?

11. In the workplace, is your boss a woman? Have you ever been treated poorly by her? If you were a man, would you be treated with more respect? Does she show favoritism toward you because you are a woman?

12. Are you paid less than you would be if you were a man?

13. If you are a child-care worker, do you feel that you are adequately paid?

14. How does being a child-care worker affect your self-image?

15. How do you feel about the mothers who leave their children with you?

16. Do you think the position of child-care worker is a respected one in this country?

Feminism

1. What is your definition of feminism?

2. Do you consider yourself a feminist? Why or why not? In what ways are you a feminist? At home? On the job? Among friends and acquaintances?

3. Is the word *feminist* distasteful to you? Why or why not?

4. How do you think feminism and feminists are regarded by most of the people you know?

5. Do you think that feminism today is no longer an important issue?

6. Do you believe that women have achieved the equality they have been struggling for?

7. Do you believe that women and men should have equal opportunities?

8. Can a woman with a "raised consciousness" still relate to men?

9. Should the next phase of the feminist struggle include men? Why or why not?

10. What are some of the most pressing issues that you think women should struggle to resolve?

11. If you are a feminist, do you believe you are better off because of it, or does it make your life harder? If so, in what ways?

12. Do you like women better than men? Why or why not?

13. Do you ever feel isolated from other women?

14. Would you describe yourself as active in any way in the effort to improve conditions for women in this country? If not, do you wish you were?

15. Do you think most people in this country still regard women as worth less than men?

16. In what ways would your life be different if the Women's Movement of the late 1960s and early 1970s had never existed?

———

NOTES

1. Grace Baruch, Rosaline Barnett, and Caryl Rivers, *Lifeprints* (New York: Plume Books, New American Library, 1983), p. 236.

2. Kathleen Gerson, *Hard Choices* (Berkeley: University of California Press, 1985), p. 4., citing the work of Louise Kapp Howe (1977) and Valerie K. Openheimer (1970).

3. Judith Hole and Ellen Levine, "Women's Liberation," *Rebirth of Feminism* (New York: Quadrangle Books, 1971), p. 131.

4. From the *Redstockings Manifesto*, published July 1969.

5. Hole and Levine, *Rebirth of Feminism*, p. 149.

6. Jo Freeman, "The Women's Liberation Movement: It's Origins, Structure, Impact and Ideas," *Women: A Feminist Perspective* (New York: Mayfield, 1975), p. 459.

7. Patricia Lone and Anita Shreve, *Working Women: A Guide to Fitness and Health* (St. Louis: C.V. Mosby, 1986), p. 55.

8. "Brainwashing and Women: The Psychological Attack," by a Redstockings Sister, mimeographed leaflet. This passage reprinted in Hole and Levine, *Rebirth of Feminism*, p. 140.

9. Susan Brownmiller, *Femininity* (New York: Linden Press, 1984), p. 51.

10. Daniel Goleman, "Sex Roles Reign Powerful as Ever in the Emotions" (*New York Times*, August 21, 1988).

11. Shere Hite, *Women and Love, A Cultural Revolution in Progress* (New York: Knopf, 1988).

12. Irene Peslikis, "Resistances to Consciousness," *Notes from the Second Year*, Shulamith Firestone and Anne Koedt, eds.; Radical Feminism: New York, 1970.

APPENDIX

Suggested Topics for Consciousness-Raising

(Reprinted from a typewritten handout, distributed by the New York Radical Feminists, *circa* 1972.)

It is helpful at the first meeting for each woman to briefly discuss her reason for wanting to be part of a consciousness-raising group and what she expects to get from the group.

BACKGROUND INFORMATION

1. ***Childhood training for your role as a woman***
   a. Were you treated differently from boys?
   b. What toys did you have? What games did you play?
   c. What activities were encouraged? Discouraged?
   d. What did you think it was going to be like to be a woman?

2. ***Early childhood sexual experiences***
   a. What experiences did you have with children your own age? With adults? How did you feel about these experiences at the time?
   b. Did these experiences affect your view of sex? Did they affect your view of yourself as a woman?

267

3. *Puberty*

a. How did you feel about your bodily changes? Breasts? Body hair?

b. What happened the first time you got your period? Were you told what to expect beforehand? Was it a surprise?

c. What attitudes did you encounter toward your bodily changes from your peers? from adults?

4. *Adolescent social life*

a. How did you spend most of your time? How did your parents feel about how you spent your time?

b. What sort of relationships did you have with girls? Did you have a best friend? How did you feel about girls your own age? What did you talk about with other girls? What were your activities? Were there older women that you admired and wanted to be like?

c. What sort of relationships did you have with boys? Did you date? Was there pressure from your peer group to date? What were your parents' attitudes toward dating? How did you get dates? What kind of boys did you date? What kind of boys did you want to date?

d. How were your relationships with girls affected by your relationships with boys? Which was more important?

e. What were your adolescent sexual experiences? Did you "neck," "pet," "make out," "go all the way," etc.? Were you concerned about your reputation"?

5. *First adult sexual experience with a man*

a. What did/does your virginity mean to you?

b. Describe the first time you had sex. What did you think it would be like? Did it live up to your expectations? Was it voluntary? Was it planned? Were you raped? Seduced or pressured?

c. Did you want to do it again?

d. How did you feel about yourself afterward? Your partner?

e. Did you tell anyone about it?

6. *Education*

a. What were your parents' attitudes toward education? Did you feel they had the same attitude for girls as they did for boys? What were your parents' academic expectations of you?

b. What were your teachers'/guidance counselors' expectations of you? Did you feel they had different expectations of female and male students?

c. What were your own aspirations? Were there courses that you wanted to take but were discouraged from taking? What subjects interested you most? Did these interests change as you went through school?

d. What kind of student were you? Were you competitive? With whom did you compete?

e. Were you involved in any extracurricular activities?

f. Was your education relevant to what you do now?

7. *Religion*

a. What part did religion play in your childhood? Does it play the same part now?

b. What effect did it have on you as a woman? What was your religion's view of women?

ADULT EXPERIENCES

1. *Masturbation*

a. Have you ever masturbated? If so, when did you begin? What connotations did masturbation have for you?

b. How often and under what circumstances do you masturbate? How do you masturbate? Do you have an orgasm? Do you fantasize?

2. *Orgasm*

a. Have you ever had an orgasm? Have you ever faked an orgasm? If so, why?

b. How do you feel if you don't have an orgasm?

c. Describe what brings you to orgasm. Can you describe your feelings and sensations during orgasm? Compare the orgasms you have during sex to those you have during masturbation.

d. To have an orgasm: Are you physically aggressive? Do you communicate to your partner what will bring you to orgasm? Do you depend totally on your partner?

e. Is it necessary for you to have an orgasm in order to enjoy sex? Is it necessary that your partner have an orgasm in order for you to enjoy sex? Do you feel that your orgasm is as important as your partner's? How important is orgasm, anyway?

f. How do you feel about the following: vaginal orgasm, clitoral orgasm, simultaneous orgasm, frigidity?

3. Contraception (withdrawal, rhythm, pills, diaphragm, condom, foam, IUD, vasectomy, hysterectomy, tubal ligation, etc.)

a. Do you use contraception? If so, what method? Have you ever used any other? How do you feel about the methods you have used?

b. Do *you* use contraception or does your partner? Are you satisfied with this arrangement?

4. Abortion

a. Have you ever had an abortion? Describe your experience. How did you feel about it? Would you have another one?

b. If you have never had an abortion, can you imagine yourself in a situation where you would want one? How do you think you would feel?

5. Lesbianism

a. Have you ever felt sexually attracted to another woman? Have you ever wondered what it would be like to have a sexual relationship with another woman? Have you ever had a homosexual experience?

b. If you are not a lesbian, how do you react when you meet a woman who you know is a lesbian? If you are a lesbian, how do you feel about women who are not?

c. What image comes to mind when you hear or read the word *lesbian*?

d. What are some socially accepted ways of expressing love for another woman?

6. Rape

a. Have you ever been raped? By a stranger, a husband, a friend, or by someone you knew? What happened? Did you feel you provoked it in any way? Did you call the police? If so, what was their reaction?

b. Have you ever been coerced into having sex? Have you ever felt pressured to have sex with someone when you didn't want to?

7. *Prostitution*

a. Have you ever had sex in exchange for money, food, entertainment, gifts, security, approval, etc.?

b. Have you ever wanted to be a prostitute? What do you imagine it would be like?

c. Have you ever used your sexuality to get something you wanted?

8. *Marriage/Being Single*

a. Are you, or have you been, married or in a marriage-type relationship? Why did you get married? Does/did being married live up to your expectations? How does/did being married affect your self-image? Did/do you find yourself operating within the traditional male/female role?

b. If you are single, how do you feel about it? How would being married affect your self-image? Do you feel pressured by your family or society to get married?

c. Do you feel more important, or different, as part of a couple, or on your own?

9. *Housework*

a. How important is it to you to have a clean home? How is your self-image related to the condition of your home?

b. If you're living with someone, who does the housework? Is it a shared responsibility? If so, is it because of an agreement, because one person nags the other, or because both feel equally responsible?

10. *Pregnancy and Childbirth*

a. Have you ever been pregnant or borne children? How did you feel about yourself during pregnancy? What was the attitude of those around you (i.e., the father of the child, your parents, your employer, other women, men)?

b. If you have not been pregnant, do you want to bear children? Under what circumstances? How would being pregnant affect your self-image?

271

c. How do you feel about giving birth? If you've had a child, was the labor and delivery what you expected? How did you feel about your child when you first saw him or her?

d. What are some of the myths of pregnancy and delivery?

11. Motherhood and Child Care

a. How does, or would, being a mother affect your self-image? How would you feel if you couldn't have children? How would deciding not to have children affect your self-image?

b. If you are a mother, what is it like? Does being a mother live up to your expectations? Whose decision was it to have children? Is being a mother different from being a father? How did becoming a mother change your life?

c. If you live with someone, do you share child-care responsibilities? If so, is it because of an agreement, because one person nags the other, or because both feel equally responsible?

d. Do you consider child care equal in status to paid work? What is your attitude toward working mothers? Working fathers? Do you, or would you, use daycare facilities?

e. What are some of the myths of motherhood?

12. Divorce

a. Have you ever been divorced or separated, or close to someone who has been? How did you feel about it?

b. If not, how would being a "divorcee" affect your self-image?

c. What is the marital status of most of your friends?

d. If you have been divorced, why did you stay married as long as you did?

13. Employment

a. What were your parents' attitudes toward work? Toward women working?

b. Did your family expect you to get married? To have a career? To get a job and support yourself? Or what?

c. What kinds of jobs have you had, if any? What did you like/dislike about them?

d. Describe your relationships with bosses or employees of lower rank, both male and female. Do you feel you have certain problems or privileges in your job because you're a woman? Do you think your job duties would change if a man were to replace you?

e. How do you feel when people ask you what you do? What do you say?

f. If you work full time, do you consider it a "job" or a "career"? Why?

g. What role does your job play in your life?

h. If you are married or are in a marriage-type situation, whose job is considered more important? Who earns more money?

i. If there were a machine that could give you any job, what button would you push?

14. Aging

a. How old are you? How do you feel about this age?

b. What age do you consider to be "old"?

c. What relationships do you have with women who are considerably older than you? Younger?

d. How do you feel about getting older? Have you noticed any changes in your body?

e. Are you satisfied with the attentions you receive from men and women of your own age? Older? Younger?

f. Do you, or have you ever, disguised your age? How do you feel when someone mistakes your age?

g. How do you feel about menopause? What do you know about menopause?

15. Medical/Psychological Care

a. Psychological care:

1. Have you ever been in therapy? Was it with a male or female therapist? Why did you go?

2. Do you think your therapist has/had any prejudices about women?

3. Did your therapist ever make any sexual advances toward you?

b. Medical care:

1. Have you ever been to a gynecologist? Have you ever had a bad experience with a gynecologist—i.e., condescending at-

titude, inadequate explanations, careless or brutal treatment, sexual advances?

2. Do you think your doctor(s) understood your problems fully and had confidence in their treatment?

3. If you've ever had a vaginal infection, how did it affect your feelings about yourself?

CONTEMPORARY ISSUES

Here are some questions that concern women. These may be discussed in any order and should be approached both from personal experience and with abstract thought.

1. How do the media present women?
2. How do you feel about your body? Fashion? Makeup?
3. Describe some patterns in your relationships with men/women.
4. What is friendship? What is love?
5. What part has competition played in your life?
6. What is femininity?
7. What is your mother like?
8. What are some of the myths of womanhood (i.e., Prince Charming)?
9. What kind of fantasies do you have?
10. How do you handle street hassles and threats of violence? Do you feel you can defend yourself adequately?
11. What makes you feel secure?
12. How do you manage money? How important are material possessions to you?
13. How do you feel about the following: monogamy, polygamy, communal living, voluntary celibacy, living alone?
14. How do you express anger?
15. What is nonsexist childrearing?
16. What are your personal goals?

THE "LIBERATED" WOMAN

1. What strengths do women have?
2. What is a "liberated" woman?

---

3. What are some of the problems/pressures of a liberated woman?

4. What is the best way to deal with a woman who is antagonistic to the Women's Movement?

5. Can a woman with a "raised consciousness" still relate to men?

6. What is equality? Is this our goal?

7. What are the goals of the Women's Liberation Movement? What are the goals of your group?

8. Is consciousness-raising a political action? Is it enough?